MIST AND SHADOW

KAYLIN WISE

WILLIAM
PRESS

Identifiers: ISBN 978-1-7373137-1-7 (eBook) | ISBN 978-1-7373137-3-1 (Paperback)

www.KaylinWise.com

CONTENTS

1

A SHADOW IN THE DARK

Daphne didn't know how she'd ended up in the passenger seat of a car she'd never ridden in before. Or who the girl sitting next to her was. Or where they were, exactly.

The driver, in fact, didn't appear to notice she was no longer alone. She was maybe a year older, nineteen at most, her thick black hair chopped at the chin. Daphne observed her with detached interest, her thoughts as tuneless as the steady whir of the tires on the wet pavement. The girl yawned widely and rubbed an eye, leaving behind a faint smudge of mascara underneath.

Daphne looked out her window for a marker she might recognize. It was difficult to see anything in the moonless dark. They were driving through thick woods that stretched on both sides of the road like an endless, narrow tunnel.

The radio dipped briefly into static.

With nothing interesting to see, Daphne focused instead on her reflection in the wet glass, her dark hair blending in with the night. She frowned. Pale gray eyes squinted back. Behind her in the reflection, the strange girl yawned again.

After several hours, though perhaps it was only minutes, Daphne became aware she was expecting something to happen.

She threw a glance at the nameless driver beside her, bracing for something her mind could not yet perceive before fixing her eyes ahead. The girl, whoever she was, hadn't moved her attention from the road. A cold wave of dread washed over Daphne. Her heart thumped unpleasantly. Waiting.

Bumps rose on her skin from the frigid cold blasting from the car's air vents. Suddenly the darkness was suffocating, looming over them like a giant that could crush the car as easily as an aluminum can. Daphne clasped her hands tightly together, trying to calm down. Everything was fine. She just needed to—

"Look out!" The yell tore out of her.

A shadow flew across the headlights like an overgrown bat, vanishing into the surrounding dark. Daphne whirled around to look out the back window as thunder cracked like a whip across the sky. The creature was gone. A blink would have missed it.

She turned forward slowly, shaking at the near miss, though at the same time unsure why. Daphne glanced sideways again. The girl hadn't reacted to the shout or shown any sign she knew the car had almost hit something—or almost been hit.

Silently, they drove into the night. Every second stretched like an hour. Daphne sat stiffly on the edge of her seat, full of dread as she watched the road in case the shadow returned.

Rain splattered on the windshield. Would it come back? Doubt crept in. Perhaps it was just an animal after all. But no, it wasn't—she was somehow certain of that. It was something dangerous. Daphne anxiously scanned the road, the woods. The radio dissolved into static.

By the time she sensed it again, it was too late.

The car lurched with a deafening *bang* as something hit its left side with the force of a charging rhino. Daphne's head smacked against the passenger window. Pain lanced through her skull. Even in the shock of the moment, the girl steadied the car, shrieking.

Daphne pressed a hand to the growing throb in her head and looked out the window, dazed. A shapeless form made of the densest, most soul-stopping black was soaring toward her.

There was no time to react. Glass shattered. Wet shards cut like fiery needles into Daphne's upthrown hands and nicked her forehead. In what was undoubtedly an instinct to flee, the girl jerked the wheel and floored the gas instead of the brake—

They lurched again just as another force collided with the car near the back. The car spun haphazardly, then, without warning, flipped. Daphne felt weightless and devoid of thought as she tumbled around, not able to scream or yell or do anything in the noise of the crushing metal and the girl's screams—

Stillness.

The car groaned to a final halt. Daphne lay curled on the ceiling, which now served as the floor. Every inch of her body ached. Thick drops of rain thudded dully against the engine above.

Beside her, quietly suspended by a seat belt, was the girl. Daphne felt the pull of her presence in the corner of her eye but did not want to look. She knew, as if the knowledge was already there waiting, that the girl was dead.

She swept aside broken glass with a shaky hand. Static spluttered out of the radio. Willing her trembling limbs to move, Daphne half crawled, half dragged herself out the smashed window and landed with a final thrust of pain on the wet asphalt.

Nausea boiled up in her throat, and blood welled from her glass-bitten hands, but she propped herself up on one of them, short of breath, and followed the beam from the only surviving headlight toward the woods.

Even as her vision turned to dust, Daphne could have sworn a shadow soared across the trees and melted into the dark.

2

OMENS

Daphne Cole moved her boot just in time to avoid stepping on the toad. It hopped onto a bright yellow leaf and stopped as if to pose.

"Stay still," she ordered, lifting a large camera. The toad kept still long enough for her to snap a shot in the dim light before it dived under a fallen tree.

The dark pall over the woods was lifting in the early morning. Daphne stood quietly for a minute, not in any hurry to move on. There was nowhere she needed to be.

A familiar nightmare had forced her awake a few hours earlier. Only when Daphne was suddenly staring at her bedroom ceiling did she remember it was only the dream that had haunted her for well over a month, since August. Unlike other strange nightmares and dreams that always slipped away from memory like sand through fingers, this one still burned into her memory vividly. Broken glass slicing open her hands. A final scream.

Daphne rubbed her hands together, reminding herself she was awake and therefore safe. The woods surrounding her house were as familiar as a favorite sweater, a place she could always come to after a bad nightmare. It was a better option than simply lying awake in bed, willing her heart to stop beating so fast as she watched the shadows change shape on her bedroom walls. To recover, all Daphne needed to do was pull on her boots and slip into the woods.

The back of her neck tingled. Daphne tensed, two invisible eyes pressing on her skin. She turned and glanced around before making out the cause above her, perched on a branch.

A large white owl with many brown markings and a pale yellow beak stared down at her from a nearby pine, almost perfectly blended in with the tree behind it. Its head glowed from the cloudy light, and its eyes—like black pits—had only the smallest fuzz of light to indicate they were not simply gaping holes.

The owl didn't move or seem bothered by Daphne's presence, as if this were a long-arranged meeting. Its dark eyes gazed intently into her gray ones. Hardly daring to breathe, Daphne slowly readied the camera.

Without warning, the owl leapt silently off its perch and soared across the trees.

Daphne's spirits sank, the weight strangely heavy. The opportunity to photograph a more interesting subject than usual had slipped away, but this was more than just disappointment.

She glanced at the silver bracelet on her left wrist: a simple silver band, connecting the head and feet of a textured owl with scalelike feathers. Two smooth, bulging eyes with dark, furrowed eyebrows. A final gift.

Some leaves rustled to her left. Daphne glanced over, half expecting to see someone emerge from behind the trees, but of course there was no one. She was alone.

An alarm beeped from her jacket pocket. Lost in thought,

she jumped and checked the time on her phone. It was already half past seven.

Daphne made her way back through the woods in a daze, almost tripping over familiar dips in the ground. A two-story white home hidden in the woods came into view, yellow light glowing in the downstairs window. She ran across the yard and leapt onto the porch, stooping briefly to collect the empty thermos of tea deposited earlier, and thrust open the front door.

"Daphne?" The call came from the living room.

"Mom?"

"Okay, just checking!"

Daphne shook off her rain boots on the entryway rug, wishing she could do the same to the strange mood now infecting her, and sprinted up the wooden steps to change her clothes. She narrowly avoided stepping on Mystique, a fluffy black cat who took up most of the top step. When she returned from her bedroom, the cat was batting something invisible with a giant paw. She smiled and long-stepped over her on the way down the stairs, then turned into the empty kitchen.

Thoughts of the owl were swept away. Daphne's mouth watered as she took in the sight of the cupcake on the table, thickly piled with frosting and garnished with a tiny cookie.

"It's cookies and cream!" Her mom came up from behind, waving her arms, cropped blonde hair askew. "I bought it on my lunch hour yesterday, from the new bakery downtown. They also sell gift-wrapped toilet paper. I thought about getting that for you instead, but..."

"Thanks." Daphne tossed the empty thermos in the sink as she went to claim the cupcake, unwrapping its shiny foil with reverence. "What's it for?"

"It's your half birthday!" her mom said with another dramatic wave of her arms. "Only six months until you're an adult!"

"I didn't know we celebrated half birthdays," Daphne said as she took a large bite of frosting. Nevertheless, it was a tradition she could appreciate.

"We don't, I guess." Her mother took a seat opposite where a binder lay open on the table. "But I wanted an excuse to check the place out without getting anything for myself."

Daphne recognized this to be a subtle self-gibe by her mother, who was an amiable and upbeat woman but rather touchy about her larger size. They were both silent for a few moments. Daphne, although focusing most of her attention on eating what she had decided to classify as breakfast, detected a slight shift in her mom's mood.

"So, were you out in the woods all this morning?" Her mom's tone was a touch too cheery, Daphne recognized. She felt suddenly uneasy.

"Yeah." She slowly set the cupcake down and swallowed.

"Any good photos?"

"A few," Daphne said, matching her mom's casual tone. "I saw an owl, but it flew away before I could get it."

"Really? What kind?"

"I don't know." Daphne rested her elbows on the table, twisting her silver bracelet out of habit. "Its eyes were completely black."

More than anything, this was the detail that stood out most clearly in her impression of the bird. Daphne was not sure why the encounter had unsettled her so much. It was like the owl had marked an event, some line crossed—but that was stupid. It was just a bird.

"Hmm..." Her mom reverted into thoughtful silence. Daphne, wishing to appear normal, took another bite of the cupcake but couldn't quite enjoy it as much as before. "So, what time did you get up?"

It was another lead-in, Daphne thought with a twist of the

stomach. A more direct one. The path of the conversation was becoming clearer.

"The same. About three-thirty, but I didn't go into the woods until five." She had turned on the bedroom lights and listened to a podcast. Unless a nightmare affected her badly, the woods could wait.

"Hmm..." Her mom's lips were pursed, the humor in her face descending into worry. Then, gently, but as if steeling herself, she began in a rush, "You know, I ran into a friend at the grocery store the other day—do you know Yvette? Dr. Sow? Anyway, she specializes in sleep disorders, and she was telling me how there's some treatment options for nightmares—"

"Mom," Daphne interrupted quietly, looking at a spot past her mom's elbow. They had arrived at the dreaded point. "I've told you before, I don't need to be treated."

"But it might help," her mom plowed on. "There's some therapies, or maybe you could get a prescription—"

"I don't need to take anything." Daphne sighed, but without anger. For the first time that morning, she felt tired. "There's...nothing wrong with me. I can deal with it. I swear."

But her mom continued to look at her with such wide and concerned eyes that Daphne felt a rush of guilt for the worry she had caused over the years. She knew the topic of treatment, broached by her mom every so often despite the fact it was always rejected, came from a feeling of helplessness. There were years of her mom bursting into her bedroom to stop the screaming clearly audible down the hall, to hold the thrashing and sobbing figure on the bed and assure her fifty times it was only a dream, a nightmare.

Daphne didn't quite know why the idea of treatment was always so unappealing, only that her nightmares had been there since she could remember, and the suggestion of getting rid of them was like admitting there was something intrinsically wrong or embarrassing about herself.

For better or worse, the nightmares were there to stay, and Daphne could deal with that fact.

"Mom, I know you worry about my nightmares, but you really don't have to," she said, trying to look reassuring as she met her mom's worried eyes. "I'm not a kid anymore. They're not...they're not as bad as they used to be." Daphne dropped her gaze to the crumbs on her half-finished plate and began to gather them with a finger. She didn't like lying.

"Are you sure?"

Daphne paused, tempted for a moment to reveal the contents of her latest nightmare, one that was so terrifyingly realistic. However, she knew the cost of confiding was more worry, more anxious questions, and perhaps silent consent to enter her bedroom in the dead of night to comfort her. That consent had been revoked for the second time at fifteen, when she had decided she was past old enough to deal with the terrors alone.

At this cost, how could she reveal her nightmares were worse than ever? Normally, Daphne could confide in her mother about practically anything, but the issue was beyond her help. It always had been.

"Yes," she replied, meeting her mother's eyes again directly. They searched her carefully, but her mom said nothing, evidently deciding the subject was worth dropping for now.

"So. What's that?" Daphne nodded toward the open binder on the table as she returned to her breakfast.

"This?" Her mother looked down, successfully distracted. "Just a photocopy of Thomas Blakely's diary."

"Who?" The name sounded familiar, like a ghost out of an elementary school lesson.

"Oh, just a businessman who used to live in Long Haven

around a hundred years ago. He lived awhile in the mansion you toured in the fourth grade."

Daphne made a noise of recognition. Although she hadn't set foot in the local historic home since then, she could faintly remember being impressed by its size and old-fashioned elegance. However, she and her classmates had found the house interesting because it was supposed to be haunted, not because of its history.

"You'll see his name around town," her mother continued. "He invested a lot into Long Haven while he was here."

"Why are you reading his diary?"

"Because it's important for early local history. Someone found it buried in their attic, so now I'm trying to type it up for the historical society. But, any-hoo, it's been difficult reading his writing." She flipped through the binder. Pages of cramped cursive flashed before Daphne's eyes. "And there's also the fact there's a lot missing from it, so it's not very cohesive. You can tell he ripped out a lot of pages. Burned them, probably."

"Really? Why?" Daphne said, now intrigued. What secrets would an early-twentieth-century businessman have to keep?

"Well, I suppose the answer's been burned," her mom said, taking on the intellectual voice that appeared whenever she discussed her passion, history. "But my guess is he had sensitive information about his business, or probably just gossip about other people he couldn't afford to have read. When you're a prominent person in the community, you can't exactly be vocal about your feelings."

"I guess," Daphne said, suppressing a yawn.

"And from what I can *ascertain*," her mom continued, in a bad British accent, "'e was well-known for being *private*."

"He kind of sounds paranoid."

"Well, he did leave town just a few years after arriving. He told everyone it was evil."

Daphne cleared her plate from the table. "Really? Why?"

"Well, his sister had just killed herself, so maybe—" She paused as the plate slipped from Daphne's fingers and fell noisily into the sink. "—he thought the town got to her."

"He thought the town *what*?" Daphne said, taken aback by the unexpected morbid turn in the story.

"I don't know much about it yet. It's been slow going," her mother said, flipping through the pages again. "Some of it's interesting, though. Maybe I'll do a book!"

"That'd be cool," Daphne said, though truthfully she did not hold the same passion for history as her mom, or—she glanced at the old photo frame propped on a shelf by the sink—as her dad once had. She suppressed another yawn.

"So, what time is Jessica picking you up?"

"Noon. We're going to lunch, then shopping." Daphne's mood was sinking back into its gloomy state, and she wondered if she should call her best friend and cancel. Maybe by the time Jessica arrived, she would feel better, and she *had* been looking forward to it. She fingered her bracelet. Maybe it *was* just that association.

"That's right, I was going to give you some money for shopping." Her mom stood.

Daphne looked at her, surprised. They were not poor, exactly, but it was an unspoken agreement that as a senior in high school, she was old enough to pay for things that weren't essential, although she'd quit her fast-food job in June without a replacement.

"You don't have to do that," Daphne said honestly. "I wasn't really planning on buying anything—Jessica's the one who wanted to go shopping."

"Nonsense!" her mother replied, regaining her comical cheeriness that contrasted with her daughter's grimness. "It's your half birthday!"

She disappeared and a minute later returned with a magenta pocketbook, thrusting a few twenties into her daughter's hand.

"Thanks, Mom."

Her mom smiled. "Spend it well."

3

MADAM MOON

"I love that store, it's so *cute*."

Jessica exited the boutique behind Daphne, peering with satisfaction into the tiny plastic bag that held her newest purchase. "This card is *so* perfect for my brother's birthday."

"You can't go wrong with barfing unicorns," Daphne answered drily.

"He'll find it funny," Jessica said, turquoise earrings jangling happily as she tucked the bag into her large purse, to join several new shirts and a necklace. They set off down the sidewalk.

"Do you want to go anywhere else?" Daphne asked, admitting to herself she hoped the answer would be no. Shopping exhausted her at the best of times, especially after nearly two hours of it. In contrast, Jessica, a heavyset Hispanic girl with a pretty face and elegant clothes, never ran out of energy. Though Daphne was trying her best to act normally, the strange mood that had come over her since the woods had returned with a vengeance after lunch. She wanted nothing more than to hole up in her bedroom.

"Mmmm..." Jessica said thoughtfully, glancing at windows as they walked aimlessly past the downtown storefronts. Daphne spotted the colorful-looking bakery where her mom had gotten the half-birthday cupcake and felt an urge to check and see if they really did sell gift-wrapped toilet paper.

"Do you want to get coffee?" her friend suggested as they passed two elderly women chatting over tea at an outdoor table.

"I don't really drink coffee." Drinking anything more caffeinated than black tea was like injecting her dreams with steroids; they became more vivid, strange, and frightening. However, Daphne had never shared the extent of her nightmare problem with friends—it felt too private. She had briefly confided in Jessica about her most recent one but suspected her friend didn't grasp how much it affected her.

"Oh, right...Tea then?"

"That's okay. You can get a latte or something if you want," Daphne suggested. She did not want to ruin Jessica's fun, but it was taking all her energy to appear at least no more serious than usual. Daphne was also mindful of the fact that a cupcake had been her breakfast and did not want to splurge on a sugary drink either.

"That's okay, I don't really want anything," Jessica said cheerfully.

They bypassed the coffee shop and, at Daphne's suggestion, dipped briefly into her favorite used bookstore. With a twenty still unspent in her pocket, she agonized over a few novels but decided against them and placed them back on a tipsy stack.

Her mood sank lower. Daphne impatiently fought against it and hoped Jessica didn't notice how quiet she had become. She felt bad, given this was the first time in weeks she'd been able to hang out with her best friend outside of school, just the two of them. They only shared lunch at school, and even then Jessica's attention was usually divided.

Lost in thought, Daphne opened the door to exit the shop and almost ran into a passerby on the sidewalk.

"Oh—sorry," she said, and looked up to empty air.

There was no one else nearby. Daphne glanced around, perplexed. Hadn't she almost collided with someone—?

"Jessica, did you see—" Turning, she saw Jessica was making her way across the street, evidently distracted by the dresses displayed in the bridal shop on the opposite corner.

"Daphne, look at the green one, isn't it amazing?" Jessica said at Daphne's approach, gazing with longing at a glittering dress on the headless mannequin. "I want to get a new dress for prom."

"Too bad it's only September; you'd have to wait to wear it." Daphne looked over her shoulder again, even though the passerby would be long gone.

"Do you think I'm getting thinner?" Jessica's voice had lost some of its cheeriness. She was frowning darkly at her reflection in the shop window.

"You look really good," Daphne said with what she hoped was supportive-sounding honesty, uncertain what to say that would not make her friend feel worse. "Have you been doing your workout thing?"

"A few times. I only did once this week, though," Jessica admitted.

"That's okay," Daphne said, keeping her voice encouraging. "I mean, I don't really exercise at all."

"You're thin, though."

Daphne shrugged. The cupcake weighed uncomfortably in her stomach. "I mean, it's not like you're obese or anything, and you're really stylish." Truthfully, Jessica possessed a glamour Daphne wished she could imitate.

It was Jessica's turn to shrug.

"So, do you know any other shops around here?" Daphne said. In her concern for getting Jessica's mind off the subject, she had momentarily forgotten her wish to quit shopping.

"What about that place?" Jessica said, after a quick scan of their surroundings. "That looks like some kind of shop?" She pointed down the side street at a sign hanging past the bridal store with an illustration of a sleeping crescent moon next to the words "Madam Moon" in scrawled cursive.

They walked to it and paused underneath the gently swaying sign. A glass door was wedged inconspicuously into the brick with a neon sign that said, "Palm, Crystal, Tarot."

"Ooh, a psychic?" Jessica said curiously. "I've never been to one. We should try it."

Daphne looked at her, alarmed. That had been the opposite reaction to her own. "I don't think—"

"You know what?" her friend continued, warming up, not hearing. The gloom from a minute ago had vanished. "We should get a reading! I've always wanted to see what it was like, but my mom would never let me."

"I think it's all fake, though," Daphne said nervously. Others likely wouldn't hesitate, but seeing a psychic wasn't something her own mom would be impressed with. Once her friend had an idea, though, it was difficult to talk her out of it.

"You don't have to take it seriously. It would just be for fun!" Jessica was growing more enthusiastic by the second. Daphne glanced at the glass door, which advertised the rate.

"It's twenty dollars for a fifteen-minute reading! On special," she added, with greater alarm. Jessica would have to see now how ridiculous the idea was. "That's kind of expensive."

"Use your half-birthday money!" Jessica said with an air of

it being the obvious solution. "You still have money from your mom, right?"

"Yeah, but—"

"So just use that!"

Daphne paused, wishing she had bought a book after all, then had an idea. "Why don't you just go and I'll wait outside?"

"Oh." Jessica glanced at the door with the first hint of fear. There was a long pause. "I don't want to go in by myself," she admitted in a low voice.

Daphne refrained from rolling her eyes. "Okay, I'll go *in* with you, but I won't get a reading."

"All right..." But Jessica looked even more frightened. She was faltering.

Indecision built up in Daphne's chest as she weighed her options. She knew Jessica meant to get a reading, and by the laws of friendship, she could not leave her best friend to do it alone. True, she could probably convince her to abandon the idea altogether, but doing so would mean ending their outing on a sour note. At the same time, Daphne did not want to waste money on something she did not believe in.

Feeling dread at the idea, and though she didn't want to give in—

"Fine, I'll do it with you," she relented.

Jessica beamed, all fear vanishing in an instant. It was much easier to be brave with a friend.

A tiny bell jingled as they opened the door. Jessica went first, and she followed close behind. Daphne's nose was immediately hit by a strange scent. She suppressed the urge to cough and glanced around.

Her first impression was of a cluttered living room crossed with a pawn shop. In the middle of the small room, two mismatched couches were arranged adjacent to each other around an antique wooden coffee table. It was far less gloomy than Daphne expected: an overhead fluorescent light brightly lit the burgundy walls. Near the left wall, a long glass case was packed with a strange assortment of small figurines and jewelry. On the opposite end, a grandfather clock ticked next to several tall bookcases stuffed full of books, an ancient CD player, and several glittering geodes.

"Where—" Jessica had just begun to say, when a woman in her sixties walked through a dark curtain that acted as a door in the back corner near the couches. Daphne thought she recognized the psychic's taste reflected in the living room decoration. She wore a billowy paisley-patterned cardigan, short black pants, and Velcro sandals. Her curly hair just covered her ears and was dyed the color of red wine. A glittering purple rock wound lightly with string hung over her loose shirt.

"Good afternoon," the woman said in a somewhat stately tone as she stopped before them. Her voice, Daphne noticed, was mildly husky, like a smoker's. It added to the mystic atmosphere.

"Hi!" Jessica replied breathlessly. Daphne thought her enthusiastic greeting was enough for the both of them and said nothing. "Are you Madam Moon?"

"You may call me Claire," the psychic said regally. She had a gaudy type of elegance, Daphne observed, but it suited her. "How may I help you today?"

"We both wanted to do a reading," Jessica said, with a hasty side glance at Daphne. "The fifteen-minute one."

"Of course. Which one of you girls would like to go first?"

The psychic's dark eyes slid inquiringly from Jessica, full of suppressed excitement, to Daphne, who stared back impassively. The keen glance jolted her. *She knows*, was Daphne's first thought. Somehow, the woman could tell Daphne didn't want to be there at all. The eye contact lasted barely a few seconds, however, before Jessica spoke up.

"I'll go, I think."

Claire's eyes moved belatedly to Jessica. Daphne felt as if she'd been released.

"Follow me to the back," the psychic said, and turned and disappeared through the curtain. Jessica followed her and paused briefly to smile nervously at Daphne before following the psychic behind the sheet.

Daphne watched the curtain fall into place before settling onto the one couch that wasn't an ugly floral. There were no magazines on the coffee table, and her phone was almost dead. Therefore, with nothing to do, Daphne took to staring at the room around her from her safe position on the couch.

Madam Moon's also doubled as a shop—she spotted price stickers on glittering geodes (there seemed to be plenty of rocks) and CDs of music for meditation. The glass case turned out to be mostly full of jewelry. Daphne itched to smell a few of the incense sticks in the display on top of the case, but her desire to have as little as possible to do with all of it was more powerful than her curiosity over which stick smelled the worst.

With each passing minute the clock ticked by, her regret increased. After all, Jessica had only wanted both of them to get a reading because she had been afraid to enter the studio alone. When her friend came out, all Daphne had to do was say she'd changed her mind. A little rude, perhaps, but with luck she'd never see the strange woman again.

The fifteen minutes finally passed. Jessica reentered the room first, her excited smile showing the session had met every expectation. No doubt Daphne would get a full account later. A burst of nerves flashed through her stomach as she stood up. This was it. She'd just have to say she'd decided against it.

"Your turn!" Jessica said cheerily, bouncing toward her.

"Actually—" Daphne began.

"C'mon, Daphne," Jessica said, giving her a little push. "It's your turn! No backsies!"

The psychic stood in front of the curtain, waiting without expression and yet imposing. Daphne's resolve collapsed.

"O-Okay."

Daphne walked reluctantly toward Claire, who pushed aside the curtain to allow her to go through first. They were now standing in a small, dark hallway leading off to several rooms. One of them, Daphne could see through the half-closed door, was a cluttered office with an overflowing desk.

Claire led the way into an open room, pushing aside strings of red beads. Daphne hovered in the doorframe.

This room was far neater than the others and less perfumed, softly lit with floor lamps. The walls were also painted a dark red, like the rest of the studio, but covered in shadows and decorated simply with a gilded, slightly tarnished oval mirror. A house plant stood in one corner, and another was occupied by an ornate white shelf displaying porcelain angels, a cheap box of tissues, and a small wooden box arranged with dried flowers.

"Have a seat," Claire said, gesturing to the round table covered with a deep blue tablecloth sparkling with silver crescent moons and stars. Electric candles were arranged in the center with a handful of polished stones.

Daphne obeyed silently. The strange reality of what she was doing had suppressed her ability to speak, as well as the irrational thought that the less she said, the less she was a part of it. She wished fervently the session would be over with quickly.

The psychic settled down on the opposite side of the table with a businesslike air and grabbed the pad of paper off the table, pen poised. Daphne stiffened.

"So tell me, what is your name?" the psychic said conversationally, looking down at her paper.

Daphne answered. Underneath the table, she clasped her
hands tightly. Claire made a note.

"And what is your age?"

"Seventeen and a half," Daphne mumbled, then winced at
the specificity, brought on by a brief vision of that morning's
cupcake. Claire scribbled *seventeen* on the pad. Daphne
glanced at it warily, wondering, as she had with her mother,
where these questions would take her.

"So you attend Long Haven High School?" the psychic
inquired further.

"Yes." Daphne shifted in her chair. She was determined to
be polite, whatever her reservations about the session, but the
questions were making her nervous, like an oral exam she
would know soon whether she had passed or failed. The
woman gave off the impression of a strict schoolteacher. "I'm a
senior," Daphne added reluctantly, feeling she might as well
give the psychic something to work with and move the session
along.

"I see, so you are applying to colleges?" the psychic said,
looking up for the first time. Her eyes were very dark.

"Yes."

"UVA? Or somewhere else?"

"I'm starting out at the college here, to get my associate's
degree first," said Daphne impatiently. Was the psychic simply
going to keep asking her questions? She waited with resignation
for the rest of the trifecta of college small talk, as she termed it:
what her intended major was, and what exactly she planned on
doing with it after graduating. Did all psychics work like this?

Claire didn't bother to make a note, folding her hands
together with the pen. A cloudy moonstone glimmered on one
of her rings. "That's a wise decision."

Daphne made the barest nod.

"So tell me, is there anything you would like to focus on in our session, or know?"

"I...don't know. No, I guess." The woman must be growing impatient too, Daphne thought. Surely the psychic had sensed by her brief responses how little she wanted to be here.

Claire peered at Daphne impassively, like the owl had in the woods. It took all of Daphne's effort not to squirm under the gaze as the psychic seemed to study her for signs of deceit. She stared back, determined not to speak first. She could just hear the ticking of the grandfather clock in the other room.

"Has anything been bothering you?" Claire asked in the silence, her voice soft.

Daphne didn't immediately know what to make of this question. There were any number of things that could bother a person, and this was not a therapy session, after all. Intensely, she wished again she could be anywhere, anywhere else. "Not anything major, I guess," she began carefully. "I mean, I have a French test on Monday I haven't studied for, but I don't think— that's not really..."

She trailed off, squirming inwardly again, and instead began to study a tiny rip in one of the glittering moons on the cheap tablecloth, twisting the silver bracelet around her wrist underneath the table.

"I see," the psychic said, then leaned slightly forward, as if she hadn't heard what she wanted and was determined to do so. "And what about your dreams?"

Daphne looked up instinctively, like a confession. "My dreams?" she said quickly. The sound of crashing metal echoed in her memory. She was not going to tell the psychic about her nightmares. No psychic was going to give her a contrived meaning for her latest dream when it was meaningless.

"Is there a dream you would like to talk about?" the psychic persisted. "Or several?"

Daphne did not know how to answer, but she stared at a star so intently, it was likely to burn with new life.

"Or not dreams, but, perhaps...nightmares?" Claire prodded.

She looked up again, her heart beginning to beat faster. "I... don't have nightmares," she lied on impulse, yet she was not sure what she feared. No doubt it was a routine question. Maybe the psychic just liked to interpret dreams. There was nothing to suggest—

The psychic leaned even closer, staring intently at her face as if she knew it was a lie. "Not any? Not even one?"

Daphne stared. Something was off. Why was the psychic acting like she knew the answer? Had Jessica mentioned something about her nightmares, and this woman was taking advantage of that? And was this even how sessions usually went? She had pictured tarot cards, or a palm reading at the very least. *Your heart line shows a concerning lack of romance.*

"Maybe there's one nightmare you keep having," Claire said. It didn't sound like a question. One of the old lamps flickered briefly, casting a shadow across her face. Daphne felt frozen, a fear she didn't quite comprehend spreading across her heart. The air between them stiffened.

"Perhaps," the psychic said in the stillness, "in this dream, you see a young woman, and a crashing car."

Immediately, Daphne's fear vanished. Understanding hit her heart like a dull blow. She felt angry, mostly at herself. The woman had obviously done her research during Jessica's session. Daphne shouldn't have done the session at all. Did the psychic really think she was so easy to fool?

"Jessica told you about that," Daphne said, keeping her

voice neutral. But instead of looking defensive, Claire's face softened in satisfaction, and something like relief.

"No," she said simply, leaning back as if her interrogation was over. "She didn't need to. When I saw you, I suspected you were like me," Claire explained, looking at Daphne intently, "but it seems you don't know it."

Daphne stared, not having the slightest idea what the old woman was talking about. What did Claire mean, she was like her? What didn't she know?

"I...I'm not a psychic," she said, as if she were reasoning with a madwoman. Which, honestly, she couldn't be sure Claire wasn't.

"True, but that's not what I meant," the psychic said. "Have you ever wondered about your nightmares? Why you have them?"

"I don't...I just have them," Daphne said, overcome by the urge to leave as quickly as possible. "And I—I have somewhere I need to get to, sorry."

She stood up and walked out of the room. Claire followed. Despite herself, Daphne stopped, not looking at the psychic's face.

"When you have seen enough," Claire said quietly in the darkened hallway, "come find me."

Daphne didn't respond but walked away as fast as she could. Entering through the curtain to the main, well-lit room felt like emerging from a dark cave into sunlight. She tried to return Jessica's smile, who had glanced up from her phone upon their entrance.

"Finished already?" she asked, standing up.

"Yeah," Daphne answered, trying to sound normal but aware of Claire's gaze on her back.

"Well, thank you!" Jessica said brightly to the psychic, rummaging in her purse for a twenty. "This was fun!"

Daphne dug into her own pocket and handed her money to Jessica as she passed, then walked to the glass door and waited, feigning interest in the incense sticks.

Jessica joined her. "Bye!" her friend said with a small wave, and walked past Daphne through the open door.

"Goodbye, girls," answered Claire solemnly.

Daphne turned to follow Jessica, but while stepping over the doorframe, she felt the urge to look back. The psychic was still standing where they had left her, watching them go.

For a moment, their eyes met, dark irises boring into pale. Then Daphne closed the door behind her with a jingle, severing the connection.

4

GLOOM

Her feet flew over ash-colored leaves and mangled tree roots, drawing her farther into the dark. The sky was an eerie red above the spidery tree limbs. Shapeless bodies of mist shuffled out of the way as Daphne tore her way through the endless woods, but she could spare no thought for them, nor the stitch splitting a chasm in her side. Distraction, any slack in her breakneck pace, meant death.

Still, she was not fast enough. At the edge of her awareness, Daphne could sense the presence of the unseen creature that pursued her. It would surely catch up soon. She could not outrun it forever.

Her feet navigated the maze of tree roots and pockmarked trees the texture of black chalk that she dared not touch. The only sound was her heavy breathing and the sound of footfalls crushing leaves into dust as she ran in the dim light. A half-fallen tree appeared suddenly in her path.

Daphne registered it just in time and fell backward to avoid it. Her feet skidded across the ashy ground. Footfalls rippled in the distance, but she did not immediately get up, entranced by the sight before her.

A giant white owl half her height was perched on the fallen tree. Its deep black eyes were each the size of two fists, staring soulfully at her sprawled figure. There was still hope.

"Help me!" Daphne wheezed, pressing a hand against the roaring stitch.

The ground tremored. Desperation seared through her, for help, for air that was not pale and still. The owl had not moved to help, only stared, beautiful and terrible.

It was also crying. Black liquid ran like congealed ink down the owl's brown-flecked feathers in a growing stream. The substance was not tears, Daphne realized in a sickening flash. The owl's eyes were melting, leaving behind two gaping pits.

Out of one came a small, thick black spider.

Daphne scrambled away in revulsion, unable to tell whether the tremor came from the ground or her own body. The spider scuttled along the edge of the hole, then climbed down the owl's feathers and across its claws before vanishing into the darkness of the fallen tree.

To her horror, another spider emerged from the depths of the giant owl, then another. They came from the deep, moving with military precision to the ground. She made out a line steadily making its way across the gray leaves. Making its way toward her.

Daphne unfroze herself and scrambled to her feet, backing away into a tree.

Its roots sprang to life. Like snakes, they curled around her body, her hands. Daphne screamed and wriggled uselessly against their chalky iron grip.

The spiders poured from the eyes of the owl, crawling all over its stained feathers. She looked down and cried out at the sight of the first spider as it reached her, as it climbed up over her shoe. Another followed.

Daphne jerked harder than ever but could not move. The roots bound her in place. Her breaths were as short as they had been when she'd been running. Around her, the woods and red sky seemed to close in.

At the first whisper of legs on her neck, Daphne clamped her lips so tightly she almost gagged and screamed silently under the darkness of her eyelids. Spiders were swarming over her neck, her cheek, her mouth. Daphne suppressed a sob. She was covered with spiders, a thousand tiny legs.

A solitary spider found its way into her nose, and Daphne could not help it—she opened her mouth and screamed, a spine-shattering shriek that would surely alert the creature she'd been dodging. The earth beneath her feet shook with heavy footfalls—

Daphne dumped her backpack into the locker and yawned.

Around her, students shuffled with a fatigue that plainly meant it was Monday morning, chatting in groups or lingering alone outside classrooms for the first bell. She spotted Jessica down the hallway, chatting animatedly with Veronica, and grimaced. Gathering her books, Daphne slammed the door shut and steeled herself to approach.

Though she considered Jessica her best friend, Veronica was different altogether—a pretty fellow senior Daphne had only known by sight before Jessica brought her to sit at their lunch table. It hadn't taken long to dislike her, both for the way she dominated Jessica's attention and the group conversation, and her overall cattiness. More often than not, Daphne was silent for most of lunch, forced to listen to Veronica gossip about everything.

It would have been okay, Daphne thought, except for the fact that she and Jessica shared no other class period. Now the only time she was able to spend with her friend without Veronica around was outside of school. That had been the main reason why she had looked forward to Saturday's shopping so much.

"Hey," Daphne said once she'd reached them. Jessica was in the middle of a story.

"She took the card, and I can't remember what it said, but then she was like—"

Too late, Daphne realized her friend was recounting their visit to the psychic on Saturday. She cringed at the thought of sharing any greater details from her own session, especially with Veronica, who would no doubt probe her to death. They were not enemies, exactly, but definitely not friends.

"Hey, Daph—you remember what I said the card said?"

"Something about love?"

"No, that was the other one. Whatever, doesn't matter—so then she asked me if I preferred small dogs or large dogs, and I said—"

Daphne let her attention wander, having heard most of the story on the car ride home. Even from the slanted way her friend had told the story, her impression was that Jessica had done most of the work. She had managed so far to avoid talking in detail about her own session, disturbed by the memory of the psychic's penetrating stare as she recounted the details of a nightmare that came almost every night.

Though Daphne knew psychics had methods of cold-reading their clients, she hadn't asked Jessica anything about the dreams. The likely explanation was Jessica had somehow been prompted to let slip a few details. The psychic had then used that information for dramatic effect.

Although Jessica hadn't been paying too close attention at

the time, Daphne had shared with her at least a little about this latest nightmare. However, most of her friends over the years were never even aware she had bad dreams, that they were the reason she had shunned their childhood sleepovers.

Of course, she could have just asked Jessica for an explanation on the ride home, but that would invite questions into what had happened in those long minutes Daphne had squirmed on the cushioned chair. If anything, Jessica's story of her session only highlighted all the strange things about Daphne's. Claire, from the sound of it, had asked Jessica a bunch of questions and then essentially made up a story with the information. What had Claire asked her? Her name, age, education, and then about her dreams—but as if she'd already known the answer.

"So, do you really think I'll end up living in Connecticut with a Pekingese?" Jessica finished. Daphne wrenched her attention back to the conversation.

"I could see you with a Pekingese," Veronica said thoughtfully. "What about you, Daphne? What dog did *you* get?" It sounded condescending but also friendly enough to make someone doubt it wasn't just a simple question.

"I'm more of a cat person," she said evasively, bracing herself for more questions.

"So what kind of *cat* would you get?"

"I don't know. A black one," she said, thinking of Mystique.

"Wait, V, isn't that him?"

"That's him," Veronica said, and flipped her long, highlighted hair over a shoulder. A classmate with dusty brown hair swept in waves off his forehead walked past them, silently following a group of boys Daphne recognized as part of the cross-country team.

"I was right, he *is* in Euro with me," Jessica noted. She was in the nonadvanced version of the class, while Daphne and

Veronica shared an AP class. They watched silently as he disappeared down the hall. "Aw, he's *cute*." She nudged her shoulder.

Veronica giggled. "Shut up."

Though she agreed with Jessica, Daphne noted that Veronica's crush hadn't looked all that happy. She suppressed another yawn as the first bell rang.

"...with the Protestant Reformation came social changes..."

The lecture floated around Daphne's ears and dissolved into the hazy background. Pens wiggled over notebooks, writing down important facts, but her mind had drifted. Instead of listening, she doodled underneath last week's detailed notes on European history.

"The German princes helped Martin Luther because they could better control the church if it was Protestant, and they also didn't like Charles the Fifth telling them what to do," intoned Mr. Burnes, a young and rather skinny teacher with dark sideburns that stretched halfway down his cheek, "which leads us to another important date you'll need to know for the AP test..."

Daphne scribbled down 1517 and returned to filling in the iris of the eye she was intricately sketching.

The rest of the class, comprising mostly juniors, except for a handful of seniors like Daphne, jotted down notes on the Diet of Worms. Luckily, her middle spot was out of direct sight from where Mr. Burnes was standing. She wondered if he knew students called him "Mr. Sideburns."

Daphne saw Ashley Zhang was also doodling over her notebook in the front row. Ashley was good at faces...

"So, like, *why* didn't Luther like the revolt?" said a voice from the right wall. Daphne didn't have to look over to know it was Veronica's.

"I'm getting to that," Mr. Burnes said, somewhat testily. He hated to be interrupted. "Luther's goal was *religious* reform, not social. Although he was *against* peasants' suppression by the ruling class and *condemned* the massacre, he saw the peasants' revolt as an act of evil."

"Oh," Veronica said.

Thomas Blakely had thought Long Haven was "evil," Daphne thought, gazing unseeingly at a classmate's scribbling pen.

"So, as I was saying, the peasants felt betrayed by Luther..."

Boring, maybe, but not evil...

"...turned to Anabaptism, which was..."

She was drifting...

"Daphne? What are you doing?"

The words didn't register. Daphne had leapt noisily out of her seat, heart thumping. She was standing in the middle of the classroom. There had been—and then there wasn't—

"Daphne," Mr. Burnes said again, in a stiffer tone.

All at once she felt the heat of twenty-three pairs of eyes. Daphne glanced around briefly at the staring class and fought to find a way to break the silence, which was swelling—

"I-I thought I saw—" She cast around wildly and landed on last night's dream. "A spider. There." She pointed at a random spot on the floor. The girl next to the spot peered over in alarm, inspecting the area. A boy in the back laughed.

Daphne looked at Mr. Burnes, who was frowning, but she could tell by his offended air that he was not going to respond.

"Sorry," she said, heat touching her normally pale face, and sat down with as much dignity as she could, keenly aware of the class's amused smirks. Out of the corner of her eye, she saw

Veronica lean back and whisper something behind her hand to the girl sitting by her. They both giggled quietly. A hot surge of anger flared inside her at the sight. Ashley Zhang was still drawing.

"Okay. Let's continue," Mr. Burnes drawled pointedly, with a final look at Daphne, but he had evidently decided to let the matter drop. "So, the Münster Rebellion of 1534 you won't need to know—"

Gradually the awkwardness of the moment settled underneath the steady drone of Mr. Burnes's voice. Daphne, however, could no longer pretend to take in the lecture. The shock of what had happened now filled every particle of her mind. Of what she had seen.

Someone had been standing over her desk. Then they'd disappeared.

Daphne thought back, trying to remember even as the image faded, and maybe her sanity as well. While drifting off, she had noticed a person standing next to her, looked up in confusion, and—nothing. It had happened too quickly to tell what the person looked like.

Had she been dreaming? It was possible, but she had been daydreaming, not sleeping. There was the fact, too, that no matter how realistic her dreams seemed, upon waking she could always separate them in her mind. Real or dream. The figure had not felt like a dream. It had been *there*.

She tapped her pencil eraser on her notebook. Panic was spreading through her veins like frost, not helped by the exhaustion from the night before. It had not been the first time someone disappeared in front of her—there had been the man she'd almost run into outside the bookstore. Though she had written that off, what if she was starting to hallucinate? Then her mom *would* take her to get treated, for if Daphne was seeing things, that was more concerning than a few nightmares—

When you have seen enough, come find me.

Out of her harried thoughts, the psychic's words floated to the surface. Daphne almost tossed them away. Then, to her own surprise, she stopped.

Whether it was a hallucination or something else, *someone* had been standing over her desk. Yet Daphne recoiled at the thought of telling her story to a doctor. She did not want to be proven insane. The psychic would at least be an alternative, but Daphne didn't want to take this lead.

A large part of her felt her initial opinion of Claire had been right—she was a fraud who'd heard the details of the dream from Jessica, and the rest was just theatrics.

But a hidden doubt came to the surface: why would the psychic take it so far, and ask Daphne to come back? To spook her into paying for more sessions? It didn't make sense. She hadn't done the same to Jessica, who was the more likely target to become a repeat client.

No. If there was the slightest chance there was someone out there in whom Daphne could confide, who could offer an explanation other than insanity, she had to take it, no matter how little she liked it.

With a calming sense of purpose, Daphne refocused her attention to catch the rest of the lesson, but she felt again the sensation of being watched. She turned her head—Ashley was frowning at her. But the moment their eyes met, Ashley quickly looked away.

5

PERCEPTION

Shortly after school, Daphne found herself standing underneath a sign with a sleeping, cratered quarter moon and looking at a door she had never thought to enter again.

Despite her feverish plan of the last two hours, Daphne had no idea what to expect beyond this point, or what she would say to Claire. But she had at least determined she was not going to hand over any money, as a test of the psychic's honesty: if Claire asked for payment, Daphne would know it was an act once and for all, and she could still get home before her mom came home from work at the public library.

Just get it over with, Daphne thought, steeling herself. She pushed down on the tarnished gold handle and walked into the room to the jingle of bells. Immediately, her nose was assaulted by that strange, heavy scent, which, nervous as she was, felt suffocating. But she was relieved to find the room empty. There was time to think, or to abandon the plan altogether.

An imagined conversation played out in her mind as she walked to the dark curtain separating the main room from the hallway. Maybe Claire was in her office, or with a client? She gingerly pushed aside the curtain and looked into the gloom. Voices came from the session room, and Daphne hastily withdrew her hand and returned to the couch.

When the grandfather clock had ticked away a full minute, Daphne, unable to sit still, stood up and wandered to the display case. She stole a quick glance at the curtain, then removed a heather-scented incense stick from its cardboard cup and sniffed it. Recoiling at the pungent scent, Daphne returned it to its cup and sat back on the couch.

Several more minutes passed, and with every tick of the clock, her doubt increased. Was she so sure it hadn't been a dream? And Claire wasn't just playing her? Maybe—

"Hello, Daphne."

Daphne started violently and sprang to her feet. Claire had silently appeared through the curtain, today wearing a shawl with the same glittering amethyst necklace as before, a bill in her hand. She was followed by a tall, unshaven man with flyaway blond hair and overlarge eyes. Daphne took in this scene silently, struck anew by the sharpness of the psychic's gaze, which x-rayed her inquiringly.

"Until next time," Claire said to the man, who nodded and walked trancelike to the entrance, then disappeared with a violent jingle of the bells, without so much as a glance at Daphne. The door shut.

Daphne's stomach writhed in the expectant silence. Every word from her imagined conversation flew from her mind, but before her mouth had opened a millimeter, Claire spoke first.

"Follow me," she said, and walked back through the curtain again.

For a second, Daphne paused indecisively, watching the swaying curtain, but then she followed Claire into the hallway. Claire held aside the red strings of beads over the opening to the room where she did readings.

"Have a seat. I'll be with you in a moment."

Daphne nodded once, still unsure what to say, and ducked through the created opening. The beads swung back and forth as the psychic released them and retreated into her office. Daphne settled herself in the same cushioned chair as her previous visit and glanced around with a strange sense of unreality. The fake candle flickered. In the dim, lamplit room, it could have been any time of day.

A deck of mystical-looking cards sat neatly on the table, having evidently been used in Claire's last session. What had Jessica's cards been? One had been about love, or relationships. How that had led to owning a Pekingese in Connecticut, Daphne could not remember.

Curiosity tugged at her, and she lifted a corner of the top card, but Claire's footsteps sounded in the hall. Daphne hastily dropped her hands to her lap. The psychic emerged through the clinking beads, holding a folded piece of paper and something else clenched in her fist.

"I believe this is yours," she said with a smile, pushing a bill across the glittering tablecloth as she settled into the opposite chair. Daphne reached for it automatically and then paused, blinking down at the twenty with bemusement.

"I—thank you," she said, heat touching her face, and put the money away in her pocket as Claire settled into the chair opposite. Despite her embarrassment, Daphne could not help but recognize the significance of the gesture. Not only was Claire not demanding any payment, but she had refunded the money from Daphne's last session. Was this a sign of trust, or manipulation? Already the visit was going nothing like her imaginings. Claire didn't respond but folded her ring-clad fingers on the table with an air of polite expectation.

Daphne untied her tongue.

"Last time," she began slowly, speaking to a silver moon on

the tablecloth instead of addressing the psychic, "you told me I should see you again when I had seen...enough."

"Yes," Claire said with an encouraging nod.

"I—" Daphne stopped. It was more difficult than she'd expected to describe what had happened, but there was no turning back now. She twisted the silver bracelet on her wrist, her gaze now fixed on the plant in the opposite corner. "I was daydreaming in one of my classes, and then I saw..." Daphne closed her eyes, trying to recall what the figure had looked like. "Someone was standing by my desk, and I looked up, but then they weren't...they weren't there," she finished lamely.

"I see," Claire said. Daphne glanced up. There was nothing there to suggest she was moved at all by this story.

"I mean, I know I could have been dreaming," Daphne added hastily, hoping to establish herself as someone with some semblance of sanity, if only to herself. The memory of it was almost like a dream, and yet heat touched her cheeks again at the more vivid one of jumping out of her seat, and Veronica's smirk. Now she had told her story, yet the psychic appeared to be expecting something more.

"Do you think you were dreaming?" Claire asked quietly.

"I..." She considered carefully. "No. I know the difference, and this felt...real." Daphne felt something in herself resolve, provoked by Claire's silent gaze. A desire to understand—once and for all.

"Last time, you told me I was like you, but I didn't know it," she said, looking directly into the dark eyes of the psychic, which were a direct contrast to Daphne's own pale gray ones. "What did you mean?"

To Daphne's surprise, Claire closed her eyes and gave a small sigh, as if resigning herself to an unpleasant task. Then she nodded shortly and stood up straighter, businesslike.

"Last week when you were here," the psychic began, "I asked whether you had nightmares. Do you?"

"Yes," Daphne confirmed, deciding to be entirely honest, "but what does that have to do with—"

"Do you ever wonder why?"

It was the second time Claire had asked the question, but Daphne still felt taken aback. What did her nightmares have to do with what she saw in class?

"No. I mean, I've had them ever since I could remember, but most of them aren't—they don't make any sense." Briefly, she felt the whisper of a thousand tiny legs on her arms.

"You were upset when I mentioned the dream with the car crash," Claire said. Daphne squirmed, mildly ashamed. "A dream, I assume, that you have every night."

The sound of shattering glass seemed to echo through the room. "How do you know about that nightmare?" Daphne asked, afraid of the answer.

"Because," Claire said shortly, "I have it too."

Daphne blinked once. "What?"

The psychic smiled unexpectedly. "Yes, every night since August, that dream has been haunting my sleep as well."

"But how—how can we have the same dream?" Daphne asked skeptically. She didn't rule out the possibility the psychic was untruthful. This was, after all, technically her living.

As if guessing what she was thinking, Claire grabbed the paper off the table, which Daphne realized was actually two sheets folded together. "Perhaps I should show you this first." She unfolded the sheets and handed one over. "It will help you begin to understand."

Daphne took the paper with some hesitation but saw at first glance it was merely a newspaper article printed from the internet. The headline read, "18-Year-Old Woman Dies in Saturday

Car Accident." It was dated to early August, nearly two months prior.

She glanced at Claire. "What is this?"

"Read it first, and you'll know," Claire responded with a nod at the paper, leaning comfortably back in her chair. Daphne turned her attention again to the article, not sure what to feel. So far there were more questions than answers.

Aware of the psychic's gaze, Daphne forced herself to push her thoughts aside and concentrate on what she was reading. Phrases jumped off the page and swirled into a disorienting picture: *rural road south of Long Haven...rolled car...alcohol not a factor...extensive damage...pronounced dead on scene just after 4 a.m....*

The article led to an idea Daphne was not sure she could comprehend. "Are you trying to tell me," she said, a sense of unreality descending again over her mind, "this is the car crash I've been dreaming about?"

"Yes," Claire said simply.

"But how do you know?"

"Here, look at this one."

Daphne took the next sheet, a follow-up article that announced the name of the victim and that she was a recent graduate of the high school. Daphne felt a shock through her skull at the photograph accompanying it.

"That's...that's...that's the girl in my dream." She looked up at Claire, numb.

Though she had never gotten a full look at the victim's face, between the girl's dark bob and sharp chin, the features were enough to match the picture. It was the girl from the nightmare.

"Yes," Claire said, smiling sadly. "Heather Grey."

Daphne looked at the picture again. Her mind felt blank, unable to think. She had seen this girl—Heather—die. Her final minutes had been repeated every night like a sick film for

Daphne to watch, helpless. She was real. The nightmare was real. The screams, the blood.

"How can she be real?" Daphne said, staring at the photograph. Heather was smiling shyly, a small gap between her front teeth. Her eyes were a striking hazel, rimmed with long, coated eyelashes. If her nightmare was real, Daphne thought, that meant the old comforting words were gone. It was no longer *just a dream.*

She looked up at Claire. "Why do I see her?"

The psychic leaned forward intently. "Because," she said, "you can *perceive* what others cannot see."

"What do you mean?"

"Think about what you saw in class," Claire said, sounding like an impatient tutor. "Pretend, for a moment, someone really was standing there. What do you remember?"

"I don't know," Daphne said, growing impatient herself. "I just saw someone. I already said."

Claire was nodding. "Yes, and then that means..."

"Are you saying it was a ghost?" Daphne answered incredulously.

"A shade, as I call it," Claire said calmly. "One that knew you could perceive it."

There was silence. Daphne had sought out the psychic again for an answer, and this was it. Was it the right one? Claire had no motive to lie to her. It was possible the woman was crazy, except for the fact that evidence to the contrary was printed before her. Could it be real?

Daphne had been convinced getting an answer would bring relief, but she felt the opposite. "It was—You're saying what I saw was—"

"A spirit." Claire nodded.

"But if I can see spirits," Daphne said, deciding to play along for the moment, "why did it vanish? I barely saw it."

"My guess is you are still developing your perception. It seems only when your mind is relaxed and unguarded, like it was in class, are you able to let yourself perceive."

"Let myself," Daphne echoed.

"Perception is a strange thing," Claire said. "Once you are aware of something, once you understand it, you can't become ignorant again—except, perhaps, through an enormous amount of willpower. You have a logical mind, Daphne. It's difficult for you to see what's not there."

Daphne ignored this accurate assessment of her character to say, "But I haven't seen anything, not until now." Even then, she realized it was not quite true. There had been small incidents over the past few weeks she'd dismissed, willed to be normal: vanishing passersby, the strange feeling of being watched in the woods sometimes.

She looked up and saw Claire watching her with a knowing look. "It seems you have, if you think about all the moments you've ever tried to explain away. I think you were beginning to perceive anyway, though I'm afraid I gave you a little push up the path. I told you there was something more to your nightmares. That was the trigger. After all, we don't always see what's right in front of us until someone points it out—then it's impossible to stop."

"And you can see—shades—too?"

"Yes. Everywhere, in fact."

Daphne breathed deeply, choosing to avoid thinking about this for now. "But what does seeing shades have to do with my nightmares?"

"Like me, you are a perceiver, as I call it. Your mind is more perceptive, sensitive to the world around you, seen and unseen. Stronger dreams are a natural consequence of that," Claire said.

"So that's why I have nightmares," Daphne said. The room

went out of focus as the implications of this hit. Her night-mares, which had haunted her nights since childhood. Her mom's earnest face as she suggested they go to the doctor. Her own refusal and her acceptance of what had always seemed a part of her. It wasn't the nightmares that had been natural. It had been her ability to perceive what went unseen by others.

Daphne waited to feel relief or satisfaction that she had been right not to seek treatment. But the explanation she'd just been given was far more complicated. And it meant there was a reason for her dreams after all.

She realized Claire was looking at her closely, and with a great will of effort, she focused.

"It's partially why. And I should add that most of your nightmares are likely meaningless," the psychic said.

Daphne glanced automatically at the small inset photo of Heather again. Her stomach twisted unpleasantly. "So it's like having a vision," she said. The smile was disconcerting, compared to her strong mental image of the girl hanging upside down, blood in her hair.

Don't think about that.

"But if it was real, then..." The deafening bang echoed in her memory again, Heather's shrill screams. "In my nightmare, something hit the car. Or did I just dream that up?"

"You mean, did she *actually* swerve to avoid hitting an animal?" Claire said wryly, with a nod at the article on the table. "I'm afraid not."

"Then what hit us—her?" Unlike Claire, Daphne could not yet disassociate herself from the dream. She felt almost as much a part of the scene as if she'd actually been there.

The psychic frowned in thought at a spot behind Daphne's shoulder, as if considering what to say. "There is an evil in this world," she began carefully, "an evil most people don't see, because they cannot see as we do. I wish the article were right, and it was merely an animal Heather tried to avoid that night, but I'm afraid not. What attacked her was far worse and more dangerous than you or anyone will have ever encountered before."

Daphne stared with growing dread, sensing that whatever the psychic was about to reveal would change everything, more than it already had. She glanced at Heather's photo. *What did you come across that night?*

"The thing that hit her," Daphne said, recalling the blur of concentrated darkness that had been no bigger than a small animal yet had inspired so much fear. "It was small."

"Yes, but very strong, as you saw. And I know what it's called, and I'm well aware of what it is," Claire said, now brisk. "What attacked Heather is a spirit of sorts, called a dyszoon."

"Diss-zoon?" Daphne repeated, trying out the odd word on her tongue. "I've never heard of that before."

"No, they're not ever recognized, given they are mistaken for demons. For, like demons, they are strong and evil and even have the ability to possess."

"But what are they?"

"They were once human," Claire said, with a twist of her mouth.

"So they're shades?"

"No, shades are fundamentally good, though a shadow of their living selves, I should add. I suppose dyszoons could be considered to be a kind of spirit, but unlike the spirits you and I have seen—shades—they no longer retain any essence of their humanity. They are like lesser demons—much less powerful, but still entirely evil and very strong, especially when they are fully formed."

Daphne's mind whirled. "They used to be human? But how could they become those...things?"

Claire paused, seemingly to gather her thoughts, or perhaps she was merely used to providing dramatic effect.

"While they lived," she began, "they were some of the most terrible human beings to walk the earth, committing atrocities and leading godless lives, so when they died, they were damned to the worst punishments in Hell, to be tortured in the flames for all eternity. However, not every soul can become a dyszoon," Claire continued. "They are recruited based on the amount of evil already in them. Only the most evil would do. I'm sure those souls leapt at the chance to end their agony by exchanging it for what might be considered another, to become soulless entirely and the servants of an evil impossible to imagine."

Daphne absorbed all this in a horrified trance. The woman's voice seemed to have an ethereal quality, wrapping around them like smoke and forming unspoken visions in the haze. It was almost as though the psychic had transported them both into the depths of Hell, and Daphne could see the roaring flames and hear the agonized chorus of a multitude of damned souls: desperate, pleading for help.

She shuddered. "They're recruited? By who? And they're turned into those—dyszoons?" Daphne added. She could not imagine the process.

"I don't know."

"And by Hell, you mean..." She inclined her head meaningfully.

"An actual, literal Hell, yes."

Daphne nodded once to show she understood. It wasn't so much that she hadn't believed there was a Hell—she'd spent her entire life attending a Protestant church—but she had never liked to think about it. It was easier not to.

"How are they changed?"

Daphne realized immediately she had triggered something

painful. Claire's face collapsed in on itself, as if a frame of memory, a ghost of a nightmare, had passed across her eyes, displaying some unseen horror.

"I'm sorry—You don't have to—"

"It's all right," Claire said, giving her head a little shake. Her wrinkles smoothed as the memory faded away. "Some things are better left unknown. I hope that nightmare never comes to haunt you."

Daphne was eager to move forward. "You said only the most terrible humans could become dyszoons. So, someone like Hitler would be a candidate?"

"Perhaps. I imagine dyszoons were those throughout history who fed off evil, were seduced by it and worshipped it, without redemption."

In the contemplative pause that followed, Daphne struggled to imagine what evils someone might have committed to be eligible to become a dyszoon. She was aware she possessed somewhat of a naïveté of the world. Intense grief over losing a parent might have matured her, made her grimmer and more serious than her peers, but that wasn't the same as being worldly, as knowing and experiencing just how terrible people could be to each other.

Claire pursed her lips. "I've met one already."

"You have?" Daphne said, startled out of her thoughts, which were struggling to comprehend the enormity of the information so far. "Where? Did you get rid of it?" Even as she said it, she struggled to imagine Claire, who had to be over sixty, fighting with a demon-like creature from Hell itself.

"Yes. The dyszoon that killed Heather didn't disappear after the accident. I had the nightmare of her for the first time that very night, as I'm sure you did too"—Daphne's memory confirmed the dream had started around that time—"and then I sensed the dyszoon come out. I drove out to look for it straightaway."

"And you found it?" Daphne said.

"I did. It was very weak from its attack on Heather. I'm sure in a few days, it would have dissipated on its own, back to Hell, but I couldn't take the chance it wouldn't harm anyone else. Even the weakest dyszoon still has some strength. Once I sensed it lurking in the woods and found it, I banished it.

"It put up a little struggle, of course," Claire said casually, as if it were merely an annoying fly she had once swatted. "But all in all, it was easy to defeat. Luckily, it was very under-formed, otherwise it would have been extremely difficult to get rid of, probably beyond my current ability." She examined her long, fuchsia-colored nails as if remembering power flowing from her fingertips.

Something occurred to Daphne. "But the dyszoon—if it's from Hell, it can't have always been here. Someone else would've gotten hurt before Heather."

"I'm glad you brought that up, for it brings me to the most important thing. Have you ever been out on the road where Heather died?"

"I don't think so," she said. "Besides the nightmare, anyway. It's out of the way, isn't it? I always take one of the main roads out of town."

"Well, I don't suppose you'd have been able to see it anyway," Claire answered thoughtfully. "Maybe you could now."

"Seen what?" Daphne was growing used to Claire's round-about way of getting to a point, but it was still irritating.

"A portal of sorts. A veil between Earth and Hell, through which the dyszoon could enter."

Daphne stared blankly.

"I'll explain. First, you should understand, it's not easy for evil entities to enter our world. They need a vessel of some sort, a point of entry. This is only possible with human help."

"But why would anyone—"

"Because people mess with things they do not understand," Claire said fiercely, though Daphne knew the anger was not directed toward her. "How many of your friends have played with Ouija boards? Most of the time, nothing happens, but maybe at some point, something strange and possibly evil can communicate. A dyszoon, in the right circumstance, could get through this point of entry that was created."

"So someone used one, and it got through," Daphne said, trying to follow along.

"No. The portal I'm talking about is different. The link is permanent, not brief," Claire said. "It's a kind of veil between our worlds. I don't know how long it's been there, or if there are others like it in other parts of the world, but there's been a Veil in Long Haven as long as I have lived here, so at least nine years."

"So this...Veil," Daphne said, thinking hard. "If something like that has been open so long, how come no one else has been hurt? Or have they?"

"As far as I know, and I believe I *would* know, Heather was the first victim," Claire said. "Since I've been here, the Veil *was* too small to let anything through. My purpose in moving up here from Florida was to watch it closely, but it never disappeared or changed in any way."

"*Was* too small," Daphne echoed. She was starting to see the edges of a bigger picture.

"Yes, you might have already guessed: it expanded in August, enough to let a dyszoon travel through and attack the first human who happened to be on that road."

"So Heather's death was an accident," Daphne said, feeling angry at the injustice.

"She was in the wrong place at the wrong time, like many victims are," Claire said with a sad smile.

"But why did it expand *now*? The Veil?"

"The only explanation is someone—someone who had our abilities, that is—deliberately widened it, at least for a moment, to let one get through. But who that person is, or why they did such a thing, we can only guess. There is evil at work in Long Haven."

They sat in thoughtful silence as the grandfather clock in the other room began to faintly chime four. Once it was done, Daphne spoke.

"But if this portal thing is bigger, doesn't it mean more dyszoons will come through?"

"Eventually, they will. The Veil widened, yes, but whoever did it has discovered the passageway is still too narrow and difficult for the creatures to get through. The dyszoon that *did* get across was probably already waiting just on the other side, but it had lost much of its strength." An image flashed in Daphne's mind of a long, cramped tunnel small creatures were slowly oozing through like worms, diminishing in form as they lost strength along the way.

"But why open it if it wouldn't work anyway?" Daphne asked.

"Maybe it was only an experiment. Or maybe the Veil can only be widened a little at a time. I don't know how to control it, or who has found out how to do so, but in the meantime," Claire continued, "I think we can say no more dyszoons will get through until it is widened further—when *that* will be, I have my guess. If I'm right and someone *is* hoping to continue opening the Veil, then it means more dyszoons *will* come through."

"Can't you close it somehow?" Daphne said, feeling this would be the obvious solution.

"No," Claire said. Daphne's heart sank. "It's impossible. A passageway like this, you would need to be connected to it through a blood sacrifice. They would need to do some kind of ritual."

"So that's how they widen the Veil too? Through blood rituals?" Daphne shuddered at the thought of what this would entail. The gleaming side of a knife flashed in her mind, followed by the pain of a deep cut and strange, guttural chanting underneath the full moon.

"Yes. But that's not something I know how to perform—not that I would, in any case. It's an act of evil, and there's no guarantee that it would work."

There was a long pause. Daphne blurted out the question hovering over their conversation, over every explanation. "How do you know all of this?"

"About dyszoons? Mostly through my nightmares," Claire answered. "For shades, I've had almost a lifetime of experience."

Daphne nodded, then glanced at the beaded doorway. Out there, beyond it, was a world she had navigated but never seen. She had come into this room searching for an explanation, and armed with it, she would venture out into a new world. One that was more complicated than she could have ever imagined. Her head felt heavy, but there was also a weight lifted. For despite it all, Daphne knew the explanation given was the right one. It was as if a knowledge she had long hidden away had revealed itself again.

"If you think whoever is doing this will try again to expand the Veil," she said, staring at the gently swaying beads that separated them from the hallway, "then more dyszoons will come through."

"I'm afraid so, and that is why I need your help, Daphne."

Daphne looked at Claire quickly, but it was without

surprise. Claire could not be telling her all of this for her own sake. "You want me to fight the dyszoons," she guessed.

"Yes," Claire answered, and in her eyes was a strange depth. "It will not be easy, I confess. First, you will have to improve your perception, but that will come naturally."

"But what can I do? You know a lot more than I do," Daphne said, full of doubt. "I wouldn't know how to fight these...things."

"That's something that can be remedied," Claire said shortly. "Beginning to enter this world is difficult. But let me explain further: when you first walked into my studio, Daphne, somehow I thought there was the slightest chance you might be perceptive, so I decided to ask about your dreams, to tell for certain—not something you were comfortable with."

Daphne smiled sheepishly.

"It was understandable. Perhaps I went about it the wrong way, but it was necessary to know for sure and confirm my hopes. I've been saddled with this problem for nearly a decade, you realize, and bearing the responsibility of that knowledge alone. But I knew if five dyszoons, let alone an *army* of them, came through the Veil, it would be impossible for me to defeat them by myself. Therefore, I would need another perceiver."

"So you're recruiting me," Daphne said, making sure she understood completely.

"Yes," Claire said simply. "I wish, of course, shades were the only thing you had to think about, but the circumstances are different. Something evil is at work in Long Haven, and I will need your strength as well as mine if there is to be any hope of matching it."

"I understand, but I don't feel very powerful." Daphne felt it was best to be honest about her shortcomings, even as in her heart, she accepted the challenge.

Claire leaned forward, fixing her with a stern stare that was rapidly becoming familiar.

"No one, not even those with natural ability, can improve without practice. Being perceptive—that's something you are born with, but it has to be developed, like anything else," Claire said matter-of-factly. "Once you've learned how to let yourself perceive, I have no doubt you'll become very adept."

"How will seeing shades make me better at handling dyszoons?"

"Because," Claire said patiently, "there are both good and evil spirits, and we can interact with both. Being a perceiver is a unique position, Daphne. We can see shades, but seeing shades is just one element of our ability. We are also stewards. There is an invisible evil, and so it is our responsibility to battle that evil, since the world can still be harmed by what it cannot see."

"And there's no one else who can help us?" Daphne asked.

Claire laughed. "You're the first person I've met who can perceive like myself. The odds aren't good I'll find someone else."

"You've never—"

"No," Claire answered, shaking her head once. "Not one. I don't know how many people can perceive the spirit world, but I've never knowingly met someone who could see spirits besides myself—and now you."

Daphne wanted to ask more of the questions unfurling continuously in her mind. But Claire seemed to think she'd imparted all of the essentials, for she sighed and stood up, signaling the end of the meeting. Daphne stood too.

"I would like to meet with you again soon. There are other things you will need to know if we are going to get anywhere."

"There's more?" Daphne asked with a little trepidation, wondering if there was some other evil she knew nothing about.

Claire smiled with understanding, as if she knew exactly

what Daphne was feeling and thinking. "I've given you more than enough to think about. Soon enough, though it won't feel like it for a time, all of this will feel normal."

Daphne doubted this. She felt as if she'd aged twenty years in the course of an hour.

"What will we be doing?"

"Practicing," Claire answered, but did not elaborate.

Saturday morning was settled on. Daphne entered Claire's personal number into her phone.

"So," Claire said, walking her out, "before we meet again, I'd like for you to see the Veil for yourself. I'm sure you will be able to perceive it, as long as you let yourself."

"Okay," Daphne promised, but with half a mind. The other half was wondering what she was getting herself into, and if it wasn't the beginning of a long and difficult journey.

6

BENEATH THE VEIL

Daphne stirred the lunch on her tray without seeing it. Last night, her surroundings had dissolved into hot, bubbling tar that pooled around her shackled feet, melting away the rubber soles, eating into her flesh...

It had been difficult to concentrate on classes again that morning. Since meeting with Claire four days ago, she couldn't help but feel like an actor in a play only she was aware had changed its lines, while everyone else acted out the same parts. Everything had changed, and yet nothing had.

There was still much she didn't understand. What did it mean to fight a dyszoon? How would they close the Veil? Or was Daphne destined to spend the rest of her life fighting those creatures? When would she begin—the thought caused a little tremor of fear—seeing shades?

On her left, Jessica was chatting with Veronica, who sat opposite her at the end of the lunch table. Daphne kept tabs on the conversation with half an ear. The topic tended to fall into mundane territory anyway, with Veronica steering the course.

"I don't really like my last name; it's too long. Ver-on-i-ca Slow-i-kow-ski," she enunciated.

"I don't know, I like it." Jessica shrugged. "It's better than mine."

"What's wrong with yours?"

"Everyone pronounces it *R*oman."

"Oh. At least it's short," Veronica replied with a theatrical sigh. "I hope I marry someone with a short last name." She brightened as if struck by a thought.

"Why don't you change it legally? You're eighteen."

"My grandfather would kill me," Veronica answered wryly. "He's one-hundred-percent Polish and super proud of it."

Daphne wondered, not for the first time, what the lunch hour would have been like without Veronica. She'd have better conversations, to start. Yet, it was impossible to escape to another table. The sixth-period lunch hour was packed, and moving would mean upsetting the seating arrangements established since the start of the year—something others were always touchy about.

And whatever her dislike of Veronica, Daphne thought switching seats would be like admitting defeat in an undeclared war. She refused to be shut out, even if that meant enduring Veronica's personality.

"Hey, Daphne. Daphne!" said a voice as if from a great distance. A gentle elbow dug into her arm—Jessica.

"Yoo-hoo! You awake?" Veronica waved a hand rudely in front of Daphne's face. "I was just telling Jessica about the *spider* you saw in class."

"O-kay," Daphne said slowly, in a tone she hoped sounded extremely uninterested, as her insides began to simmer. She'd known the topic would be brought up by Veronica sooner or later.

"Do you, like, have a phobia?" Veronica blinked her fake eyelashes innocently.

Daphne had discovered through experience that the best way to deflect Veronica's probing questions was to answer with her own. "Doesn't everybody?"

"*I* don't," Veronica said with a little laugh, as if the fear of spiders were something strange. "What about you, Jessica?"

Her friend shuddered. "I *hate* spiders."

"Oh." Veronica deflated a little, glancing down the table for an ally. Beth, a lean girl with short red hair, was absorbed in chatting with three of her friends Daphne didn't know well. But Ashley Zhang was only sketching, looking out of place in a baggy sweater and frizzy black hair. Daphne observed her with curiosity. She hadn't figured out yet how Ashley had come to sit at their table, except for maybe a minor friendship with one of the others. Ashley spent every lunch period silently drawing in her sketch pad and ignoring the food at her elbow.

"Hey, Ashley! Olivia, can you poke Ashley? Hey, you were in Euro yesterday. Are *you* afraid of spiders?"

Ashley looked up moodily. "No," she said stiffly, returning to her drawing.

Daphne yawned pointedly. "Happy?"

Veronica bristled. "It *was* pretty funny."

Daphne discreetly returned Beth's rolled eyes, and as Jessica was distracted, Veronica could not continue the "joke" any longer. Another audience would have to be found elsewhere.

Returning to her lunch with greater concentration, Daphne reflected again on the shade she had seen during class. Although she had poked her head with anticipation into the empty classroom a few times that week, the shade passed off as a spider was not there. Secretly, she was glad of this. Daphne

dreaded seeing it again, and spiders could only be a one-time
excuse for jumping out of her chair in the middle of a lecture.

"Her shoulders always bother me," Jessica commented,
glaring at the bony back of a tall girl passing their end of the
table. "It's like, eat a doughnut already!"

Veronica smirked, but Daphne squirmed inside. She knew
Jessica, although pretty, was sensitive about her size and had a
meaner side to her sometimes. Her sharp comments about rude
customers had helped grow their friendship when they'd
worked together as fast-food cashiers. But was that bond
fading? She wasn't sure.

"Hang on." Veronica straightened her posture and flipped
her blonde hair over a shoulder. Daphne didn't have to look to
know who was coming.

The three of them were silent as Veronica's crush passed
with his half-empty lunch tray, Jessica quivering with
suppressed laughter. In contrast, Daphne thought Veronica's
nervousness must be contagious, noting the flutter in her
stomach as she also followed his progress.

I'm just on edge today. Besides spending almost every spare
moment analyzing everything Claire had told her, Daphne was
also occupied by her plans for later that day.

After leaving the psychic, she had considered following
Claire's instruction to see the Veil straightaway, but she didn't
think she could face it. She also hadn't wanted to arrive home
after her mom finished work and have to lie about where she'd
been. If Daphne had appeared particularly quiet and brooding
that Monday night, her mom had passed it off as nothing
unusual and given her introverted daughter space.

It was unclear even to herself why it had to be secret.
Daphne normally told her mom most things, but how would
such a conversation go?

Hey, Mom, I went to a psychic, and she told me one of my

*nightmares was real and then something about being able to see
ghosts and evil spirits from Hell. Can I have the TV?*

That's wonderful, Sweetie, but do your homework first.

Daphne would be meeting with Claire the next day, but
she had yet to go see the Veil. While she believed that Claire
was telling the truth about everything, a large part of Daphne
was reluctant to receive final proof. A small part of her
admitted she was afraid.

Before Claire's explanation, there had been comfort in
being able to explain things away. When Heather visited her
dreams, it wasn't until Daphne shook awake that reality swept
in again. But it was no longer a dream she could erase with the
comfort that it was *only a dream*. Every night, she was
witnessing the violent final seconds of a life at the close, and the
victim hadn't moved on.

Once home from Claire's, Daphne had pulled out all her
high school yearbooks to find Heather Grey in the pages. No
recollection came to her of seeing Heather at school, but there
were over a thousand students. It was impossible to know all of
them.

With the help of the yearbook photos, Daphne began to
draw a limited portrait in her mind of what Heather had been
like while alive. Heather's hair was long last year, not the short
cut she'd tried out after graduating high school. With a pang,
Daphne came across a photo of Heather posing with her arms
around a boyfriend at last fall's Homecoming dance. Had they
still been together a few months ago? Where was he now?

She examined Heather's expression in the softball pictures,
one of them capturing Heather mid-throw. *Driven* was the
word that came to mind. Heather did not seem like a preppy
girl, or lacquered up like Veronica, but down-to-earth. Someone
she might have liked. It was still difficult to connect her with
the girl in her nightmare.

Daphne could not find any kind of social media account for Heather, but the obituary posted online revealed Heather had had ambitions to become a veterinarian.

In lieu of flowers, memorial donations could be made to the Long Haven Pet Shelter.

The bell rang and Daphne jumped, glancing at her own unfinished food. The lunch period had never passed so quickly.

The rest of the table left to join the slow-moving crowd of students loudly heading to their next class. Daphne stood more slowly, dread increasing with each step as she headed to the kitchen to drop off her tray.

In just a few short hours, she would see the Veil for herself.

And it would prove things once and for all.

"Turn left on Laurel Road."

Daphne obeyed the woman's voice coming from her phone, steering her car onto a narrow rural road south of Long Haven. The car straightened with an air of finality. This was the road where the Veil was located, according to Claire.

Woods stretched far on either side, gloomy underneath the cloudy October sky. Daphne drove onward, expecting to see the bridge Claire had directed her toward over each passing hill.

The music on her radio became static. Daphne turned it off, realizing she was retracing the steps of her nightmare. She searched for a sense of familiarity without success. It had been dark that night, after all, and the woods were ordinary.

A small bridge came into view at the bottom of a long hill. *This has to be it*, she thought with a combination of thrill and dread as she drove down the long slope and parked to the side.

Daphne unbuckled and let the seat belt whiz back into place. The silence was heavy with anticipation. This was where she would see the Veil, if it could be seen. She exited the car as a great gust of wind blew through and violently shook the trees.

Impatiently, Daphne drew her black hair out of her face and walked hesitantly toward the bridge. Despite the expectation that had stretched tight in her imaginings, there was nothing out of place. The bridge was old, made of cemented stone that gracefully formed three arches across the wide creek. She drew a hand across the lichen-covered ledge and paused to look over. Dark water trickled tranquilly between rocks and disappeared around a bend in the distance.

She itched to take photos. There was something melancholy about the location in its isolation, under a dome of gray sky, but her digital camera was at home. After taking a few photos with her phone, Daphne put it back in her pocket and frowned at the bridge, uncertain.

If there was a passageway to Hell, shouldn't it be obvious? Maybe she had misunderstood Claire's directions and the Veil hung over a different bridge. Yet, how many bridges could there be on Laurel Road? It had to be this one.

Which meant she just couldn't perceive it.

That was one thing Claire had neglected to explain when she'd said it would be difficult for Daphne to let herself perceive. But if perceiving was only possible when her mind was unguarded, Daphne thought with irritation, how was she going to overcome that barrier on purpose?

The only time she had seen a shade, her mind had been drifting into a daydream. Maybe that was the key. If she relaxed her mind again, whatever portal she was supposed to see would appear. At worst it wouldn't work, and she would have to try again at a later time with better direction from Claire.

Daphne walked back to her car and faced the bridge. Hoping no cars would pass by to observe this strange

behavior, she closed her eyes. The temptation to open
them immediately was overwhelming, but Daphne resisted
and instead focused on the sounds around her: the creek
trickling nearby, the swirling wind rushing through the
trees.

After a minute, her heart slowed. Little by little, her harried
thoughts did the same. And for the briefest moment as she
opened her eyes, she forgot why she was there.

Daphne stepped back in shock.

Where before there was just empty air, a black circle about
a yard in diameter hung directly in the center of the bridge,
high out of reach. No light reflected off it or shone from its
depths. If the wilderness around it was an iris, this was the
pupil. It was pure shadow.

Daphne's heart hammered between her ribs. She could not
tear her gaze away from this sudden blip in the sky. The fact
that the Veil looked insignificant made it seem more frightening. It shouldn't have been there, and some core part of her
recoiled as if the circle radiated poison.

A long minute passed.

The first shock began to drain away. So Claire really was
telling the truth. Not that Daphne had doubted any longer, but
here was proof. Daphne took a cautious step forward. Some
line had been crossed, she sensed, and there was no turning
back.

It took some willpower for Daphne to force herself toward
the Veil. As far as she knew, the Veil was not dangerous by
itself. Claire would not have sent her out here if it was. With
that thought, Daphne stepped onto the bridge, staying along
the edge and keeping her eyes on the Veil, which hung at least
twenty feet above her.

As she walked, the circle began to slim. Then, as she passed
the center of the bridge underneath it, it disappeared. Daphne

walked backward. The Veil appeared again as a sliver and gradually assumed its round shape.

So it's one-sided, Daphne concluded as she stopped at the edge of the bridge where she had started. She imagined a dyszoon flinging like a slingshot from the Veil's depths, slinking along the road until it reached a lone car that sped along, unwittingly, toward danger.

The hair rose on Daphne's arms.

However calm it looked, the Veil was dangerous. Even far out of reach, it repelled her. A dyszoon had emerged from it and killed the first person it met. At some point in the future, she would have to stare down the Veil and battle whatever came out of it. There was still much she did not know.

Minutes blended together as she stared back at the pupil. Vaguely, Daphne was aware she could no longer hear the wind, though the branches around her still swayed. A strange ringing filled her ears. It grew louder, no longer inside them but a shrill noise caught from some other place.

Screaming, Daphne realized dully. Horrible, piercing shrieks that expressed an agony that didn't require words for one to understand its depths. Her arm lifted toward the circle. The Veil was so close now, no longer far away but just before her, drawing her in with a mixture of curiosity and revulsion. The screams grew louder.

Daphne leaned toward the sound. She had to look past the door to see who was screaming so loudly. Her finger trembled as it strained toward the lightless gate. She could sense its edges. She was inches away—

Daphne touched it.

A flash. A sharp, split-second vision her mind couldn't comprehend in so small a second. Then a force slammed into her body. Daphne's feet were no longer on solid ground but kicking helplessly in the air. Backward she flew, five, ten feet, until her heel touched the pavement. She fell onto the road with a smack.

Sound returned at once. Slowly, painfully, Daphne propped herself on her elbows. Her long sleeves had protected her from any scrapes, but no doubt she would be bruised tomorrow. She looked at the Veil, now back in its original place and no longer inches from her touch. The imaginary eye around the pupil that was the Veil narrowed in malice. Dared her to try again.

The sound of a horn burst through her skin.

Jumping violently, Daphne scrambled to her feet and leapt from the middle of the road. A moment later, a black truck flew past so close she could feel the air ripple. The driver honked again angrily and drove across the bridge, then around the bend and out of sight.

Daphne exhaled. She was so used to the road being deserted, she hadn't bothered to keep an ear out. Another second and she would have been a ghost herself.

Limping a little, Daphne walked to her car and opened the door, resting a hand on the top to look one more time at the Veil. Her aversion to it had been correct. The circle by itself looked unthreatening, but it was dangerous. It had lured her in, played with her. They would not be able to touch it without getting harmed.

But the Veil could not stay there forever. Someone was working to open this gate between Hell and Earth, and that made it dangerous. What they would do about the Veil if—when—they defeated the dyszoons was an unspoken question, one Daphne didn't want to think about yet. She slipped gratefully into the car and shut the door.

7

MEMORIAL

Daphne watched the circle in her rearview mirror as it disappeared over the crest of the hill, relieved now that its gaze was no longer on her.

She would have felt dumb about her fear if not for the ache in her back and arms, proof her wariness had not been unwarranted. It was doubtful that Claire had expected anything like it to happen, but Daphne could not help feeling a little resentful. Surely the psychic could have warned her, or at least explained the nature of the Veil more. But Daphne had walked in blind, left to figure it out for herself. The throbbing in her arms where she had broken her fall added fuel to the feeling.

A flash of white on the side of the road put it on pause. With a jolt of excitement at what the cross might be for, Daphne instinctively slammed on the brakes. She had missed the marker on the way to the bridge, but coming from the other side, there was no mistaking it, the only indication that something had happened at that spot. Exiting her car, she quietly stepped toward it.

A well-made cross painted white stood a little crookedly in

the grass. Daphne knelt to read the words engraved into the wood. It was with a strange, reluctant triumph that she read the name *Heather Grey*. The site of the nightmare ended here.

Daphne looked around, attempting to feel some recognition but without success. Even the memorial felt distant from her, as if it were for a stranger and not someone whose final moments she had watched a hundred times.

Underneath Heather's name, in smaller letters, was *Psalm 23*. Maybe it had been a favorite, or more likely it had been chosen as a common verse for such an occasion. *Though I walk through the valley of the shadow of death, I will fear no evil...*

Objects were scattered at the base. Underneath the bouquet of fake violet flowers was a beanie lizard, ragged from rain and sun, and a scattering of smooth stones. Daphne caught a glimpse of writing and picked one up, feeling slightly guilty at disturbing the memorial. The name *Nathan* was written artistically in paint. Who had he been? *Who is he*, Daphne reminded herself, trying to recall the long list of names from the obituary. The rocks were proof: somewhere in Long Haven, a family was mourning.

She gently returned the rock to its spot, next to *Noah* and *Mom&Dad* and a scattering of other names. Heather, in a way, had not been the sole victim of the dyszoon's attack. Maybe there were friends represented here, other family, a boyfriend.

Daphne again wondered what Heather had been like, beyond the brief, violent glimpse in her nightmare. All she knew were facts, and facts did not make a person. Heather was, or had been, a year older and a recent graduate. A summer that was no doubt full of expectation for a bright future had instead been brought to a crushing halt. Daphne saw the shadowy forms of an imagined family. Would it be better for them, knowing the truth of how Heather died? That it hadn't been her fault?

Her neck prickled as if in warning. A gust of violent wind blew leaves around her feet as she stood warily.

Someone, or something, was in the woods.

Though not sure how she knew, Daphne felt a presence like a caress at the edge of her mind, as certain a sign someone was there as the snap of a twig. The desire to leave was her first instinct, to avoid the presence, which did not feel like a living human and probably wasn't.

She glanced at the memorial, struck by an idea. If the Veil was visible to her now, that must mean other things were too. The presence...What if that was a shade, the last ghostly remnant of Heather herself, haunting the place of her death?

The thought chilled her. Daphne didn't want to see shades, especially one in the form of Heather. But the moment would have to come anyway. Claire had mentioned they were every-where. They could not be avoided, so she would not try.

Daphne swallowed once, then walked with determination into the woods. She wove around the trees, not following any particular path across the dead leaves. If there was a shade in the woods, she would meet it now rather than later.

The edge of the woods vanished. Daphne had wandered in farther than she'd intended, lured by her curiosity and the sense of something close. The woods felt different during the day. It was gloomy underneath the cloudy light. She stopped and looked over her shoulder uneasily. The presence was nearby, but where was the shade?

"Is anyone there?" she called. The sound stuck close to her, as if it, too, were afraid of moving forward. "Hello?"

Daphne steeled herself and started walking again. There was a large tree root sticking out of the ground that acted like a step down a small hill. If only her perception were more devel-oped, Daphne thought as she stepped over it, she could prob-ably pinpoint—

The ground underneath her step exploded.

For the second time that day, Daphne was thrown backward. Something small and dark rebelled against her descending foot and shot into the air with an ear-piercing shriek. Dirt showered over her. As she lay on the ground, Daphne's mind felt sluggish, her thoughts full of fog. Through the disorientation, however, she registered an important detail—

The thing was coming back.

Daphne rolled out of the way just in time for the ground to explode again where her head had rested. Her shriek matched the creature's as she leapt to her feet and stumbled away. The thing had flown off, darting like a pinball about the trees.

She needed help. Blindly, Daphne felt into her jacket pockets for her phone and came up short—she had left it on the front seat of her car.

Her car. Wildly, a plan formed: she could get to her car, drive for Claire, and come back later to defeat...whatever it was. Daphne didn't want to say its name. It could not be. Claire had said she'd banished it.

Daphne took a step in what she hoped was the direction of the road. The tinny shriek became louder, and she dived away just in time. The trunk of a nearby tree was partially shorn off in an explosion of wood as the dyszoon tore through it, and Daphne stumbled to get out of the way, tripping backward onto the ground. The small mass approached from above. There was no time to think—

She threw up her hands to protect her face. Like a bird hitting a window, the creature bounced off an invisible barrier, screaming in violent rage. Stunned, Daphne could not move her hands, even as it returned for another attack.

The dyszoon pounded into the barrier, a shapeless mass of black spreading itself like smoke over glass, its shrieks of rage piercing her ears as it was repelled again and again. Terror held all her limbs in ice, and Daphne didn't know what she had created, or how, but knew with a horrible certainty it was perhaps the only thing between herself and death.

For the thing wanted her dead. Daphne could feel that the dyszoon hated her with a fervor that was like an entity in itself, an invisible poison that strengthened the hopelessness spreading through her like cancer, a small voice whispering the futility of fighting.

The shapeless creature pelted itself once more into the barrier and then seemed to give up, bolting away with another ear-piercing scream of frustration, out of sight above the trees. Daphne lay frozen on the ground. Her hands were still lifted protectively in front of her. She flexed them once and then stood, her legs rubber. She didn't know where the dyszoon had gone but could sense it was out there, it was close—

Daphne spun around to a blur of black. Pain exploded in her left shoulder as the creature struck it with tremendous force, almost knocking her to the ground. She screamed at the lightning pain that exploded in the spot and fell sideways against a tree. The dyszoon flew away and out of sight.

As quickly as the pain had come, the worst passed. Gritting her teeth, Daphne gingerly moved the joint. Somehow it was not broken, though it throbbed horribly. It seemed the dyszoon could not harm her like it could the tree. Daphne absorbed this fact in the precious few seconds given to her before she turned her attention to sensing where the dyszoon was.

A heavy tree limb in her line of vision tore off cleanly with a sound like a gunshot.

The dyszoon flew straight for her. Daphne knew she must deflect it again, but to her horror realized that she had no idea how. Her mind blanked as she took a step back, her shoe hooking on a hidden root.

The trees tilted. Daphne threw out her arms in a vain attempt to protect herself just as the dyszoon approached—

Like glass being hit by an ax, the dyszoon shattered into black sand. The cloud suspended bizarrely over her, then fell, vanishing into nothingness.

A renewed calm returned to the woods. The presence was gone. Daphne lay still, branches swaying above to match the swirling in her head. Then, she rolled to her side and retched. Nothing came up. When the urge passed, Daphne lay down again. Every limb had turned useless.

After several minutes, Daphne forced herself to stand, feeling still like she might become sick, and brushed off the leaves and dirt clinging to her. The tree that had been partially shorn was nearby. She limped over to it.

The bark was stripped off. Daphne placed a hand on the raw wood with a sense of disbelief, even as she touched the carnage. What disturbed her more was the branch. Slowly, she made her way to it, glad to feel a little strength returning to her legs as she crouched down beside it and fingered the splintered end where the dyszoon had torn it off. That would have taken enormous strength.

In the back of her mind, the crash of metal echoed. And yet, the dyszoon had not been able to do the same damage to her shoulder as it had to Heather's car. Why?

The more pressing concern was that a dyszoon had been roaming the woods. If it was the same one that killed Heather, had Claire been mistaken, when she thought she'd defeated it?

Unlikely, Daphne thought, noting the empty stillness that had fallen over the woods after the battle. Claire couldn't have walked away without feeling the dyszoon's presence. So did that mean this one had come out of the Veil more recently?

And how, exactly, had Daphne managed to defeat it?

8

THE CEMETERY

Early on Saturday morning, exactly one week from their first meeting, Daphne drove to a cemetery located on the outskirts of town to meet with Claire again.

There was a strange familiarity, like reenacting a memory, as she passed the redbrick pillars at the entrance underneath a metal arch that read "Long Haven Cemetery." She drove up a long asphalt lane into an expansive sea of headstones. Spotting a solitary red car far ahead, Daphne pulled up behind it.

Painful memories were reawakening at her return. Daphne hadn't confided in Claire when they scheduled the meeting, but her dad was buried somewhere on the right, underneath a slab of granite with a death dating back four years ago. The silver owl bracelet gleamed on her wrist. She hadn't set foot in the cemetery since the funeral.

Daphne exited the car rather stiffly. A brilliant blue-and-yellow bruise had blossomed across her left shoulder, but it was hidden underneath her shirt.

In the day since the dyszoon attack, Daphne had managed to regain a sense of calm. She wasn't dead, anyway. Perspective.

Although, in the hour before finally falling asleep, she had relived the short battle and embellished the creature to make it scarier than it was: like an overlarge bat or a black comet. It was difficult to believe it had once been human.

Daphne squinted against the light, which was bright despite the cloudy sky, and slammed the car door shut. Anticipation tingled in her stomach. Claire hadn't said why she wanted to meet here, but given the location, Daphne was sure she was about to see a ghost. Also, Claire was not yet aware of the second dyszoon attack. That news would have to be related.

Daphne looked around briefly, taking in the scene. Though she avoided cemeteries, she admitted there was still a tranquility in the neat rows of stone, shaded here and there by trees that were just beginning to turn color.

She spotted Claire walking slowly along a row near the path with her hands clasped behind her back, reading a gravestone with interest before passing on to the next one. A vivid memory intruded on Daphne's mind of her father's urn being placed into the dirt before a similar auburn gravestone. A firefighter turned to ash.

Daphne shook those memories away and approached Claire, who looked up. It was strange to see her outside the studio. She had exchanged her sparkly rock necklace for a large jade stone and dark chiffon shirt. Oddly, the color worked well with her curly red hair.

"Hello, Daphne," Claire said. "I'm glad you could make it. I hope it's not too strange a place to meet."

"It's fine," Daphne answered. "Though my mom's the one who likes cemeteries." Realizing the strangeness of that statement, she quickly added, "She uses them for research, sometimes." Briefly, she wondered what her mom would say about the truth of where she was and made a guilty mental note to keep quiet about it.

"A friend of mine likes cemeteries. Is your mother a professor?"

Daphne hesitated. She didn't know Claire well, and she felt reluctant to reveal too much. "Librarian. But she helps with the archives, and she's in the historical society, and she also writes the history column for the newspaper." She stopped abruptly. Her nervousness was making her ramble.

"Oh! Your mother is Laura Cole?" Claire said, comprehension flashing across her face.

"Yes," Daphne said, taken aback that Claire had made the connection. Fewer people than ever subscribed to the print newspaper, but then she recalled the articles were also posted online.

"Well, tell her I enjoy her articles," said Claire.

Daphne tilted her head noncommittally and said nothing, instead glancing around the empty grounds.

"So, did you manage to see the Veil?" Claire asked.

"Yes," Daphne answered, turning to face her. Adding *and I got attacked by a dyszoon* seemed too abrupt, somehow. "It wasn't really what I thought it would look like."

"No, it doesn't look very significant, does it?" Claire stepped off the grass, which needed cutting, and started walking up the patched road farther into the cemetery. Daphne strode quickly to catch up, relieved that they were heading in the opposite direction from her father's grave, which she remembered was near a tilted white obelisk.

There was still the incident with the Veil to talk about. Daphne decided to break the lesser news first. "Something happened when I saw it. It was like it drew me in, and I tried to touch it. Then it threw me."

Claire looked at her, stopping abruptly. "The Veil *threw* you? Is that why you're limping?"

"Was I?" Daphne said in surprise. She hadn't thought it was noticeable.

"Are you all right?"

Seeing the psychic's worried face, Daphne felt the last of her resentment fade away. Claire obviously hadn't known what dangers the Veil would pose. "I'm fine," she said, shrugging. "Just bruised."

The psychic observed her closely, then said, "I knew the Veil was magnetic, but I never suspected it would draw you in like that. I'm used to it myself, but I imagine to someone who's never seen it before—"

"It's fine," Daphne said hastily. "Really."

They resumed walking, Claire in troubled silence. More to postpone the moment she'd have to awkwardly broach the subject of the dyszoon attack, Daphne spoke first. "Why are we here?" she asked. "Is Heather buried here?"

"I don't know if she is, actually," Claire said. "But there's someone I want you to meet."

"Are we here to see shades?" Daphne jogged a little to keep up with the psychic's brisk pace.

"Yes, but there's just one in here."

"There's only one shade?" Daphne said in surprise.

"Yes." Claire smiled. "Cemeteries aren't the great haunting you might expect. People rarely die in them, or feel very attached to them."

"Oh." Daphne screwed up her courage, giving the sleeve of her thin gray sweater a nervous tug. "Claire, there's something else I need to tell you too. When I went out to see the Veil, I... sensed there was something in the woods, so I went to see, and then I was—*attacked!*"

Daphne hadn't meant to say it so bluntly. But her foot had just sunk into an unnoticed pothole, and she wobbled and only just stopped herself from falling over. She'd had enough of that.

Claire stopped abruptly. "What? You were attacked?"

"I debated whether or not I should call you," Daphne said, bending over to massage her ankle, adding it to her growing list of injuries. "But I thought maybe I'd better wait until meeting you in person—"

"Daphne, tell me what happened." Claire looked especially grave as she listened to a short account of the way Daphne had investigated the strange noise in the woods and then tried and failed to fight off the dyszoon before accidentally managing to banish it.

"And I threw up my arms to block it, and I felt like I had managed to hit it, but without even touching it. And then it was gone."

Claire didn't speak for a moment. Her brow was furrowed in thought, mouth tightly pressed as she weighed this new information. Daphne, however, felt like a weight had been lifted. She'd been dying to confide in someone about what had happened. Withholding such an important development in her life from her mother, whom she usually could talk to about practically anything, had had a price.

"Could you have been wrong when you thought you banished the dyszoon?" Daphne suggested.

"No," Claire said distractedly. "No...it definitely was gone..."

"Could it have gone through the Veil again?"

"That wouldn't be possible. The Veil's not opened enough right now. It would have needed to be held open like last time—but I would have felt it."

"So the opening in August," Daphne broke in. "That wasn't permanent?"

"No," Claire said, brow still furrowed. "I believe that was only a test. Whoever tried to expand it will continue to work on strengthening their connection to the Veil before trying again, perhaps to make it permanent next time."

Daphne watched the psychic think, unsure what to do. No helpful ideas came to her.

"Unless..." Claire said distantly. "Unless *two* came out together, and *both* attacked the car."

"You mean there might have been another dyszoon?"

"I never sensed a second one after the first one came out. Therefore, I assumed there was only one. But perhaps, if they came out at the same time—"

"You wouldn't be able to tell how many came out," Daphne finished.

"Exactly." Claire looked around and appeared to spot what she wanted, for she stepped off the road and started to journey into the headstones.

"How do you think mine held on for a month and a half?" Daphne asked as she followed, something like respect growing in her for the psychic. Now that she had actually faced the creature herself, Daphne knew how much bravery it would have taken for Claire to willingly confront it without having faced one before. "I thought you said the dyszoon would have disappeared on its own eventually if you hadn't banished it."

"Eventually, yes. But I never knew how long."

Daphne looked at Claire in surprise. She'd been under the impression that Claire knew everything, could answer every question about the world Daphne was slowly entering. Apparently, this was not the case.

"So maybe they both attacked the car, then one wandered away far enough that I couldn't perceive it. It would have been too weak to travel very far..." Claire was rambling distractedly by now. "And if it just stayed in the woods quietly, then perhaps it would have enough energy for one last...I'm so sorry, Daphne."

"You don't have to apologize," Daphne said, touched. "It wasn't your fault. I fought it and survived."

"Yes. And that's an achievement in itself."

Daphne knew that Claire was talking about the battle, not the surviving, although in her opinion, that was a good thing as well.

"So. How did it go?" Claire asked.

Daphne explained the particulars of the battle, her clumsy attempts to avoid it, and her accidental success. At the mention of the dyszoon's hit, Claire's eyes flashed in alarm.

"It's fine," Daphne said, rolling her shoulder. "Just a bruise. It doesn't hurt unless I press it." She decided not to mention the soreness in the rest of her body.

They wove around headstones, some decorated with flowers or a tiny American flag, others with personal items that reminded Daphne of Heather's roadside memorial.

"I'm glad, in any case, that it wasn't a fully formed dyszoon," Claire commented. "Both of ours were weak."

"It didn't seem very weak," Daphne mumbled, remembering the crack of the tree branch. The memory of the dyszoon's hate lingered like poison over her skin, but she did not bring it up. Out of all her impressions, this one stood out the most vividly. It had hated her with all its being. Hated her for existing.

"In a manner of speaking. Anything stronger might have been too much for you to fend off at this point, or it could have caused greater damage."

"Why didn't it? It cut off a tree branch. I should have a broken arm."

"Rules of engagement," Claire said thoughtfully. "It seems dyszoons can't touch humans in the same way as nonhuman. Plus, it was severely under-formed, so it couldn't do as much direct damage."

Daphne nodded. "And how was I able to fight it?"

"As you discovered—earlier than I intended you to—dyszoons can only be banished with a mental strike of sorts, rather than a weapon," Claire explained, tilting her head slightly. "I've had to push away some bothersome shades, and I had guessed the same principle could be used on the dyszoon I encountered. I suppose you could call your shield a longer version of that hit."

"But how did I do it?" Daphne looked down at her fingers as if they held the answer.

"Instinct. Just as you're beginning to perceive things without conscious thought, you can accomplish things without knowing how you did so. As your perception becomes stronger, you may find the answer. It's not something I can teach—or honestly know much about, myself." They walked several yards up the path before Claire spoke again. "Well, there's nothing for it now. We're one for one, Daphne, though the time may come when you surpass me."

They continued walking in silence. Daphne followed Claire unconsciously, for her mind was drifting into deep thought. Truthfully, she hadn't dwelled much on the practical side of perceiving. Fighting dyszoons—on purpose—seemed to belong to a distant future she couldn't envision. Her brush with the one yesterday was an accident, never to be repeated.

But Claire had said she needed help. More dyszoons would come out of a passage they did not yet know how to close, and Daphne knew that because she was younger, she wouldn't suffer as serious an injury when she fell, which would likely be often. Her encounter yesterday was proof of how dangerous it was to battle a dyszoon.

Daphne would need to grow in her ability to perceive. Of course, that was why she was meeting Claire in a graveyard. To focus on building up her strength. To prepare for battle.

"She's over there," Claire broke in, stopping to point. "Do you see?"

"What?" Daphne wrenched away from her thoughts. She was surprised to see how far they'd wandered into the cemetery. Their cars were now distant behind them, across a field of granite.

Daphne squinted in the direction of Claire's finger and thought she could make out some faint white mist about a hundred paces away near one of the larger headstones, which was shaped like a Celtic cross. It seemed to hover, shapeless, looking nothing like a "she."

"I think I can see something by the cross," Daphne said, uncertain.

"Hm, let's try and get closer."

Completely unafraid, Claire navigated purposefully through the headstones toward the strange mist. Daphne hesitated a moment and then followed. Truthfully, she'd been happy to keep her distance.

They walked until the mist was mere feet away, tall as a person and separated from them by only two rows of headstones. Daphne stopped, feeling a stab of fear. Of course, she had known this was coming, but it was quite another thing to have it arrive at last. She was going to see a shade.

"Is it moving?" she asked, trying to sound casual.

The white mist had drifted and then paused a few feet away, as if contemplating them.

"Yes, she's looking to see what we're doing," said Claire. "How much can you see of her?"

"A white mist, that's all."

"Really? Couldn't you see the Veil?"

"Yes, but it took a few minutes," Daphne said, defensive. Perceiving was still difficult, and Claire was expecting too much of her. Hadn't she just defeated a dyszoon on her own?

"No matter," Claire said, and Daphne felt soothed. "Those were different circumstances. Maybe the Veil is a stronger presence."

Claire looked from the mist, which hadn't moved again, to Daphne, who tried quickly to hide her apprehension. She didn't need to be afraid. It was just a dead person.

"Perhaps it would be easiest to do what you did with the Veil. If you try too hard to use your physical sight, it makes it harder to perceive."

"Okay." Daphne closed her eyes, but reluctantly. She'd felt safer keeping an eye on the mist. Even without seeing it, though, she thought she could feel its faint presence. It was like sensing another person in a dark room.

Feeling Claire's eyes as well, Daphne concentrated on the sounds around her. Her hearing gradually sharpened to the sounds of distant birds, every passing car.

After a minute, Daphne opened her eyes again. The white mist had not moved. More importantly, it was still a mist.

"Can you see her?" Claire asked, flicking her eyes between Daphne and the shade.

"No," Daphne said baldly.

"Try again."

Impatiently, Daphne closed her eyes again. But it was actually relaxing, she had to admit as her heartbeat slowed, doing what basically amounted to meditation. Her heart beat faster again as she began to discern the faint presence growing stronger. Daphne opened her eyes—

"Why can't I do it?" she exclaimed in frustration. The shade was still a mist, though a hopeful part of her thought maybe it was denser than it had been. "I'm sorry."

Claire seemed to be contemplating something.

"Yes..." the psychic said to herself. "Perhaps that would be the best way."

Daphne waited, arms crossed, feeling angry with herself and looking at the mist helplessly. Why was it so hard? She'd done it before, albeit in special circumstances. How long was it going to take?

Claire walked up to her. "Hold out your left arm," she ordered, offering her own.

"What are you going to do?" Daphne asked warily.

"I'm going to help you. Roll up your sleeve."

Daphne inched back her sleeve and lifted her arm toward Claire like they were about to shake hands.

"Show me your forearm."

"Okay..." Daphne turned it over. Now it looked like she was expecting Claire to give her something. "So what—?"

Claire did not stop to explain, but with a purposeful strength, she clasped Daphne's exposed forearm with her right hand.

Immediately, a bolt of energy passed through Daphne's body like an electric shock. It was fire—and power. Daphne felt more aware than she'd ever been in her life, and invincible. If another dyszoon had shown up, defeating it would be laughably easy—

She wrenched her arm away. "What did you *do*?" she gasped, gripping her arm. As quickly as the bolt had come, it was gone—yet some remnant of it remained.

"I transferred some of my energy to you," Claire said calmly. "Just a small amount, to help you perceive. I'm sorry it comes on rather strong."

"You...gave me...your energy?" Daphne panted.

"Think of it as a boost to your perception. It's not permanent, although it *is* rather tiring." Claire's eyes did look less energetic. "I'll be fine after a nap. Now," she continued, businesslike. "Can you see her?"

"Can I see...?"

Daphne straightened up and looked at the white mist—except it wasn't mist anymore. Instead of being on fire, her mind was now numb with shock.

Staring at her mournfully was a woman. She was not transparent, yet there was a softness to her appearance, like a photo just out of focus, that made it seem like she was not fully present. The shade was young, not more than twenty-five, with stringy brown hair reaching all the way to her waist. Her jeans were baggy, and she wore a loose, sixties-style shirt. Looking at her narrow face and dark eyes, Daphne thought the woman was pretty, albeit in a haggard, drawn way, as if she'd skipped too many meals. What looked like tendrils of smoke drifted softly off her body and hair and dissipated into the air.

"She's a...she's a...hippie," Daphne managed to say.

She felt the urge to scream, bolt, or possibly faint. One did not see ghosts, after all, every day. But she made a mental effort to compartmentalize the fear, to force down the part of her that screamed she was seeing something out of the ordinary, possibly dangerous, and she should flee. Instead Daphne gazed at the shade with what she hoped came off as impassive interest. If Claire was not scared, she decided to try not to be either.

"Her name is Robin Whitworth." Claire was acting as if she were showing her nothing more exciting than a name on a tombstone. She obviously had a high opinion of Daphne's nerves, or else was so used to everything the initial fear had been forgotten.

"Wh-When did she die?" This seemed like the next important question.

"1967. September."

"How?" Another important point.

"Overdose. This was a popular spot in the sixties for drugs and such things. Her friends abandoned her when they discovered she was dead—afraid, I suppose, of getting arrested."

The shade—Robin—seemed unmoved by this discussion of her life. She was still staring at them, looking mournful but unconcerned.

"How do you know this?" Accustomed as Daphne was to Claire's general omniscience, she doubted the information was buried in a newspaper archive somewhere.

Claire smiled. "I asked her."

"Shades can talk?"

"Yes." As they watched, the shade of Robin turned away from them as if bored and walked down the row. "But there are several important things to remember about shades. One is they are terrible companions. They are shadows of their living selves, unconcerned about everything except the reason they still remain, and remembering only the basic details of their lives."

"Why do they stay?" Daphne asked, peering down to see whether the shade's sandaled toe floated or touched the ground. Blades of grass poked through Robin's feet, unbent. It was a strange sight.

"There are plenty of spirits that stay behind with unresolved business or emotions before they can allow themselves to continue on, though some stay because they are simply too traumatized by the manner of their death," Claire explained knowledgeably—which she probably was, Daphne reasoned. She had probably seen thousands of shades over her lifetime. "There are different kinds of shades, with different levels of awareness. Most are like Robin, here, but others are unreachable, even with our abilities."

"And we're the only ones who can see them?"

"This clearly, yes. The second thing to remember," Claire added with a nod at Robin, "is that shades will respond to your will. They owe what you might call a rent to the living, for continuing to reside where they do not belong anymore. That is why they will respond to what you say, when you ask it. It's their payment—to assist."

"They'll do what I say?" Daphne said, wondering what on earth one could use a shade for.

"Yes. Try it."

Daphne was alarmed. "But I don't—What do I ask her?"

"Something simple. Shades can still physically touch things. Ask her to pick up something for you."

"O-Okay." Daphne walked toward Robin apprehensively, taking care not to show her limp. The shade had now drifted, and Daphne stopped within a couple feet. The air seemed to get chillier, but Daphne thought this was less to do with the shade than her own fear.

"Robin? Robin?"

The shade turned in midair to face her, expression grave.

Daphne's panic increased, but she forced it down. "Would you mind...grabbing those flowers there?" She pointed at a small nest of fake flowers leaning against a gray headstone.

Robin didn't speak but looked where Daphne was pointing. Slowly, she walked toward the headstone and bent down, light hair falling around her shoulders. The shade's misting fingers grabbed the arrangement and tried to lift it, but the flowers only nudged a small amount. She tried again patiently.

Daphne hurried forward, feeling guilty. "That's okay... Robin. You can leave them there."

The shade straightened and looked at Daphne impassively with dark eyes. Mist rose off her shoulders, but it was startling how alive she seemed. Frightened by their closeness, Daphne backed away, almost tripping over a headstone, and hurried back to Claire.

"She couldn't move it," she said, not able to keep a slight note of accusation out of her voice. Claire had surely known that would happen.

"No," Claire said, smiling, hands clasped. "Shades can touch physical objects but can't move them well."

Daphne looked at the shade again. "Like in ghost stories."

"Exactly. It doesn't take a perceiver to realize something has moved on its own, even if they can't see what's causing it."

The broken tree branch flashed in Daphne's mind. "So dyszoons can move things, but shades can't?"

"Dyszoons are more like creatures," Claire reminded her. "Shades are barely present."

They watched Robin sidle listlessly down the row, no doubt as she had done for decades. Daphne was struck by a sadness she didn't quite understand. Only she felt it would be a terrible thing, to be so troubled as to remain behind. To forgo bliss, when it had been within reach.

"Is there a way we can help them?" Daphne asked solemnly. "You know, to move on?"

Claire smiled, but wryly. "Sometimes, but in most cases what's keeping them on Earth can't be solved, because those reasons have long passed and are now out of reach. Much pain could be avoided had they learned to let go of the things of the past and moved on from them." Claire nodded toward Robin. "But here they are."

Robin had stopped again. For the first time, Daphne's stronger emotion was pity, not fear. Had the shade stayed behind because she was traumatized by the sudden end of her young life? Or was it something more complex?

As if she knew what was going on in Daphne's head, Claire said, "I should warn you, Daphne. I understand the desire to want to help shades, but doing so is trickier than you might imagine. Whatever feeling keeps them on Earth is strong, and it won't have a simple remedy. In most cases, it's impossible. Even if there is a way to help them, it's best to leave them alone."

"Have you ever tried to help them?"

Something like bitterness pursed the psychic's mouth. "Yes, I have," Claire said, sounding almost sharp. "But in every case, it was better left alone."

Daphne did not press the matter further. She understood, vaguely, what Claire meant. But what was the purpose of perceiving, if not to use the ability to help the things they could see were in distress? Was Daphne's power to be used only to battle dyszoons?

Claire yawned. The act of transference, giving away some of her energy, seemed to have tired her out.

"I think this will be all for today. Once the transfer wears off, you'll find it difficult to see shades again, but I hope it will give you a start."

"So you want me to practice?" Daphne interrupted. She wondered what Claire's helping hand had done, and if she would see more shades—wherever they were.

"There are plenty of shades around Long Haven, in places you might not expect," said Claire. "Practice seeing them until you can do so clearly. That's my new homework for you."

"And the better I can see them," Daphne said, watching Robin walk aimlessly down the row, "the better I'll be at fighting dyszoons?"

"Yes, because the better you see, the stronger your perception will be overall. Eventually, perceiving shades will take no effort—sooner than you might expect. In the meantime, we'll pray the Veil stays as it is for a while." Claire yawned again. "Now, I think I'll go home and take a nap before I open, to get some of that energy back."

They navigated their way back through the headstones. Claire began to chat about ordinary things. Daphne, as she listened, could not help but glance in the direction of her father's gravestone. Someday she would be able to visit it, but not today.

She had not told Claire her father was in the cemetery. Their relationship so far had been built almost exclusively on the task set for Daphne. Despite this fact, she was beginning to feel a bond with the shrewd and intelligent woman next to her, however much she disapproved of her profession.

Daphne looked back at the shade once more. Robin was staring after them, watching them go. Again, a strange sadness welled up inside her. No matter what Claire had warned about shades, there was a part of Daphne that felt a sense of duty to them. To help them, just as they were bound to help her.

9

OLD HAUNTS

In the darkness, Daphne spotted her.

Standing directly underneath the curious pupil in the sky was a young woman in a white nightdress, like a pale phantom in the night. A long, brown braid lay over one shoulder. What Daphne could see of her shadowy face was blank, devoid of expression, and yet somehow menacing.

The woman slowly lifted a hand and beckoned with a finger.

Come...come to me...

But Daphne did not want to come. Did not want to walk toward this woman, whose strange appearance filled her with dread. Yet it was her duty, for she was responsible. She could have prevented this.

Daphne looked behind her shoulder, paranoid someone would emerge from the shadows, when she wanted to settle this quietly. She turned back. Her lungs turned to ice. The woman's face was no longer cast in shadow but lit with a terrible light, and her nightdress was black as dusk. Its torn cloth flowed around her like snakes.

As Daphne watched in a trance, the woman raised her arms and ensnared Daphne's gaze with a white-eyed stare. The corners of her mouth tugged upward in an evil grin.

It was terrible, and yet it was Daphne's responsibility to save her. She *must* force her feet forward. Her foot took a step, and the asphalt cracked and split. Daphne was conscious of laughter, but it came from deep within the earth, harsh as spiked steel. The woman stood there, silent, as everything tilted, and Daphne stumbled and fell forward into darkness—

She landed face-forward against a solid floor. A crackling sound filled the air. Fire engulfed the walls of the small room, and yet there was no smoke. A flaming beam fell through the eaten floorboards above and crashed inches from her head with a heart-stopping bang, showering the cement floor with sparks. Daphne gasped at the near miss and looked up at the figure looming over her.

A man was standing there, wearing charred black rags and observing her with what was left of his burned and blistered face. He wore a black-rimmed hat that hid most of his burnt hair. Soot filled every crevice of his skin, caked into the linings of his fingernails.

"Daph-ne," he coughed. Ashy smoke billowed from his mouth. Behind him, part of the wall collapsed. The pieces smoldered on the floor.

"Dad!" she shouted over the crackling flames, scrambling to her feet with difficulty. Her body was heavy. So heavy.

"Help me." He took a shuffling step toward her, kicking the still-flaming beam. Sparks flew. The heat shivered between them like a shield. "Help me!"

"I can't," she rasped. The heat was oppressive. "You know I can't."

"Help me, Daphne!" he cried more earnestly, stepping clumsily over the beam. She took a heavy step back but stopped as the man doubled over and coughed into his fist, blackening it with soot.

"*I can't!*" Daphne shouted, watching in horror as he wrenched his other leg over the beam and limped toward her against a backdrop of fire, one hand raised in desperation, the other clutching his stomach.

"Please! Help me!" he begged. His skin began to blacken and flake away, and Daphne felt her heart do the same. She could not save him.

"I—"

"HELP ME!" he screamed.

"*I can't!*" A sob shuddered through her. Daphne was now moving backward as fast as her leaden body would allow. "I'm sorry! Dad, I'm so sorry!" Her back hit the wall. Engulfed in its flame, she was frozen there, powerless to move from the enemy's embrace, as the figure before her collapsed to his knees, holding his disintegrating face and screaming in agony while sobs of *I'm sorry, I'm sorry* became just another crackle in the fire—

Daphne awoke still shouting.

"I'm sorr—!"

The final apology reverberated in the silent bedroom and extinguished in a hiss. Her breaths came heavy; she was gasping in the newly present oxygen, eyes confused by the darkness, when the room she'd just left had been so bright with flame.

Slowly, her breathing steadied. It had been a nightmare, Daphne realized, cool air brushing against her damp face. One that hadn't haunted her for at least a year.

Understanding was a relief. The nightmare wasn't real. Its rules no longer applied. Daphne rubbed her forehead, feeling thirteen again. Of course it wasn't real. That wasn't how he had died, or even where.

Daphne glanced toward the door, hoping fervently her mom hadn't woken up. Even if she had, her mom had kept to her promise to not come running, a habit conditioned by years.

Lying still was impossible. Daphne dressed silently by lamplight, then tiptoed down the hall. A pause outside her mother's closed bedroom door revealed she still slept soundly. Daphne, relieved, stole quietly down the wooden stairs, avoiding the knots that groaned, and walked into the kitchen.

Her routine was automatic by this point. Once the electric kettle bubbled, Daphne poured hot water into a silver thermos with a black tea bag. It was the most caffeine she ever allowed herself, otherwise her nightmares would be even worse. In another minute, she slipped into her rain boots and a dark coat and exited the silent house.

The early Sunday air was cool, peaceful. Something tight within her chest loosened as she crossed the yard purposefully and entered the woods to the sound of crickets, the soft rustle of leaves. Daphne directed the beam from her flashlight while her other hand clutched the thermos. The spice-scented steam was soothing.

Daphne slowed to a slight pace, stepping carefully over dips in the ground and fallen branches. As she'd hoped, the fog of the nightmare was giving way to cold sense. The dream was an old one. No doubt her visit to the cemetery for the first time in years had triggered it somehow.

She moved along aimlessly, not following any particular path, only the light, as she wove deeper into the woods. After several minutes, a faint touch like a finger caressed the edge of her mind. Daphne stopped abruptly and directed the flashlight beam to the left.

A young boy stood several paces away, one hand clutching

a tree as he gazed at her curiously, unaffected by the light. His image swung between faint and solid, mist rising and curling slowly off his body like the thin steam from her thermos. He wore overalls, a tiny fringe of dark hair carelessly swept across his small forehead. Daphne opened her mouth to speak, then—

He turned and fled.

"Wait—stop—" she began, but the boy had vanished through the trees. Daphne dropped her tea and hurried after him.

There was a small break in the trees, and the boy ran to where a man was standing. At a glance, Daphne knew immediately he was also a shade, even before she noticed the mist rising off his shoulders or that he, too, drifted in and out of focus, solid and then transparent. She slowed to a stop a comfortable distance away as the boy reached the man's side and turned around to face her.

Somehow they were not mere mist. Although Robin from the cemetery had appeared clear, not faded, Daphne acknowledged the progress she'd made. Apparently, Claire was right about the effects of her energy transfer, although Daphne did not feel any different. Just more receptive. Willing.

It was with surprise that Daphne realized she did not feel any fear, only a familiar, strange sadness, as she took in the youthfulness of them both. All the shades she'd seen so far had been young.

At her click, the flashlight went out. Darkness filled the corners of the woods once more.

Even without light, the shades were visible, glowing with the faintest silver like a moon, just enough for Daphne to see the man's features. He was tall and very thin, wearing a simple but filthy shirt only half tucked into his pants. Dirt smudged his face. Unkempt, wheat-colored hair hung almost down to his shoulders. Daphne noticed he wore no shoes.

Maybe they had died nearby, she guessed, or perhaps they had sought refuge in the woods once their haunts had been swept away by time, seeking the peaceful feeling she found underneath its branches. The shades continued to cycle, fading and solidifying with the timing of a gentle wave.

"How did you die?" Daphne asked softly, voicing aloud the first thought that had come from looking at the boy. He was the one who troubled her the most.

His voice was high and childlike. "I got run o'er by the tractor." He did not seem disturbed by this fact.

"That's..." Daphne was at a loss what to say. Claire was right about shade relations being complicated. They didn't seem to require a response, or sympathy. She settled for an apology.

Daphne wondered where the boy's family had farmed, and when. There were any number of farms around Long Haven. Was she right in thinking the boy had moved here with the times? Long Haven was a growing community. Maybe his family's farm was now underneath a parking lot.

Another wave of melancholy swept over her. Daphne found she could talk to the boy no further and turned her attention to the tall shade. Despite his appearance, he seemed approachable.

"What's your name?" Daphne said to him, deciding to start with a more conventional question.

A long pause. "Frank."

"How...did you die?"

As if in answer, his appearance flickered. Blood was splattered down the front of his ripped shirt. Bruises blossomed over his exposed arms and blackened both eyes, one swelling shut. The knuckles on both hands were violently split apart. Daphne stepped back, her heart thundering wildly.

"I was murdered," he said calmly. In another moment, the bruises faded, and he appeared normal again.

Daphne stared. She hadn't realized shades could change their appearance, and was glad she could not perceive well enough yet to make the image any more graphic. Her heart raced, and she hoped the boy would not show his death injuries as well.

It was too much to take in. Abruptly, Daphne left the two shades and walked away in a half-trance, pausing only to pick up the dropped thermos. She reached a damp log and sat down weakly.

There was more to her ability than she knew. Perceiving meant seeing not only shades themselves but also traces of their story, their pain. They were quiet shadows, wisps on the earth, and still they were human: their stories made them so. Daphne clutched her thermos tightly. The reality of that knowledge, of what she could now see...She was not prepared.

There was guilt. She hadn't bothered to find out the boy's name, or even asked if she could help them. However, that was exactly what Claire had warned her against. Helping shades was difficult, most likely impossible. Given their old-fashioned appearance, no doubt what was keeping them on Earth, in the realm of the living, was long ago and therefore out of reach of remedy. Claire had said as much.

But as she stood up again, the terror of her nightmare momentarily chased away, Daphne could not shake the image of the man and child wandering forever in the dark and cold of the woods.

It wasn't until six that Daphne made her way back to the house. A light was visible through the windows. As a morning person, her mom got up early even on Sundays.

She opened the front door and stepped inside the entry-way, wary but determined.

"Hi, Daphne!" her mom called from the living room. Daphne shook her boots onto the ratty entryway rug and walked toward the sound. Her mom's blonde head was visible above the armchair in the lamplight, facing toward the empty fireplace. Coffee steamed near her elbow. Mystique lay contentedly on the armrest.

"Mom? Are you busy?" Daphne said, indecisive. If her mom hadn't woken up when she called out, maybe it would be best to forget it all.

"I'm booked," her mom said, holding up the historical romance novel she was reading. She shifted around in her armchair to look over the top of black-rimmed reading glasses at her daughter. "What's up?"

Daphne sat down on the couch, playing for time. Her finger traced over the textured owl on her bracelet. "Did I wake you last night?" she asked as a way of opening, staring at the steam rising from the coffee mug, so like the kind that rose from shades.

"Nope." Daphne felt rather than saw her inquiring look. "Why?"

"It's just, I..." The moment stretched on tenterhooks. *I had the nightmare again.* It would be so easy to confide. And yet the look on her mom's face, as if some theory was being confirmed, was more than Daphne could deal with. "I know I called out, is all," she finished.

She stood up to go, stretching over to give Mystique a quick scratch to cover the awkwardness. The resolve of a week ago to keep quiet about her nightmares had reared its head again, the desire to shield her mother from the worry of knowing *that* nightmare had reappeared, after its long absence. Also, Daphne wasn't sure she could face bringing up a past that was painful for both of them. She'd put her mom through enough.

Her mom's expression was steadily growing serious. "Are you sure you're feeling okay?"

"Yeah," Daphne said, faking brightness as she walked away. "I'm fine."

"All right," her mom said with a sharp look, and Daphne did not see her return to her book as she exited the living room and bolted up the stairs two at a time. She should have said nothing...

Her foot hit the landing. Daphne looked down the hall, heart skipping a beat. Something had moved, she was sure of it. But had it just been her moving reflection in the mirror at the end of the hall?

Still, nothing was there. Daphne paused warily a moment longer and then moved on, hoping to have half an hour in which she might rest without ghosts.

10

THE GHOST IN THE HALLWAY

Daphne pulled out of the driveway the next morning with some anticipation.

She had met two shades just around her own house. If her ability to perceive shades was improving, what kind of changed world was she headed toward?

Oddly enough, the prospect of coming across more shades was not as frightening as it had been just a few days ago, especially since the encounter with the two shades in the woods. Judging by the nonchalant way Claire spoke about shades, Daphne assumed perceiving them was something she could get used to with time.

The sky was patchy, casting gloomy light on the passing fields. Daphne glanced around for any person that was out of place.

Fortunately, the nightmare in the burning room had not returned last night. She hoped fervently that its appearance on Saturday night was just a fluke and the dream would never return. Though hardly better, Daphne knew she would take Heather's final moments over his any night, even in those terrible moments upon waking when the dream still enveloped her mind. He had been able to help with that, once, but that comforting embrace was now ash under stone.

A lone figure drew her eye.

A woman wearing a high-collared work dress stood in the field on the left. As the car drew level, Daphne looked into the woman's hard stare, at the grim lines set into her face and gathered at the corners of her mouth. Loose strands of lifeless brown hair flew alongside gentle tendrils of smoke off the woman's shoulders. A tremor traveled along Daphne's arms. With effort, her eyes wrenched away and floated down to the scythe resting casually in the shade's hands. Red stained the curved blade.

Daphne craned her neck to keep looking as she passed, uncertain whether she was actually seeing properly, but the woman was now past her window. The encounter had lasted only a few seconds. Out of necessity, she turned her attention back to the road.

Just in time to see the man standing in front of her car.

Daphne screamed and jerked the wheel to the left, knowing at the same moment it was too late to avoid hitting him. Instinctively, she closed her eyes and braced for the thump of metal on flesh. A moment later, she forced them open. The car shuddered to a stop. Daphne settled back into the seat with a thump.

There was a hammering in her chest, and she could feel where the seat belt had dug into her skin. The expected sound of impact hadn't come. With trembling hands, Daphne unbuckled and fumbled for the door handle, hoping against hope she had somehow missed the man, despite how close he had been to her vehicle.

Daphne stood and anxiously scanned the road behind the car, painted with new black lines from her sudden stop. Not only was there no one in sight, but the woman in the field had vanished too.

The realization hit her all at once. Of course. The man she had hit was a shade.

Only when a passing car honked did Daphne stop staring at the spot where the man would have died, had he been alive. *It was just a shade.* Weakly, Daphne ducked back into the front seat and drove off again, not looking left or right.

"Hey, D—"

"Holy—" Daphne's books tumbled out of her arms onto the backpack hanging in her locker. Hastily, she fell against it to stop them from falling to the floor.

Jessica laughed. "Are you jumpy or what?"

"Sorry." Daphne straightened and gathered the textbooks into her arms, cheeks warm. "Kind of."

"How was your weekend?"

A vivid black blur crashing against her shoulder flashed through Daphne's mind. "Didn't do much. You?"

Jessica shifted her books to her other arm. "Me and Veronica just hung out at her house—"

At this, Daphne felt a pang, though she would rather have faced off against another dyszoon than join them, if invited. Which she had not been. But she listened to Jessica talk as if from a distance, knowing she could not share anything about what had happened with the dyszoon, the Veil, or the growing responsibility she felt.

But it didn't have to be like that *all* the time, Daphne reasoned. Despite being able to see shades everywhere, she didn't have to let the new world she was beginning to perceive affect every part of her life. Next weekend was open, and they could take the opportunity to do something fun without worrying about the Veil or the growing distance between them.

"That's cool. Hey, would you want to do something this—"

"Jessica! Hey, guess what?" Veronica skipped toward them, clutching her books with suppressed glee. Neither noticed Daphne roll her eyes and sigh.

"What?" Jessica answered, matching her excited tone.

Veronica lowered her voice and said giddily, "He added me. Nathan did."

"Oh my gosh!" Jessica squealed. "Really?"

Daphne stared.

"Yes!"

"On his own?"

The grin faded a little. "Well, no, I added him first. But...he accepted almost right away!"

"Oh my gosh, that's so great!" Jessica said. "I'm so happy for you!"

"Thanks!" Veronica giggled again. "I was so excited! I was fanning myself, like—"

Past them, Daphne saw Beth busily hanging up artwork in the display case on the wall outside the art rooms, with the aid of a small cart. Beth always struck her as mature and driven, and she was one of the few people she could talk to without feeling drained by the experience. Unnoticed by either girl beside her, Daphne left them to work out Veronica's chances and approached.

"Hi, Beth, what are you doing?"

Beth turned from the painting she was hanging. "Oh, hey, Daphne. I'm just switching out the artwork for Mr. G."

Daphne looked at the half-empty display case, a mixture of paintings, drawings, pottery, and jewelry. "Are any of these yours?" she asked.

Beth pointed to a copper ring fused with leaves on a small

stand, which Daphne admired. "I made that one. I'm taking Jewelry this semester." She grabbed a pencil drawing off the cart. "Are you in any art classes?"

"Just Photography." Daphne shrugged.

"I've heard that class is fun," Beth said, tacking up the landscape scene with efficiency.

"Yeah," she answered absentmindedly. As Beth lifted the next painting off the pile, Daphne's attention was caught by a vivid flash of red. She recalled Ashley Zhang's busy pen at lunchtime, the portraits of which she sometimes caught a glimpse. Now Ashley's face gazed at a point past her shoulder, expertly drawn in bold, sweeping black lines in the style of a comic character against a billowing background of vivid red. The ink eyebrows were deeply furrowed, the mouth open in an expression of outrage, disgust. Daphne admired the realism as much as she was perturbed by the expression, which seemed to capture the simmering anger sometimes visible beneath Ashley's moody surface.

Without realizing it, Daphne held the drawing up so she was face-to-face with it. The clash of black against red recalled her nightmare of lifeless black trees lit by an eerie crimson sky.

"Daphne? Can I have that one?"

Daphne started, then held it out to Beth. "Oh—yeah, sorry."

Beth filled the last of the space with satisfaction. "It's good, isn't it? It's like a graphic novel."

"That one's Ashley's?" Daphne asked. The glass was shut and locked, containing a little of the drawing's vibrancy.

"Yep, she's really great at portraits. I'm more of a 3D artist, you know. It'd be neat to be part of a real exhibit, sell a few pieces." The first bell rang. Beth took hold of the empty cart. "See you at lunch?"

Daphne smiled, and before the crowd of students could

carry her off, she took a final look at the red portrait. Though she could not have said why, it was a relief to see that anger locked in its cage.

The rest of the day passed uneventfully. Daphne entered the history classroom for seventh period with some wariness, but the shade she had almost seen there did not appear. Nor had she seen it anywhere else.

By the time she arrived at her locker after school, having stayed behind after the final bell to speak with the teacher about an assignment, the hallways had trickled down to a handful of students. Daphne threw materials haphazardly into her backpack and swung the load over her shoulder, cursing the French workbooks that added considerably to its weight. The other shoulder was still too bruised to put the strap around.

Checking her phone, Daphne saw with a leap of anticipation that Claire had left her a message.

She considered what the psychic might want. They had just seen each other Saturday. Could something have happened with the Veil? Maybe another dyszoon had arrived unexpectedly and Daphne would be responsible to stop it—but no, that would be impossible, she reassured herself. Claire had said the Veil was still too small to let any of the creatures through, and in any case, they would sense if it expanded and when the creature arrived. Unless her own senses weren't developed enough yet...

The hallway was empty. Daphne slammed the locker shut, dimly aware of the presence of another person nearby as she lifted the phone to her ear and turned to leave. Briefly she glanced upward, wondering vaguely why the person was standing so still and at the same moment struck by a familiarity.

A sliver of ice traveled to her stomach. The woman's shoulders were edged with rising mist. The shade stood in the middle of the hallway several yards away, watching her silently. Daphne looked closer at the woman's face and froze.

"Hi, Daphne, I was wondering if you would be able to meet this Friday—"

Daphne lowered the phone. Claire's voice finished the message and went silent.

There was no mistaking the girl from her yearbook. The one whose death each night she was powerless to stop.

It was Heather Grey.

Daphne dropped her heavy backpack to the floor and walked closer to the shade. The only emotion that could edge into the shock was surprise—for the calm in her voice as she broke the silence.

"You're Heather," Daphne said.

The shade nodded, impassive.

Daphne stared, at a loss for words. Only a few months ago, Heather had walked through this same hallway, alive. Now here she was, a remnant. Her appearance faded and sharpened, but with less intensity than the shades in the woods. Heather wore the same clothes as she had just before her death: a dark long-sleeved shirt and leggings, with a silver necklace. Eyeliner and mascara emphasized her strikingly large, hazel-green eyes, a bob of heavy black hair framing a heart-shaped face. She was tall, Daphne noticed.

Even though the shade was obviously Heather, Daphne scrambled to fully comprehend that this was the same woman who had sped obliviously toward death in her nightmare. Although Daphne hadn't known the living Heather for comparison, she thought the shade was strangely diminished, a mere shadow of who she had once been. Heather did not smile. Her expression was focused, drawn, as if attempting to work out a difficult problem.

Daphne realized something. "You tried to talk to me before, during class. Why?" Maybe the shade had even tried to get her attention every day, without her knowing.

"I need to help my brother," Heather said. A strong wave of unreality swept over Daphne. Though she could never get Heather's attention in her dream, to warn her, here they were now. Heather's story had not ended with her death.

"Your brother?"

"His name is Nathan," the shade said earnestly, her hazel eyes now stained with worry. "I have to help him."

Daphne recalled the stone she had picked up by Heather's roadside memorial with *Nathan* written on it. "What do you mean?"

At the soft sound of footsteps, she turned around quickly. A sophomore headed up the hallway, absorbed in his phone, and turned the corner out of sight. Daphne's heart pounded at the thought of what the scene must look like to everyone else. If someone saw her standing alone in the middle of the hallway, backpack on the floor, talking to herself...

"He hasn't done well since my death," Heather said softly. "I can see it, when he's here. He seems fine, but I know him. We were close."

The shade looked unseeing, as if lost in thought. Mist rose continuously off her shoulders and dissipated.

"Your brother goes to school here?" Daphne asked. She hadn't carefully examined Heather's entire obituary, her list of survivors, having been more preoccupied with the other details. That Heather had a younger sibling who could be a classmate hadn't occurred to her.

"He skipped Homecoming," the shade answered faintly, still gazing into the distance. "His last Homecoming."

"Nathan's a senior?" Daphne said, trying to connect the name to a face without success. There were over three hundred students in her class. It was impossible to know them all. But if he was a senior, then—

She was struck dumb by the connection.

He added me. Nathan did.

It was *him*. Veronica's crush. Nathan Grey. She almost wanted to laugh, but the urge passed as Heather focused again and took a step forward. Daphne resisted the impulse to move away. She still didn't like to be too close to shades.

"Could you help him?" Heather said. The closeness of her large hazel eyes was disconcerting, their gaze intent on Daphne's face. The sudden request startled her. It was the first time a shade had asked her for something.

"What do you mean?"

"He's being distant from his friends. I've watched him."

An image of Nathan's dead sister observing him at school, unseen, flashed unpleasantly through Daphne's mind.

"They don't understand. Can you help him?"

The piece of ice felt like it had melted in her stomach. Daphne thought she understood, for the first time, what Heather was trying to say.

"He needs a friend," Daphne said distantly. "Someone who knows what he's going through."

Heather was asking her to be what no one had been for Daphne, when she had lost her father. Nathan needed someone who understood, who crossed the gulf when everyone else didn't even know there was one.

She couldn't be a counselor, but she could be a friend.

Heather nodded.

Whatever feeling keeps them on Earth is strong, and it won't have a simple remedy...Even if there is a way to help them, it's best to leave them alone.

It was like the voice from her phone, spoken clearly in her ear. Daphne remembered Claire's words, resonating with personal experience. Warning her. And yet...was battling dyszoons the only purpose to her ability?

A vivid image of the ragged lizard by Heather's memorial leapt before her eyes. If anything, the memorial marking the spot of the crash had made Daphne recognize in a tangible way that there were consequences, should the evil remain unchecked. A family had already been torn apart. If there was some way she could help Nathan, she should at least try, shouldn't she?

Daphne looked at Heather, whose love for her brother had kept her from moving on.

"Will you help him?" the shade pressed.

Daphne remembered Claire's words, the bitterness in her face. Saw the white cross and the items at its feet. Painted onto stone, his name. *Nathan.* Daphne turned back to the girl of her nightmares.

"I will."

11

DEADLINES

At seven on Friday night, Daphne descended the stairs. The sound of a tapping keyboard came from the kitchen, and Daphne entered the room to find her mom sitting at the table, wearing a deep frown above her reading glasses. The thick photocopied diary of Thomas Blakely lay next to the laptop.

"Hey...Mom? I'm going to stop by Jessica's house," Daphne said lightly, ignoring the guilty squirm in her stomach. *Lie.*

"Okay," her mom said slowly without looking up, immersed in her project. "Could you do me a favor?"

"What?" Daphne said warily.

"What do you think this word is?" Her mom pointed to the paper. Daphne walked over and bent down to look.

"His handwriting is really bad," she noted as she tried to decipher the cramped cursive. "It looks like maybe...Henderson?"

Her mom brought the sheet up close to her eyes and peered over her glasses. A sudden flash of comprehension lit her face. "Oh! I thought it was 'hinders,' but that didn't make sense."

"Glad I could assist." Daphne smiled. "I'm going to get going, then."

"What?! Where?" her mom said in mock surprise, and chuckled at the eye roll Daphne gave her. "All right, have fun. I'll just be here...all by myself...lonely..."

"Have fun with that, then," Daphne said, and left to the sound of her mom's laughter.

Guilt returned as Daphne drove into town. Outright lying didn't come easily to her, but revealing she was going to see Claire would mean explaining all she had concealed about her nightmares and abilities. It had been difficult enough accepting the truth of it herself; how would someone who couldn't see shades possibly believe it?

She looked forward to seeing Claire, odd as the feeling was compared to two weeks ago. For the past few days, Daphne had practically burst with the desire to call Claire and tell her about meeting Heather's shade, but it didn't seem like information that could be told over the phone.

Traffic became heavier as she reached downtown Long Haven. At the sight of the cars and an unusually large crowd walking past the bars and restaurants, Daphne hesitated. What if someone she knew, especially Jessica, happened to recognize her car parked by the studio?

No doubt lying had made her paranoid, but it was easy enough to walk the short distance to see Claire. She turned a block early and parked along the road.

The air was chilly. Daphne put her hands in her jacket pockets and walked to the corner. Bars and a few restaurants were open, their windows alight like beacons. Although it was Friday night, Daphne wondered at the large number of people roaming the sidewalk. She halted and stared at the sight before her, realizing why.

The sidewalk was full of shades.

Side by side with the living who could not see them, men and women strolled up and down the street, pausing now and then to stare listlessly into the air. Their clothes spanned hundreds of years of known history. Women in jeans and full skirts and short shorts. Men wearing tall hats and flat hats and ball hats.

Daphne stood blinking at this scene for a full minute, startled by the transformation of a street she'd known almost her whole life. The sight was eerie—she had never seen so many shades gathered in one place. Although she saw them clearly now, Daphne realized she could sense their forms in a way that didn't need sight, although she couldn't have explained how.

On the opposite side of the street, it was the same story. Unless she wanted to take the trouble of parking elsewhere or taking a chance on the back alley, Daphne would need to walk through them.

"You can do this," Daphne said to herself sternly. "It's only a block."

Steeling herself, she took a step into the light and shadows of the path before her. A shade passed, a misting Black man in eighties clothes, and Daphne hurriedly stepped aside to avoid the massive stereo perched on his shoulder. A woman in a bustled black dress, buttoned high, glanced curiously at Daphne while briskly walking past.

At least there wasn't any difficulty in knowing which people were living and which were dead, even without the telltale signs of smoke rising off the shades. Daphne skirted around a couple holding hands who were unaware they had just passed through a giant man wearing a suit and wide striped tie.

She halted halfway down the block, entranced. A procession of soldiers, wearing what looked like World War I uniforms and hats, was marching down the street through oncoming traffic. There were large gaps in their procession, but the marching handful had apparently kept their original places. They marched past Daphne.

She was jostled and quickly stepped out of the way of a pack of chattering college students.

"Sorry—"

Daphne focused with an effort. The end of the block was near. She passed a shade leaning casually against a brick wall, a man in eighteenth- or possibly nineteenth-century work clothes who stared at her solemnly under a shallow cap. As she passed, the man's face and hands became shriveled and black. A burn victim.

Daphne's heart jumped and she hurried away, touching a finger automatically to her bracelet. She could feel the shade's eyes on her as she moved on. Parking down the street had been a mistake.

As if she were in a spotlight, more shades were taking notice of her. They moved in closer, like moths attracted to light. A small group of shades ahead observed her approach, and Daphne hoped they would move out of the way. Instead, they drew in suddenly around her, talking all at once.

"M'dear, there was no help for him, no money to pay—" a middle-aged woman said, undaunted as Daphne avoided her and was immediately confronted by another woman, young, with frizzy red hair, who all but shouted, "My children? Who will take care of my children—?"

Alarmed, Daphne shrank away from the shade. The burn victim had peeled himself from the wall and joined the small crowd forming behind her, like an entourage, of men and women in clothes whose times she could not identify in her haste to disentangle herself, only registering a few likely dated before the country itself. As they surrounded her in a crescent, their voices jumbled together as all of them earnestly pleaded their case. Only snatches of it reached her clearly.

"—my eight children—"

"—I love her. She *must* know I love her—"

"—They had to saw off the arm, the bullet had—"

Laughter came from inside a brightly lit bar. Shortly past it, mercifully, was the side street where Claire's studio was located. She only had to get through the shades to reach it.

Then the only remaining gap closed, blocked by shades. The voices had risen to shouting, each shade clamoring for her attention.

"I'm sorry, I can't—" Daphne said, unheard, and they drew even closer, tightening the small circle they had formed. The dead were merging in. Out of the corner of her eye, Daphne saw a misting hand reach for her own—

"*Don't!*" she cried, sweeping her arm instinctively to shake off the shade. To her surprise, she felt a push, as if against her mind, and the shades on her right backed away impassively, now silent. Daphne turned and strode forward bravely, praying the shades would move aside and she would not have to walk through them.

To her immense relief, they did. The path was clear, and Daphne broke through, feeling the wide space surround her like a breath of fresh air. A glance over her shoulder revealed that the shades, as if on cue, had dispersed and continued their routes. In her haste, Daphne didn't have time to contemplate what she had just done, or how. Shaking slightly, she hurried the rest of the way down the sidewalk and diagonally crossed the empty street to the studio. The entrance to Madam Moon was awash with yellow light from a nearby streetlamp. It was much quieter at this section: the sounds of drunken laughter had faded, and—thankfully—there were no shades in sight.

Through the glass, a faint glow from the hallway light escaped the curtain separating the two rooms. The studio had closed at six.

She tried the door handle, but it was locked, no doubt to keep out farsighted customers who'd disregard the CLOSED sign. Daphne glanced upward: the waning full moon loomed large in the sky. She grimaced and raised a fist to knock.

A faint presence touched her mind. Daphne lowered her hand as a hulking figure tottered toward her. As it came closer, it became apparent the old man, bundled in a heavy black over-coat, was a shade. His smoking cane tapped the ground sound-lessly. As she watched him wobble past, the man raised a stiff arm and touched a glove to his hat in salute. He continued down the side street before vanishing into the dark alley.

Her knock sounded more urgently than intended. Daphne bounced on her feet as she waited, glancing anxiously at the spot where the old man had vanished.

Claire appeared through the curtain and unlocked the door, and Daphne almost fell through in her haste to get inside, feeling she'd arrived at a fortress, the door acting as barricade. The perfumed room had never looked more welcoming.

Apparently Claire noticed. "You look a little run over," she said, locking the door again.

"I was," Daphne said breathlessly. "By shades, I mean. Just now."

"Ah," Claire said. "I take it you can now see all the ones on Main?" She chuckled, to Daphne's exasperation. It did not feel funny. "Well, let's head to the other room."

Daphne followed the psychic through the curtain for the third time, calmer now that there was increased distance between her and the shades outside, and thought how it had been only been two weeks, almost exactly, since she had met Claire. It seemed much longer.

"Do you drink tea?" Claire asked, pausing outside her office door.

"Yeah."

"I'll join you in a minute, then."

Daphne brushed aside the strings of red beads and entered the room where Claire saw clients. Although there were no windows, the room felt more mystic at night than it had during the sunny afternoons when she had always visited it. She sat in the chair facing away from the doorway.

Claire returned, bearing two steaming white mugs of machine-brewed tea.

"It's chamomile," she said, setting one down on the starry tablecloth before settling into the opposite chair. "I hope you like it."

Daphne lifted the mug and tried a sip. "It's good," she commented honestly.

"It's what I drink instead of coffee," Claire said, her long magenta nails wrapped around her mug. "Seems to help with the nightmares, or at the very least, doesn't make them any worse."

Daphne nodded, lifting her own mug again. The tea had a soothing effect, and she felt herself recovering from the claustrophobia of being surrounded by shades. Yet Daphne felt mildly ashamed at the way she had panicked and pushed them away.

"So I take it you've been more successful at perceiving shades?" Claire asked. The edges of her dyed hair glowed red in the lamplight situated in the corner behind her, and her necklace gleamed: a thick waning crescent moon of polished silver and gold on a short chain, embedded with three tiny diamonds like stars.

"Yes," Daphne answered, moving her gaze away. "They're

not as clear as in the cemetery, but whatever you did to me worked."

"Transferring to you some of my energy would have helped, but I'd give most of the credit to yourself." The psychic nodded over her tea. "Once you start to become more open to your abilities, it's a natural progression."

"I'm seeing them everywhere now," Daphne said, thinking of the shades in her woods. "One of them showed me his injuries. I—didn't know shades could do that."

"Ah," Claire said with a wry smile. "I should have warned you, but I didn't think of it. Sometimes that will happen. I once met a shade in France whose stomach was cut open, and his organs—" She gestured outward with a hand, then shuddered at the memory. Daphne was glad no shade with such a graphic level of injury had shown itself to her. Though the murder victim and the burned man hadn't been pleasant, and the child...

The idea of it disturbed her. "One of the shades I met was just a kid," Daphne told her, biting her lip.

"Shades that are children are very rare," Claire said compassionately. "But I've found most shades are young."

Daphne nodded, and it was with difficulty that she asked, "Why would a kid stay behind?"

Claire seemed to consider the question carefully. "I think... the emotion that leads someone to stay behind as a shade is very strong. Certain experiences would affect a child more deeply. It's hard to say without asking them, if you could even manage a straight answer."

Daphne nodded again, thinking of the shades who'd had no difficulty explaining their problems to her just a few minutes ago. "The Main Street shades," she began, determined not to reveal how much the shades on Main had rattled her. "They were more—active—than the other shades I've met."

"It depends on the shade," Claire explained. "But they're all harmless. All you have to do is order them to go away, and they'll obey."

"I pushed them," she mumbled.

"That's necessary sometimes," Claire said seriously, then, as if she guessed Daphne's thoughts, added, "It's useless to feel guilty about it, Daphne, trust me. Those shades came to you because they knew you can perceive them, and whatever problem keeps them on Earth consumes them. It is, almost literally, all they think about. Of course, if you ask, they can tell you a few things about themselves, but they no longer live. They owe a rent, remember. You are not being cruel by having them obey you, or establishing boundaries."

Daphne felt better. The shades hadn't been hurt, after all. And in the safety of the room, the encounter with the shades seemed much less frightening. She was never in any real danger, though the thought of passing through a solid-looking person was still unpleasant. "You know, it's weird, but they don't really scare me much anymore," she observed truthfully.

"No?"

"It's more like..." Daphne cast around for words to explain. "They make me uneasy, like when I saw the Veil and I knew it wasn't supposed to be there—I mean, obviously, but on a deeper level, I guess." Daphne looked at the beaded door, thinking of the shades out in the world. They all had a history.

"Yes, shades are a strange existence," Claire said. "Even though they are a shadow of who they once were, they are a little like time capsules. And if time is a cushion from the past, a shade, I suppose, is like a needle through that cushion—a reminder that history is only forgotten, never lost."

It sounded like something her mom, an amateur historian, would agree with. Daphne had hardly begun wondering if the two women would get along when a thought hidden in her mind, purposely unacknowledged since she had first learned of shades, appeared in its full form: what would she do if her dad suddenly appeared as a shade? It was always possible... The idea was like nails in her stomach.

"I hope no one I ever knew stayed behind," she said in a small voice. Absentmindedly, she twisted the silver bracelet around her wrist under the table and watched the lamp in the corner casting its light on the dark red walls.

"That's very wise of you," Claire said approvingly. "Many people would wish otherwise."

Daphne stopped twisting the bracelet and settled her hands back on the table, forcing those thoughts away. "Well, like you said, they wouldn't be the same."

"No," Claire agreed with a grim smile. "They wouldn't."

She thought of Heather, the reason she had been eager for this meeting, and the way the shade was reduced to a fraction of herself. It wasn't worth seeing a loved one only to have them appear as a shadow. It would be like a photograph in a frame but with the face missing: a vital component wasn't there.

"Claire, do you remember," Daphne began, "when I told you about what happened in class, and you told me it was a shade?"

"Yes?"

Her heart pounded. "I met her. I met the shade."

Daphne related the particulars of what had passed between herself and Heather, and the request that had nagged at her mind. Her promise.

However astonished Claire was by the information, having shared the nightmare, she bore it well enough that Daphne, who was well past the first shock, felt safe adding, "And I know you said helping shades was difficult, but doesn't this mean I have, I don't know, an obligation to help him? I don't need to tell him about Heather. Actually, I *wouldn't* ever tell him about Heather," she corrected herself, rubbing her forehead.

Claire folded her lacquered fingers together on the table, her mouth set in a grim line. "I understand the sentiment, Daphne," she began carefully. "There have been times when shades have asked for my help for whatever problem keeps them here. Sometimes I gave it, but it is a difficult thing, helping them, even when the death was recent. Their issues are always complex, and they are always consumed by them, as I've said."

This was the answer she'd been afraid to hear. Daphne could not explain why she felt so strongly about helping Nathan, and Heather. Maybe it was because she had dreamed so often about Heather's death, helpless to change one detail, and this was one way she could finally make a difference.

Claire continued. "So. My advice to you is the same: it is better to let things run their course. Eventually, Nathan will move on, without your help."

Silence fell. Daphne bit her lip, busily thinking of some way to prove her point, to show how difficult it would be to do nothing, to stand by while someone struggled. It was already becoming impossible not to observe Nathan in the limited amount of time he came into her sight, during the lunch hour, so she was sneaking glances at him almost as often as Veronica. She hadn't been able to judge his state of mind from those glances. But if she *did* notice things were bad, would she really be able to turn away and trust the situation would work out on its own, without interfering?

Yet Claire had a point. As grieved as she had been over her father's death, Daphne had slowly been able to gain a new normal. But a sliver of memory came from the depths of that hidden well: the memory of isolation, apartness from her peers. Having someone who knew what it felt like to lose someone close or who even just actively sought her out when the effort was too much on her end would have been an enormous benefit.

Claire sighed. "I can see you will need to discover this on your own. My advice is the same, but if you feel you must help him, you should do so."

The arguments climbing over each other in Daphne's mind collapsed like the scattered stones on the table. She was relieved. "It might not need to come to anything, anyway," she said reasonably. "I don't know exactly what I'm supposed to be doing."

"I suppose you'll find out," the psychic said, looking resigned, but Daphne took it in stride. As much as she would have liked Claire to approve of her plan of action, at least it wouldn't be secret. She had enough secrecy at the moment. She recalled the bitterness that had flashed on Claire's face when the psychic had first spoken about helping shades, but still did not feel it her place to ask what had caused it.

"I suppose I should also tell you why I called you here this evening," Claire added after a few seconds' pause while they both silently drank tea, lost in thought. "There are some things we need to discuss, now you are mastering your abilities a little more. The first is, I will be out of town next week, to visit my three sons in Miami."

"You have sons?" Daphne asked without thinking. Somehow she had thought of Claire as alone, without family.

"Yes." Claire smiled fondly. "And my first grandbaby, too, next spring. Two of my sons are married."

Absorbing this, Daphne asked, "If you're going to be away —what if something happens with the Veil? I'm not sure I could fight dyszoons by myself—"

"I wouldn't expect you to," Claire broke in reassuringly. "I don't think anything will happen to it while I'm gone, or I wouldn't go. But I'm afraid this is the last time I'll have the opportunity before it expands further."

"Do you think that'll be soon?" Daphne asked, alarmed. She had been under the impression they still had time.

"Yes. You see, I've been thinking a lot about that lately," Claire said. "And I believe I have a good guess."

"You do?" Daphne said in surprise, having expected to hear it was impossible to know the date.

"Well, first, you must understand it's no easy thing, creating a portal like that. I imagine it's just as difficult to change its dimensions. The attempt in August only succeeded in opening it just enough to let two dyszoons through, and nothing more."

"But I thought that was just a test?"

"I believe so, because there were only two, along with the fact that one of the creatures—yours—wasn't put to any purpose but abandoned to fade slowly in the woods. But I'm certain another attempt will be made soon."

"But when?" Daphne said anxiously. "Nothing's happened to it since summer. What are they waiting for?"

"I have considered the same question, and I have a theory. There's no reason I could think of for waiting to expand it, except for a day that might help them accomplish what they need, given the difficulty of what they're trying to do. And the closer we get to it, the more reason I have to believe I'm correct."

"You don't think—"

"Yes," Claire said. "The Veil will expand on Halloween."

"Halloween." Daphne choked on her tea. "That's in...three weeks." It was all they had. Three weeks. She had concentrated so much on trying to see shades that the ultimate task Claire had set for her had seemed so distant it was almost out of sight. Now here was the deadline. Three weeks to prepare. "But why Halloween?"

"There is a truth buried in the tradition," Claire said, straightening like a teacher about to begin a lecture. "Before trick-or-treating and so on, Halloween was a day to repel ghosts and prepare for the dark winter days ahead. On that night, the bind between the living and the dead becomes its strongest, and the line between us...blurs." She traced a finger along the tablecloth in emphasis.

"So on the night of Halloween, it might be easier to expand the Veil," Daphne concluded quietly, staring at the amethyst set into one of Claire's rings. When she looked up again, the psychic's dark eyes were as serious as she had ever seen them.

"Exactly."

The lamp in the corner flickered for an instant, and Daphne imagined creatures hidden inside that brief, fragile darkness, or outside the fragile light.

"What do I need to do?" she said, in a voice that was almost a whisper. The shadowy fog that hid her future seemed to clear just a little, but Daphne didn't want to look at what was coming, at what her part might be. There was so much she did not know.

"The same as what I told you when you came to me a week ago. I have no doubt the dyszoons will come out of the Veil sooner rather than later, and I will need your assistance to banish them back to Hell before they have the chance to harm anyone else."

Shrieks echoed from a memory of a hatred so pure and undiluted, directed at her. The hairs on her arm lifted again. And that had been just one. "How many do you think will come through?"

"If two slipped through in such a limited space, I believe there will be more this time around—maybe four, though we should be prepared for as many as six," Claire said calmly.

"*Six?*" Daphne said, aghast at the high number. "But I could hardly fight *one* dyszoon."

"You defeated that one when you were first beginning to perceive," Claire reminded her. "Now I think you would find it easier."

Daphne doubted this. "I'm not exactly sure how perceiving shades better makes me any better at fighting dyszoons."

"It won't, necessarily, but the better you are able to see the unseen world, the better you can interact with it, and practice. The closest you will be able to get to the feel of fighting a dyszoon would be to use shades."

"You mean, push them away like I did earlier?"

"In a way, yes. Your goal would be getting used to your power to deflect spirits. It's not something I can teach well, I'm afraid, but it would be the best preparation for what lies before us."

"Have you practiced on them?"

"Yes," Claire said. "Much as I am relying on you, Daphne, I plan to do my part."

Thinking of shades, Daphne was struck by an idea. "Couldn't we use shades to help us battle the dyszoons? I mean, they're both spirits, right?"

Claire shook her head. "I'm afraid not. Dyszoons aren't exactly spirits, though they were once human. They are a different type of creature, and far stronger. I tried that with mine, unsuccessfully. It seems it would take many, many shades to banish even *one* dyszoon, and only after much effort. We must be the ones to do so."

"If I can figure out how," Daphne answered gloomily.

"Three or four dyszoons will be hard to defeat, but not impossible."

Daphne looked at the gilded oval mirror hanging on the wall, reflecting only the shadowed burgundy walls, and imagined dark spirits shooting out of its surface. Walls became splinters, table legs scattered, the porcelain angels smashed into shards..."What about the Veil? Are you sure we can't close it?"

"I'm afraid not," Claire said again. "We're not connected to it by blood, remember, so there's nothing we can do but wait. The battle will come, and the only thing we can do is prepare for it the best we can."

Daphne pursed her lips, then said, "I feel like I should be doing something." It was agonizing to *know* yet be able to do nothing.

"You *are* doing something, Daphne," Claire said, sounding stern. "What you are doing now is the most important thing you could be doing. It's frustrating, yes, but you can't prevent a storm, only prepare for the damage. There is nothing to be done about the Veil except prepare for the evil that comes out of it."

"*Why* would someone want to expand it?" Daphne asked, frustrated. "Who would *want* to bring dyszoons out?"

"I think we'll get an answer to that question sooner rather than later. I have seen nothing, awake or dreaming, so it's useless to speculate at this point."

"Can't we stop them somehow? What if we got there early and confronted whoever it was?"

"I'm afraid the person who widens the Veil won't necessarily need to be at the scene to do so—we can't count on it, anyway. The best thing, and only thing, we can do is to make sure whatever comes out doesn't get a chance to harm anyone else."

They had a faceless enemy somewhere, like a dark form in the distant mist, its features as obscure as its plans. Perhaps Claire was right. It was impossible to act without more information, so they could only do what they could at present.

She took a long sip of cold tea, draining it, and commented, "I think I'll ask my mom to buy this."

Claire sipped her own and checked the small watch on her wrist, which was surprisingly plain compared to her other jewelry, with a black leather strap. From the hands, Daphne could see it was almost nine.

"Speaking of which, she's probably wondering what's taking you so long."

"I told her I was at a friend's," Daphne admitted.

"Ah," Claire said, expressionless. "You don't want her to know about your abilities?"

"I mean, I do, kind of," Daphne said awkwardly. "But I can't exactly prove it, can I? She'll think I'm going..." She twirled a finger in the direction of her brain. "It took me until I saw the Veil to really believe all of it, but she won't be able to see that." There was also the lie. Her nightmares were as bad as ever. Worse. She would not let her mom worry. She'd put her through enough.

Claire said nothing. Her silence felt disapproving.

"Did you ever tell anyone?" Daphne asked doubtfully.

"No, not for years. It was a lonely time," Claire said, her expression becoming brooding. "But that's your decision," she added briskly.

Still, a heaviness seemed to draw over the psychic, and Daphne swallowed the questions she'd wanted to ask about Claire's past. Maybe next time.

The meeting drew wordlessly to a close. Claire led her to the door and unlocked it.

"Good luck, Daphne," she said, holding it open. Before it shut behind her, Daphne thought she heard a sigh.

12

THE PROMISE

As if on cue, Daphne's eyelids snapped open in the darkness.

She had dreamed of Heather again, but this time the rolling car slowed until Daphne could have counted every piece of glass suspended in the air between her and the girl whose life was ending. She watched Heather's dark hair fly forward, obscuring her face, mouth open in a shrill scream. Then the glass and darkness swallowed her, and Daphne was not looking at Heather but her bedroom wall lit up in the moonlight.

Black-and-white photos covered nearly every inch of it, the work of years of wandering in the woods and a few historic places around Virginia her mom had dragged her to visit. Daphne's eye fell to the one of the bridge on Laurel Road. It was not a good photo—just an angled shot of the bridge and its three arches, taken on her phone camera. Where the Veil should be, there were only the black trees in the background.

In only three weeks, the Veil would expand. In three weeks, something like what she had encountered in the woods would pass through the gap between worlds and enter hers, only stronger and in greater numbers.

The deadline hung over her like a suffocating blanket. How was she going to be ready in time? She had barely managed to fight off *one* dyszoon, and that one had been a shadow of its full strength. Yet, if they failed, if they allowed a dyszoon to escape, there could be another victim like Heather.

Daphne glanced at the clock—half past three—and remembered the promise she'd made to help Nathan. A week had passed, and still she was no closer to an idea as to how to go about it. School would start in a few hours.

But today was the day, Daphne decided with determination. Somehow she would talk to him, even though the only period they shared was lunch. She would just have to find a way.

A solution didn't present itself later that morning, once Daphne arrived at her locker and checked up and down the hallway. Sometimes Nathan would happen to walk past before classes started. She was both deflated and relieved when there was no sign of him. The problem was out of her hands for a few hours. Heather wasn't anywhere in sight either.

The lunch hour arrived. Daphne glanced at him, three tables over, as she set down her tray, noticing him silently playing with his food. The shade of Heather was standing a few paces away, though her eyes were fixed on Daphne rather than her brother, who didn't know his sister stood near. She was struck by the creepiness of it.

Daphne had toyed with the idea of calling Claire to ask for advice, but the psychic was out of state. She didn't want to bother Claire on her vacation, and in any case, she already knew what Claire's opinion would be. Most likely, Daphne would be told to drop it altogether, now that she had a firsthand experience in how difficult helping shades was.

Possibilities passed through her mind. Simply walking over to talk with him at his table was not an option, not without knowing anyone else at the table. That was too weird. Unfortunately, lunch was their only shared hour. There was no chance of a group activity bringing them together, which would have been the easiest way.

Daphne looked at Jessica, who was sitting at her left. How would she approach the problem? Knowing her best friend, who was rarely anything but friendly, Jessica would likely have already cornered Nathan into a conversation in the lunch line and begun chatting effortlessly.

And Veronica? From the eager glances Daphne had seen, if Veronica had found a way to "cheer up" Nathan, she would have done it weeks ago. Now it was a predicament they shared, for different reasons. Daphne picked at her own food, torn by indecision. Maybe she could bump into him on the way out, apologize...

The conversation at the table had turned to college. Although unsure of her major, Daphne had already made the decision to start out at the local college, after seeing how much boarding would cost at the schools she had toured during the summer. Still, Daphne felt a little lame. Her classmates would be moving away from home, and she was going to be left behind in Long Haven.

"I really hope I like my roommate," Veronica was saying. "That we can, like, hang out and have fun and stuff."

"I haven't really thought about that yet," Jessica admitted. "I just want to get into a good program."

"What are you doing again?"

"I want to do pediatric nursing," she answered, confirming what Daphne had already long known. "I just love babies and toddlers!"

Veronica nodded. "I can see you doing that."

"What are you going for?" Daphne asked Veronica, despite herself.

"I don't know," she said shortly, sounding frustrated. "I keep changing my mind."

"I thought you wanted to go to the school with the criminal justice program?" Jessica said.

"That was before I saw the dorms. You should see the paint, it's so gross."

The others were also discussing colleges. Taylor, one of Beth's friends, was planning to attend a college out of state, where some of her family lived.

"—and there are tunnels between the main buildings—"

"Like gopher holes?" Beth laughed.

"Ha, no! They're like normal hallways. They say they're really nice in winter. So anyway, I might go there—"

The bell rang. Instinctively, Daphne glanced over to where Nathan was getting to his feet, Heather's unrelenting stare on her as she eerily stood near him. But what could she do?

Nathan was in a separate part of the crowd inching its way up the two hallways lining the theatre, and Daphne tried unsuccessfully to get closer. Even if she did catch up to him, what then? What could she say that wouldn't fizzle out in a second? It was agonizing.

She dropped off her tray in the kitchen and then walked with the crowd until she reached the first hallway, where most of the senior lockers were. She opened hers and saw Nathan had also stopped to gather his books fifteen or so lockers down. Grabbing the books she would need for the rest of the day, Daphne shut her locker and looked over at him, ignoring the strange glance from the girl at the locker next to hers.

Feet from Nathan, students passing through her like air, was his sister.

He was still collecting his books, oblivious to Heather's presence. Daphne noticed he was tall and very skinny, even for a cross-country runner. Was that what Heather had noticed?

The shade stared at her with solemn intensity, her message clear: *Now is the moment.*

Gripping her books tightly, Daphne swallowed. Nerves wriggled in her stomach. Walking with the slowest part of the crowd, every step closer only increased her panic. She wracked her brain for a topic, an excuse to talk. They had no classes together, so she couldn't ask anything about coursework...

Daphne hesitated, more and more agonized. She was getting closer, only feet away. The moment was coming up. Soon it would pass, and the opportunity to speak with him would again be gone.

Nathan placed another heavy textbook onto his precariously held load and reached into the locker for one final thing, just as Heather stepped forward and unceremoniously swiped at the top of the pile.

The heavy textbook fell with a loud smack onto the floor. A folder and notebook dropped haphazardly and were stepped on. His pencil bag slid across the hall and was promptly kicked farther away by a hurried stride.

Daphne stood stunned by this sudden occurrence for precisely two seconds before seizing the opportunity that Heather had given her. She hurried forward and scooped up the folder, and then hesitated, holding it out.

"Here—here you go," she said, addressing the floor where he was slowly and gloomily retrieving his things, and crouched down to join him. "I think your pencil pouch was kicked over there. I'll...go get it."

"Oh—thanks," Nathan said, glancing up briefly to take the folder, which now had a dusty footprint on the front.

With some difficulty, Daphne pushed through the crowd and found the pouch on the other side of the hall against the wall. Unsuccessfully, she attempted to calm her nerves as she returned to Nathan's locker. Heather had vanished.

"I found it." Daphne handed it over, finding it easier to look at his hands instead of his face.

"Thanks, Daphne," Nathan said again and added the pouch to his pile. Daphne blinked. He knew her name? "I don't know how I dropped everything," he added anxiously.

Daphne risked looking at his face. Like Heather's, his chin was sharp, but his hair was dusty brown rather than black, naturally stuck up and wavy. His eyes startled her—hazel, in the exact shape of his sister's. Suddenly, Daphne could see why Veronica had a crush on him.

"Too many books?" she said, forcing a smile, stomach wriggling.

"Just math and...math," he said wryly. It wasn't quite a joke, so Daphne merely nodded. She had already run out of things to say, and her feet itched to walk away as fast as possible. The number of students had become a trickle; the bell for seventh period would ring in two minutes. What else could she do?

"Well, I should get to class," Daphne said, feeling an increasing sense of failure as she turned away in the direction of her route.

But to her surprise, Nathan slammed his locker shut and caught up to her.

"I've got to go that way too," he said. "What class are you going to?"

"Euro," Daphne answered, blinking at this turn of events that so worked in her favor.

"Do you have Burnes?" he said.

"Yeah," she said hesitantly. "What about you?"

"Yeah. Unfortunately."

The next pause was agonizing to Daphne, who scrambled for something to say as they briskly turned the corner onto a long stretch of hallway, hurrying to class. Why did talking have to be so hard? She thought of Jessica again, and her bubbliness, and how easy it was for her to carry on a conversation—

"My friend's in that class," she said abruptly. "Jessica Roman. Do you know her?" Daphne winced at the lameness of it, but it was better than awkward silence.

"She sits behind me."

"I bet she talks a lot," she said, and glanced sideways long enough to see him smile faintly. The sight encouraged her.

"She talks to me sometimes before class," he said, and Daphne wondered if Veronica was behind that. "Burnes gets pretty mad if anyone talks during his lectures."

Daphne silently agreed, recalling the expression on Burnes's face when she had interrupted the class by standing up. "He doesn't seem to care, though, if no one pays attention," she said, relieved at the sight of the classroom door. If they could just keep bashing Burnes, they could make it to the end of the hallway.

"Which is hard to do, admittedly," Nathan said, tilting his head. "I'm not really a history guy."

"I'm not either—girl, I mean." Daphne cringed at the nervous correction. She again noticed the two large textbooks he was carrying. "Are you more into math?"

"Yeah, I was thinking that's what I'll go to college for."

"Accounting?"

"Not if I can help it," he said. "I'm not sure yet. Maybe a math teacher."

Daphne nodded. They were almost to her classroom, but now she was beginning to relax. Nathan was easier to talk to than she'd expected based on Heather's assessment of him. If she hadn't already seen him before, Daphne might have feared he'd be moody and wallowing in depression, beyond her ability to connect to, but he was obviously neither of those things. But she shouldn't be surprised. Grief didn't mean all function was gone, nor did it mean a personality change. It came out differently for each person.

And the fact was, Heather hadn't requested a therapist. She'd wanted Daphne to befriend him. That was all.

"Daphne?"

"Sorry, what?" She had missed what he'd said.

"Oh—I just asked what you're going for, in college."

"I'm not sure," Daphne answered, caught off-center. "Photography, maybe, but I'm not sure a degree in it is worth it."

"What do you photograph?"

"Nature. Close-ups a lot. I like doing black-and-white, stuff like that." They reached the classroom, and for the first time on their walk, she wouldn't have minded continuing with him farther. "Well. See you, Nathan."

He nodded. "I'd like to see your photos sometime."

Normally the suggestion would have made her freeze. Daphne didn't like to show her photos to other people. It was too intimate, somehow, as if they showed a side she was not willing to share. But somehow the suggestion wasn't terrible, coming from him.

"Sometime." She smiled, then, struck by another wave of awkwardness, turned and went into the classroom. The class was still in disarray, and most students were standing around talking. Mr. Burnes was in his office in the back. Veronica turned away from her junior friend, wide-eyed, as Daphne came in.

"Was that Nathan Grey you were talking to?" she asked bluntly.

"Yep," Daphne said, amused by the expression on Veronica's face. She was evidently too astonished to demand how they knew each other. Daphne passed without further comment to her desk.

Mr. Burnes came out of his office, along with Ashley

Zhang, who looked livid. Daphne caught her eye, curious. Ashley glared at her, but Daphne felt too happy to care.

"All right, class!" he barked once at the front, sideburns stretching ominously. "We have the entire English Civil War to get through today! Let's get to it!"

Amid the residual shuffling and the ring of the bell, Daphne smiled to herself in satisfaction, feeling giddy. She had finally talked to Nathan, and it had gone okay. It was not much, but maybe just talking to him did some good, even if all they did from now on was say hello when they passed each other. Veronica's reaction was the icing on the cake. Not even forty minutes of bloody revolution could dampen her mood.

The feeling of triumph had dampened by the next day.

Nathan was not at school, and in hindsight, Daphne noted their conversation seemed much less significant, full of small talk. She had meant to talk to him again if the opportunity came, but a glance at his empty place at lunch threw away those plans. Heather, too, was nowhere in sight. Did he have a cross-country meet?

Though Daphne didn't know exactly why, his absence made her feel wary. The feeling was irrational, she told herself. It wasn't her business. He could just be sick. And yet...

But Daphne could not shake off a bad feeling as she slid into her desk in history, and she was so preoccupied that she jumped at the packet of paper dropped onto her desk. She looked up blankly.

Mr. Burnes sighed theatrically, making plain her essay had insulted his sensibilities as a teacher. "Daphne," he said, "look carefully at the feedback."

Daphne glanced down and with a flush of anger saw the

written percentage, which amounted to little more than a C. She had barely passed.

He smiled tightly at her silence and moved away, handing out more essays. Daphne flicked through the packet at the scribbled notes in red ink, neatly undoing her thesis and presentation of evidence, which had seemed fine when she wrote it. Flicking back to the front of the essay, she felt Veronica's eyes on her, trying to make out the red number from a distance, and quickly placed the ruined essay in a folder, face hot.

More than usual, it was difficult to keep her mind on the lecture. A low score she could handle, but the way he had sneered made her face flush again. Again, she wondered where Nathan could be, and if he was okay.

The bell finally rang. She scooped up her books and reached the door at the same time as Veronica.

"Hey, what did you get on the essay?" Veronica smiled widely. "You looked a little upset!"

Behind Veronica, her junior friend smirked.

"I did pretty good." Daphne smiled and walked quickly out the door, wishing she could have come up with a better response. Most of the time, she could deal with Veronica and her back-and-forth friendliness, but when caught off guard... Mr. Burnes's face popped again into her mind, and she felt another flush of anger.

Her mood had improved by the time the final bell rang.

Slowly Daphne made her way through the hallway, wondering whether she should wander the woods again and practice interacting with shades. On the few times she had met other shades in the woods, they had remained frustratingly impervious to her touch. They might as well have been air.

Not, Daphne had to admit, that she really knew what she was doing.

Though not expecting to see Heather, Daphne glanced down the hall for a misting figure. The shade was nowhere in sight. In a way, that was a relief. The more Daphne saw her, the more pressure she felt to fulfill her promise.

Lost in thought, Daphne almost collided with the subject of her thoughts as he walked sharply out of Mr. Burnes's classroom.

"Nathan!" she exclaimed, hastily stepping out of his way. He stopped with an absentminded apology. "What—"

Daphne broke off at the sight of his face, which was red with agitation and something like worry. His skin was pale and wan. Deep shadows were under his eyes, as if he were ill. Someone bumped into her backpack, and Daphne quickly moved off to the side.

"Oh—hi, Daphne," he said distractedly. "Where are you going to?"

"Home. Are you okay?" she asked. "You look—"

"I'm—it's nothing, just something that—yeah." Nathan scratched the back of his neck awkwardly.

Glancing at the open classroom door, Daphne asked, "Were you talking to Mr. Burnes?"

He looked over his shoulder, too, and then, grabbing Daphne's arm, led her gently away from the open classroom door, answering as they walked along the busy hallway. "Yeah, I was just talking to him in his office about catching up, since I've...kind of been falling behind, and I thought if I explained what—yeah."

Daphne paused, forcing him to stop too. "You were trying to make up some work, and he didn't want to help?"

"Something like that, yeah. I don't remember what all he said, something about how it was my problem and he doesn't cater to slackers, if I wasn't going to put in the work—" Nathan was not looking at her but at a distant spot, swallowed by whatever emotion he was trying to suppress.

"But I'm *trying* to make up," he burst out in a rush. "That's why I've been talking to everyone today to retake my tests and stuff so I can bring some of my grades up, but I'm not doing great in history, and I can't make up the lectures, but I need the credit, otherwise I don't have enough history to graduate—"

Nathan stopped and looked at her as if he realized he had just vented to a stranger. "Sorry," he said, rubbing the back of his neck again. "I've just had a messed-up week, and after cross-country yesterday—" Again, he broke off, and Daphne wondered what his cross-country practice had to do with anything—his absence?

"No, it's fine," Daphne said honestly, and added, "I know he isn't the greatest teacher to—" She was stuck by an idea, and before she could weigh it in her mind, blurted out, "What if I helped you study the history, or something?"

Nathan did not say anything immediately, and Daphne felt startled by her own offer. The silence stretched. She kicked herself. The offer was too weird—they hardly knew each other. "I mean, I know we don't have the same class—" she added hastily, her face heating up.

"You would?" Nathan blinked.

"Yeah, if you need someone to review some of the stuff... just an idea, whatever." It was Daphne's turn to look awkward, but then his face broke into the widest smile she had ever seen him give. It wiped some of the strain from his eyes.

"That would seriously help me out," he said. "Would you by chance be able to do something this weekend? Like, Saturday afternoon?"

Daphne was taken aback. Somehow it felt strange to go from the offer to an actual plan so quickly, without thought, but she *had* offered to help. "I don't think I have anything going on," she answered, feeling as if someone else had taken over her voice and made it sound so casual, like she had people over to study every day. Or people over at all.

"Great, at your house? I don't want to make you drive somewhere..."

Dazed, Daphne exchanged numbers with Nathan and gave him her address. They parted ways, and only when she had reached her locker did Daphne realize the promise she'd made to Heather had not crossed her mind during their entire conversation. The offer of helping him study had been made on the spot because he'd needed help. It was the right thing to do, Daphne reassured herself, now regretting it.

Stop being weird. It's fine.

Anyway, what had she thought being friends with him meant?

Maybe his schoolwork was what Heather noticed was wrong after her death, and she would move on after his grades straightened out. But it didn't matter anymore. Daphne was going to help him, promise or no promise. It was the right thing to do.

She slammed her locker shut and had a sudden urge to laugh at the thought of how Veronica would feel after finding out Daphne had accomplished with Nathan what was yet outside her grasp.

13

STUDY DATE

On Saturday, Daphne rummaged through her backpack as her mom breezed into her bedroom, still wearing a bright pink shirt from the breast cancer walk from that morning, an annual event she'd participated in as long as Daphne could remember. The grandmother she never knew had passed away from the disease when her mom was a sophomore in college.

"I bear subs," she announced, handing one to her daughter.

"Thanks," Daphne said gratefully. She leaned against her bed and unwrapped it, fending off the large paw of Mystique, who'd chosen to leap off the bed and investigate. "Stop it, this is vegetarian."

"What time is your date?" her mom asked, glancing at the backpack.

"It's not a date," Daphne said, a little testily. "We're studying."

Her mom lifted up her sub in a gesture of peace. "Okay, what time's your *shtudying?*"

"After lunch, so like, one."

She checked her bare wrist. "So, half an hour? But I do really need a nap, so you'll be on your own." Daphne was glad about this. "I don't need to meet him, right?" her mom said. "He's not a psycho killer?"

"Not that I know of."

"Well, if you're sure." Casually her mom turned and observed the wall of black-and-white photos, which had not altered much since last time she'd viewed it. "Where's that bridge?" she asked suddenly, pointing.

"What?" Daphne's heart tensed, following the finger to the photos of the stone bridge tacked to the wall. She'd added the photos from the previous weekend, but the sight of it made her feel as if she were caught in a secret that could be discovered through the photos' existence. The world of perceiving shades and her normal world felt like two separate lives that could not be joined without catastrophe. "Oh, just something I found outside of town."

"It's pretty," her mom remarked, chewing thoughtfully.

"Yeah," Daphne said nonchalantly, hoping the topic would be dropped. "Bridges are...cool."

"That reminds me, we got a postcard from Uncle Lloyd in the mail today." Her mom's adventurous younger brother traveled all around the world for his career and shared Daphne's passion for photography. They did not get to see him often, but Daphne looked forward to his visits and emails and had clung to his travel stories since she was a child.

"Where is he now? Tahiti?" she asked, taking a bite from her sub out of Mystique's reach.

"Thailand. He said he might be able to come home for Christmas."

"Really?" Daphne beamed, forgetting about her impending day for the first time. "That would be great!"

"He said he was eighty-six-percent certain."

"Pretty good chance, then. I hope he can make it."

"Me too." Her mom sighed suddenly and stood up. "I'm going to go lie down, then. Wake me up if you're getting murdered, okay?"

Several minutes after one, Daphne sat at the top of the stairs, absentmindedly scratching Mystique's head with icy fingers as she waited for the sound of a knock on the front door.

It's just studying, she reassured herself. Why was she so nervous?

Because he wasn't an ordinary person coming over, was part of the answer. Without Heather's interference, Nathan would not be coming over at all. He was studying with her because of the interference of his deceased sister. That was not normal.

But the offer had been made without thought of Heather, Daphne reminded herself. His sister may have caused their first meeting, but everything after that was natural. She was helping him because it was the right thing to do.

The sound of the doorbell nearly threw her out of her skin. Daphne shot to her feet and attempted to brush the dark fur off her blue-and-white plaid shirt.

She walked downstairs to the entryway, stooping to organize the boots she'd haphazardly thrown off that morning, and opened the front door. Nathan stood just outside, wearing a backpack over both shoulders and athletic sweatpants. His wavy hair was swept up naturally, and Daphne noticed he looked healthier than a few days ago: the color had returned to his face, and the shadows under his eyes were no longer visible.

"Hi," she said.

"Hi, sorry I'm late," he answered earnestly. It was four minutes past one. "Your house was farther away than I thought."

"You're not that late," Daphne answered, amused. She stood back to allow him room to enter and closed the door behind him, dimming the light. In the small entryway, he seemed much too close, the air charged with expectant silence.

Stop overthinking.

"I...thought we could study in the kitchen," Daphne said.

"Okay," Nathan answered, turning. "This way?"

"To the left," she said, following.

He dropped his backpack on the floor next to the chair where Daphne had placed her books and tablet. As Nathan took out his materials, she opened her notebook, only to find it was full of French. Her history and French notebooks were both blue.

"Oh, I grabbed the wrong one. Give me a sec," Daphne said nervously.

"Sure," Nathan answered easily, unpacking his own notes on the table.

Daphne left and sprinted upstairs to her bedroom to get the correct notebook from her backpack, feeling anxious for each second Nathan passed alone downstairs, waiting for her. Retrieving it, she closed the door on the mess inside, in the unlikely event he went upstairs, and stepped into the hallway. She froze.

A uniformed young man was walking up the stairs, trailing mist. His baggy green pants were tucked into laced-up boots, treading soundlessly on the floor. A rifle in his hands pointed down. The soldier's face was handsome and impassive underneath a helmet covered with mesh.

The shade stepped onto the landing, not paying any attention to Mystique, who batted a paw in confusion at whatever had disturbed the air.

"Stop," Daphne whispered. The shade continued to walk toward her. "Stop!" she said, louder, but quiet enough so her mom wouldn't wake and Nathan couldn't hear from downstairs.

The man was three feet away. "Stop!" Daphne said again, stepping back, and then flattened herself against the closed door as the shade passed. She winced as his elbow passed through her like a cold breath. Every wrinkle in his jacket was visible up close.

Daphne watched him silently vanish through the mirror at the end of the hall. The last traces of mist vanished into the air. And there was only her own reflection, staring back at her in bewilderment. It might not have happened at all.

She went downstairs in a daze, only glancing over her shoulder once to see if the soldier had reappeared. Was this one on a permanent loop, forever walking up the stairs and down the hall? Had he always been there?

Nathan looked up at her approach, flipping through his own notebook.

"Would you want to go over the English Civil War together? I missed that one."

With an effort, Daphne forced herself to focus on history. The shade would have to wait.

"Sure. Do...you want a soda or something?"

"Thanks," Nathan said, clicking his pen. "Hey, the English Civil War is with Oliver Cromwell, right? Sorry, I bet that's a dumb question."

Grabbing the handle, she paused for a moment at the old magnet by her clenched hand—*Virginia Is for Lovers*—and jerked the door open. The sight of the shade upstairs occupied her thoughts, and she pushed it away with effort.

With studying to concentrate on, Daphne found her nervousness melting away as they buried themselves deeper into history over the next hour. Nathan, she discovered, was actually easy to be with, and he didn't seem to mind her awkwardness, which with any luck wasn't as obvious as she feared.

Nathan himself wasn't how she had expected him to be. He wasn't transparently sad—not that she had expected copious amounts of weeping—but instead was easygoing, and earnest in a charming way.

It was easy to forget how they had come together. In fact, she didn't think of Heather at all until Nathan mentioned his brother's band.

"You have a brother?" Daphne said, looking up. She had thought Heather was his only sibling.

"Yeah, he's older than me—twenty-four." His wavy hair stood up more than ever from his habit of running a hand into it when concentrating. "He lives on the coast now. He does indie folk stuff, mostly cover, but he's written a few songs too."

"I like indie music," Daphne said. "Is that what you're into?"

"I like classical," Nathan said, looking bashful.

"Classic rock?"

"No. Well, yeah. But I listen to classical when I run a lot. Mozart. Beethoven." He looked self-conscious and added, "I know, it's weird."

"No," Daphne said truthfully. "I mean, it's...good for relaxation." She shrugged to hide the mortification. Why was she so *awkward*? Was she always like this?

"That's why I like it," he said. "I get bored of pop music."

"Me too," she answered, and with a mutual smile that made her face feel warm, they returned to studying. Nathan was in the middle of asking her a question when Daphne heard footsteps on the stairs. Her mom burst into the kitchen, still wearing her pink shirt.

"How's it going, y'all?"

"Nathan, this is my mom," Daphne said, embarrassed. In the presence of a stranger, she didn't feel the need to impress, her mom was extra boisterous.

"Oh—hi, Mrs. Cole," he said, twisting around to shake her hand. She took it with affected formality.

"How's the studying going?"

"Fine," Daphne answered pointedly.

"Great," Nathan answered, seemingly not put off by her mom's humor. "I mean, I'm not in the AP class like Daphne, but our class covers the same stuff."

"And this is Euro? Is that the teacher with the weird sideburns?"

"Um—yeah. Mr. Burnes," Daphne said with a side glance at Nathan, who was grinning at her. "How was your nap?" she said to change the subject.

"I slept very well until I woke up. Now I need tea." Her mom turned toward the fridge and waved her hand carelessly. "You folks carry on."

Daphne glanced at her suspiciously, assuming her mom was actually there solely to scope out Nathan. "Okay. What were you asking before, Nathan?"

"Oh. I was just looking at the notes, where it says Mary becomes queen after the Glorious Revolution of 1688. Is she the same person as Bloody Mary—?"

Daphne was distracted by the sight of her beaming mother behind Nathan, giving two thumbs up in approval and mouthing, *He's cute!*

Mom! she mouthed back reprovingly, widening her eyes over Nathan's talking head.

"—but she's married to William of Orange." He looked up,

and Daphne quickly morphed her face into an attentive expression.

"No, Bloody Mary was Scottish, and not Protestant. *This* revolution happened a hundred years later." She watched her mom leave the room with an outstretched thumbs-up and a manic smile, a bottle of diet iced tea clutched in her other hand. Daphne inwardly rolled her eyes as her mom left, focusing again on her notes. "The way Burnes explained it, the monarchy was restored with Charles the second, but they didn't like him; then James the second took over, and Mary was his daughter who lived in the Netherlands—"

"Right," Nathan said, throwing down his pen with a flourish. "With William of Grape."

"Actually, it was William of Apple," Daphne replied, mock-stern.

"William of *Applesauce*."

His expression was so deadpan, Daphne couldn't help but burst out laughing. "Yeah, that." Feeling suddenly shy again, Daphne returned to her untidy notes and attempted to focus. Nathan, however, grinned and straightened in his chair.

"What did William of Pineapple do?"

"He founded a bank."

"Woo-hoo..."

It was past four before they both felt they couldn't continue.

"Well, I don't know about you, but that's all my brain can handle right now," Nathan said, rubbing his eyes and leaning back in his chair.

"At least you can sleep in tomorrow," Daphne said, closing the textbook with a satisfying thud.

"Actually, I can't. I have to get up early to run." Nathan removed his hands and smiled at her.

She smiled back hesitantly. "Why?"

"We usually run as a team in the morning," he answered. "My coach says it's so we can keep up a team dynamic for meets. It's a way to keep competitive, too, so our performance keeps improving."

"That makes sense, I guess," Daphne answered, shaking her head all the same. "When's your next meet?"

"Thursday," Nathan said, then brightened at a thought. "You should come out and see it sometime."

"Watch a meet?" Daphne said, surprised at the offer. They weren't friends, but maybe this was a casual offer for him. "I've never been to one before."

"They're pretty fun."

"Maybe. How many meets do you have left?"

"A few," said Nathan. "Some in November, then the season's over."

"Oh." Daphne thought about it. She didn't know how fun watching people run was, but part of her felt pleased to be asked. "I'll come and check it out sometime. Just let me know when they are."

"Sure," he said. Daphne recalled how, when she found him outside of Euro, she had gotten the impression something had happened during practice to make him miss school. But whatever it was, Daphne was not going to ask, despite her curiosity. If Nathan did not want to go into it, that was his choice, and it was none of her business. She didn't like talking about personal things with strangers either.

Still slouched, Nathan looked comfortably around the kitchen. "Is that your dad?" he asked with a nod at an old picture frame perched on the windowsill. Daphne glanced at it. His muscular arm around her mother's thin shoulder.

"Yes," she said distantly, putting together books without

noticing what she was doing. Sometimes, when she was caught off guard...

"Where is he?" he said, nonchalant. It was such a simple question.

The humor of the last hour vanished like an extinguished candle, the smoke lingering in the air. But it was not his fault. She rubbed a finger over the frayed corner of the textbook. "He...died when I was thirteen."

"Oh—I'm sorry," came the expected answer. There was a long pause. When Daphne could no longer pretend to straighten her books, she glanced up and saw Nathan was looking at her with a somber expression, as if seeing her for the first time. As if something had clicked into place.

"It's okay," Daphne said, and forced a smile. She was anxious suddenly to be alone again, and changed the subject. "I...hope this helped you out."

"Yeah, thanks a lot. It was fun," Nathan said sincerely, also standing up and putting books into his backpack. "It's a lot better than studying by myself, anyway."

Daphne followed him to the front door, and with a final, charming thanks, Nathan left. She sighed in relief at the sound of tires on gravel.

In the silence and dim light of the entryway, she wondered what Nathan thought of her dad's death. If there was one thing she couldn't stand, it was pity. She did not want him to treat her differently because of what happened. She did not want to be marked, apart from everyone else. But that was what she was. Between that tragedy, her nightmares, and being able to perceive shades, Daphne felt she was continually set apart.

She turned to the staircase. The shade had not appeared again.

And yet, wasn't she guilty of doing the same toward him? What about all her preconceptions because of his sister's death? The sister who she watched die every night in her nightmares?

They had something in common, and perhaps that was the reason she'd been compelled to help him. Daphne wasn't sure if losing a parent was quite the same as losing a sibling, but did it matter? They'd both lost someone close.

The crunch of gravel faded.

14

RULES OF ENGAGEMENT

Daphne stationed herself on the top step early Monday morning.

She hadn't caught a glimpse of the soldier since Nathan's visit on Saturday. If the shade kept to a specific schedule as to when he walked up the stairs, it was not apparent yet what that was.

Mystique sat in her usual spot, and Daphne scratched the cat absentmindedly.

"C'mon," she said impatiently, jiggling a knee. "Where are you?"

Minutes passed. It was getting closer to the time when she would need to leave for school. Mystique grew tired of not getting Daphne's full attention and hopped with a jingle onto the landing to find a nap spot.

"You're leaving me too?" she called after the bushy tail. Daphne turned back to the stairs and immediately vaulted backward.

The misting, uniformed shade was marching up the stairs, where a second before he had not been. The soldier stared ahead and did not react as Daphne scrambled to her feet. Maybe it was just his getup, or the fact that he was unresponsive, but this shade was frightening.

"Stop." It came out as a whisper. His boot reached the top landing, and Daphne took another step back. "Stop!" she tried again, louder, but the soldier kept walking, full of purpose, toward the end of the hall. There were only seconds until he reached it.

Daphne melted against the wall as he passed, holding her breath as his nearly solid form came into sharp view, so she could see the individual creases on his uniform. He was almost to the mirror, where he would disappear. There was no knowing when she would see him again.

"*Stop!*" she shouted in desperation. At the same time, without planning it, Daphne reached out a mental hand and firmly tugged where she imagined his arm to be.

The man lurched and stopped just before the mirror.

Daphne gaped at his back, stunned. Without meaning to, she had deliberately touched a shade. Somehow, too, she had been able to pull him out of his loop.

The shade stood completely still except for the mist curling slowly off his uniform. Daphne peeled herself from the wall and crept forward hesitantly, glancing into the mirror despite being unable to see his face. She stopped within arm's reach of the shade.

"Who—who are you?"

For a moment it appeared he would not answer, but then the soldier rotated and looked directly at Daphne with solemn eyes, seeing her for the first time. His face was handsome, clean-shaven.

"Phillip," he said after a pause, frowning as if uncertain this was correct. "My name is Phillip."

Daphne stared, more nervous now that his eyes noticed her

clearly, but she forced herself to speak. "Did you—die in a war?"

The shade—Phillip—frowned again. Daphne wondered at this; all of the other shades she'd met and spoken to had known how they had died. But she had just pulled him out of a loop. Perhaps it was like waking from unconsciousness, when everything feels confusing at first, and he would become more oriented with time.

She took a step closer. Between the long gun and his tallness in that narrow space, the shade was especially intimidating. But up close, Daphne could see he was really no older than his early twenties, at most. He was not much older than her, in a way.

"What year is it?" she improvised.

Another long pause. "1944," the shade answered, to Daphne's excitement. If he knew that answer, she could try being more specific.

"When did you—I mean, what day is it?"

He stared at her blankly. "Sixth of June."

Daphne paused. She knew that date. Her mom might be the history geek of the family, but her dad had liked WWII stories.

"So you died on D-Day," she said. Phillip gazed at her without expression. Maybe he didn't know the answer.

"Did you...live in this house?" Daphne asked. The thought was intriguing. Her mom had been drawn to the house by the fact that it was old, that it had a story. Now, here could be a talking remnant of part of that history.

"I..." Phillip frowned again. "I don't..."

The shade didn't know where he was, then, Daphne noted with interest and disappointment. Yet, maybe her mom would know more about a man called Phillip who had possibly lived in their home. Why else would his haunting be here?

"Okay," Daphne said, before deciding to ask directly. She swallowed. "Why are you here?"

His face snapped to attention, like it would given an order. "Violet," he said abruptly, no longer uncertain or confused. "I must see Violet."

"Who's Violet?" she asked, taken aback by his sudden clarity.

"I must see her. I must see Violet," Phillip said, with more agitation. Like with some other shades, it was repeated as if it were an obsessive thought.

"Okay," Daphne said placatingly, taking a step back. "Who is she?"

"Violet."

"Yes, I know," she said. "But who's Violet?"

"I must see Violet."

Daphne sighed. Talking to shades was difficult at the best of times, but with a newly woken shade, it would apparently take some time. She burned with curiosity at who Violet was, at why Phillip had spent all this time walking perpetually up the stairs. Who was Violet? Who had she been?

"Who's Violet?" she tried again half-heartedly.

"I must see Violet," the shade repeated urgently.

Daphne gave up. Likely, that was all she would be able to find out for now. Maybe Phillip would become more responsive in the coming days, once he became more used to being out of his loop. Then she could try asking him more questions.

The clock on the wall showed it was ten minutes later than she normally left for school. Daphne turned away from Phillip and sprinted out the front door, just remembering to lock it but feeling somehow a stranger was already in her home.

. . .

Daphne wrenched her locker open, anticlimactically now that she had made it to school a full five minutes before the bell. She spotted Jessica down the hall in a group that included Veronica and suppressed a smile. Normally, Daphne prided herself on not being petty, but she was satisfied knowing Veronica would be upset about the study session with Nathan, if she ever found out.

Daphne wondered how Phillip would spend his time now that he was no longer stuck on a loop. Would he stay in the house? Would he wander?

"Hey, Daphne," said a voice.

Daphne turned and looked into the face of Nathan.

"Hey." She smiled, feeling a pleased fluttering in her stomach, as well as a sudden shyness.

"What's up? What class do you have next?" he asked.

"Photography."

A flash passed over his face. "Oh, right! You were going to show me your photos."

"I was?" Daphne replied, flattered he had remembered. However, she still felt a protectiveness against showing her photos to anyone. Over his shoulder, she saw Veronica peer over, eyes wide.

"Yeah, your black-and-white ones."

"Oh. Maybe," she said evasively, selecting a notebook from the shelf and adding it to the pile in her arms.

Nathan leaned against the locker next to hers. "What do you have to take pictures of, in class?"

"Whatever we want, basically, as long as it's part of the project. Right now we're doing mood—" Daphne resolved to turn away from her books and actually look at him but broke off, her stomach lurching, at the unexpected sight of Heather, who was standing just an arm's length away from her brother.

The sentence was lost. It was easy to forget her friendship with Nathan had begun with a promise.

"What's that?"

Daphne tore her eyes from Heather's penetrating stare and into the twin of those eyes. "What?" she said in confusion before realizing he wasn't talking about his sister, who, after all, he couldn't see. What would Nathan say if he knew his dead sister stood so close? She frowned, scrambling to remember what they were talking about. "Oh, mood? It's, um..."

Luckily, though not in any other circumstance, Jessica chose that moment to appear.

"Daphne! How's it going?" she said cheerily. Jessica's hair was in its usual high, sleek ponytail, which swung back and forth as she approached. Daphne was struck by the same suspicion she'd had when her mom had walked into the kitchen on Saturday: her friend was there solely to scope out Nathan and find out why he was standing by Daphne's locker, when they clearly never knew each other before.

"Good," Daphne replied, glancing once at Nathan, who was still leaning against the locker. He'd adopted the polite smile of someone who's been interrupted and is waiting to see whether it's permanent before leaving. Then Jessica turned to him confidently.

"Hi. You're Nathan, right?"

Daphne suppressed a smile. She knew Jessica was well aware of who he was. If she had dared to glance in that direction, no doubt she would find Veronica watching the exchange.

"Yeah," he replied, more subdued under the force of Jessica's outgoing personality.

"We have history together!" she said.

He nodded.

"Everyone I know hates that class. I don't know how I'm passing!"

She could be overwhelming at first, but Jessica never faltered when it came to awkward silence, and she was smarter than her high voice made her appear. Daphne could see Nathan relax his shoulders slightly.

Her admiration turned to panic at his reply.

"I know," Nathan said, nodding. "Daphne's been helping me study."

"She has?" One of Jessica's thin eyebrows shot up in surprise. *Really?* they seemed to spell.

Helping Nathan had seemed like a part of Daphne's new, private life of perceiving shades, so she had not thought to tell Jessica about her study session with him. Now she could see Jessica struggling to digest this information. She hoped he would not mention they'd studied at her house.

"Just to review some things," Daphne put in quickly, keeping her voice casual, as if she had study sessions with definitely-not-ugly guys all the time. She was painfully aware of Heather observing the three of them. *Please go away.*

"I've been trying to catch up on some of the days I missed," Nathan explained.

"Oh! Do you need some notes or something? You can take a photo of them if you need to," Jessica said helpfully.

"That actually might be a good idea. Thanks."

"No problem."

The first bell finally rang, to Daphne's relief. Students began to shuffle reluctantly to their first classes of the week. She was in no hurry, for the art rooms were just down the hall.

"Talk to you later, Daphne," Nathan told her, and to Jessica, "See you in class." Down the hall, he turned and called, "I still want to see your photos!" and was gone.

Daphne couldn't help but smile. Her friend turned to her with a gleeful expression. "Ooh, guess who's going to be *jealous!*"

"What?" Daphne said uncomfortably, and shifted her books to her other arm. Heather still watched her.

Jessica rolled her eyes. "See you at lunch!" she said, and caught up to Veronica down the hall. They put their heads together immediately.

Daphne stood by her open locker, staring grimly after them. She was understanding more what Claire had meant by the difficulty of helping shades. Between Jessica and Veronica's interference and Heather's eerie hovering, she would be lucky to become better friends with Nathan at all. The idea of making Veronica jealous was fun at first, but Daphne could see it could become more problematic than a snide remark here and there. They shared lunch, and Jessica was both of their friend and might be forced to choose a side.

But it wasn't like she was *dating* him, Daphne defended herself. Nor was Veronica. There was no side to choose.

There was, however, one issue she could resolve right away.

Daphne turned and saw Heather hadn't moved from her spot, but was watching her. Except for the mist rising from her form, she might have been just another student. Discreetly, Daphne jerked her head, and the shade walked to her side, passing through an oblivious passerby in the process. Since there were still plenty of people in the hallway, Daphne pretended to rummage for something in her backpack.

"You need to give me a little space, okay? I can talk to him better if you're not always around," she murmured.

After a few seconds, Heather nodded. "Okay."

"Okay," Daphne confirmed, and slammed her locker shut.

It was the first time she'd given a shade an order on her own, Daphne realized as she left Heather in order to head to the art rooms. She knew Heather would have to obey, but her guilt that someone was forced to do her will was mostly suppressed by her annoyance over the shade's intrusion.

If she and Nathan could just talk without the prying eyes of his dead sister, or Veronica and Jessica, for that matter, they'd have a better chance of becoming friends.

Daphne passed the art display case, where Ashley's outraged self-portrait gazed down at her, and, almost unconsciously, quickened her pace.

15

PRACTICE

Daphne had to admit there'd been some advantages to having a house-haunting restricted to one area.

Now that he was no longer confined to the stairs, Phillip had taken to wandering aimlessly around the house, mainly the upstairs landing. She forbade him from entering any of the bedrooms or the bathroom after he once walked unceremoniously through her bedroom door just as she was falling asleep. Without meaning to, Daphne had pushed him back through the wall. It was difficult to attempt this skill deliberately, but she was improving.

This order mostly limited him to the small hallway outside, seemingly by preference. Phillip liked most of all to stop and stare at the long mirror, even though it could not reflect him.

To her initial excitement, her mom recalled a Violet who was one of the daughters of a family who had lived in their house in the forties. But she didn't know of any Phillip, when Daphne had dared to ask directly, other than the one who had sold them the house.

The timing could not be a coincidence, but any attempt

at getting Phillip to tell her anything about Violet resulted in the same circular conversation as before. Violet was his anchor, whoever she was—the reason he had remained behind. But who was she? Why had Phillip been walking up the stairs?

Daphne toyed with the idea that Violet was once his girl-friend, someone he left behind in the war. But any mention of Violet, and the shade would only repeat her name as before. Daphne did not know how long it would take, if ever, for him to answer the question.

While Phillip was intrusive, Heather now kept her distance. Daphne didn't see any sign of her at all whenever Nathan stopped by her locker before school or walked with her to history. The shade had disappeared from the lunch period as well.

Claire was now back from her weeklong visit to her sons in Florida. Daphne was relieved the psychic was in Long Haven again, despite Claire's assurance nothing would happen while she was away. The possibility of having to battle a dyszoon by herself had kept her on edge.

"Have you had luck practicing?" Claire had asked Monday evening over the phone, after relating some details of her trip.

Guilt squirmed in Daphne's stomach. "I've been trying, but it's like I can only touch them when I'm *not* trying," she admitted.

Daphne heard the thoughtful silence on the other end of the phone. "I would say to try it again anyway," Claire said. "And don't just use one shade—gather together a few. There will be more than one dyszoon to contend with when the Veil expands, and that might help."

"How?" Daphne asked, masking with difficulty the desperation she felt. Halloween was less than two weeks away. And if she didn't get better at it...

"Doing so will make the circumstances more like they will be in battle. If you can pretend, however little, it could help."

Daphne imagined a group of shades surrounding her like they did on Main Street, and she cringed at the thought of them rushing her. If she brought together four shades, that would still be four she could not deflect. But she needed to practice. Even if she were able to fight a dyszoon in the fear of battle, like she had done in the woods, she would not be strong enough to do it for long. The creature left behind in the woods to diminish was very weak compared to what she would face later, and in greater numbers.

"Don't worry, Daphne," Claire reassured her, correctly interpreting the silence. "It might not work straightaway, but when it does, you will learn quickly. Just like perceiving shades."

That was true. Seeing shades was already second nature, and Daphne had become so used to them that in a way it was like she had always perceived them. Despite her doubts, Daphne brightened. She only needed to try.

They'd ended the call by arranging to meet on Saturday morning at a house a little outside Long Haven, since Claire needed to check on her friend's cats there and could meet at the same time. As Daphne stared at the colorless photo of the bridge on her bedroom wall, she made a decision. The next day, she would start.

Three misting shades stood in front of her, glancing around indifferently at the brightly colored woods.

Phillip stood a few paces next to Daphne, looking impressive in military uniform, with his long gun held against him. It was likely the first time he'd been outside of the house since first haunting it, and Daphne thought it might be good for him.

He glanced around the forest, alert, as if chosen to be the lookout.

Late afternoon sun filtered through the trees. Straight after school, Daphne had wandered the woods, investigating any sense that told her a shade was near. She gathered three—Frank, wandering alone, whose shirt was mercifully unblood-ied, and then two women. One of them looked to be in her forties, wearing twenties-style office clothes. The other was half her age but in dress from the previous century. Whatever their backgrounds, they had all ended up in the woods.

Daphne surveyed them, uncertain. So far, she had followed Claire's advice, but how it worked from this point on, she had no idea. Were the shades even aware of the evil that was coming?

She cleared her throat, and four pairs of dead eyes turned to look at her. Daphne swallowed. She could figure it out.

"Thanks for coming with me..." She trailed off—niceties didn't matter with shades. Deciding on a different tack, Daphne started again. "I gathered you here because I need your help. I'm not sure if you know, but there's something coming—something evil."

At this, all of them stirred uneasily. Maybe they were aware of the impending battle after all.

"I know I'm new to all of this, but I have to fight those things, so, I need you to help me practice, if—if you can do that."

The shades stared at her without expression. Daphne glanced instinctively at Phillip for reassurance. He gave a curt nod, to her surprise, and she turned forward again, feeling buoyed.

"Okay, this is what I need you to do."

. . .

Daphne slowly got to her feet, rubbing the side that had fallen on a hidden stick when she had dived to the ground to avoid Frank's assault—if it could be called one, when she could barely feel any of the shades as they passed through her.

Cursing inwardly, Daphne took in the sight of the shades nearby, waiting patiently to be told to attack again. After half a dozen times, it was still a frightening sight to have someone who looked solid soar toward her, much like a dyszoon, when normally they moved like the living. The last time, she'd reacted on instinct.

Only ten minutes had passed. One by one, each had done their part to attack her. Daphne thought ruefully that her only success was the faintest sensation of a block before the younger woman had passed through her. The block wasn't strong enough to stop the shade entirely, and her misting form had swallowed Daphne and passed through unpleasantly like a cool wind.

"All right," she muttered. "That's not going to work."

The younger woman kicked her foot ineffectively against the ground.

Daphne glanced at Phillip, the only shade she had not asked to attack her. If she were being honest with herself, he was still intimidating in his uniform and meshed helmet, though despite it all, she found herself liking him. He kept his protective stance, hand firmly gripping the rifle to protect against an imaginary ambush.

Ambush...

It had seemed logical to start slow, to practice on one shade at a time until she had mastered blocking, and then work up. But maybe it needed to be a trial by fire. Daphne turned back to the other shades, then set her jaw firmly. She hated the idea, but it was necessary to try.

"I want you to attack me again. But—" Daphne hesitated. She would just get it over with. "Do it all at once."

The shades were silent. She turned again to Phillip, letting him know this time he was included, then braced herself.

"Okay—now."

With blazing, breathless speed, the shades erupted—four silver-tinted blurs raced toward Daphne. In that minuscule moment, she threw up her hands uselessly to protect herself. Then—

Daphne opened her eyes, surprised to see the shades standing silently once more, as if they had been doing so the whole time. In just seconds, it was over. The sensation of cool wind brushing through her left as quickly as it had come.

She gritted her jaw, frustrated. Terror had frozen her instead of inflamed. There had been no time to think, and yet her only reaction was to shut her eyes against the coming wave rather than defend against it. Any anger was at herself. At least the sensation of being passed through wasn't as bad as expected.

"Same thing again," Daphne told the shades. Another idea struck her—when the dyszoons did attack, she would have no control over when or how they came, in the battle ahead. "But this time, I want you to choose when."

The shades didn't nod. There was hardly any time to wonder if they had the ability to make that decision when the older woman became a blur.

She passed through Daphne just as Frank joined, doing the same. This time Daphne forced her eyes open and shuddered as his form tore into her, before the other woman soared forward too, her body like moonlit fog with a solid face. The grayish mist enveloped Daphne and faded into the air. She made eye contact with Phillip, directly in front of her, and opened her mouth to tell him to stop so she could gather her breath.

At that moment, he became smoke.

Seconds slowed. She could not turn away from his approaching face, his dead eyes filled with so much soul. Terror gripped her, and yet Daphne felt determination, a rightness, when her hand lifted, as if the fact that blood still pumped through it meant it could defend against the dead.

It couldn't. But she could.

Phillip was just a foot away and then, inexplicably, bounced away as if he had hit an invisible wall. The scattered cloud of him condensed and became the solid form of the soldier a few paces away, unharmed.

Daphne gaped at him, then realized her arm was suspended and lowered it. The hit had resembled the attack of the dyszoon in the woods when she'd made the shield it couldn't penetrate, only it was a weaker sensation, and without any malice. Her heart fluttered in excitement. For once, it had worked.

The others were waiting patiently for her on all sides. Despite her first success, the celebration would have to wait. This success was only the beginning. Spinning slowly to look at them all, Daphne readied herself, nodding nervously.

"Again."

A moment of anticipation, then—

Behind her, Daphne sensed the form of Frank and turned just in time to feebly defend herself. A faint push did nothing to stop him soaring through her. She winced and drew her attention to another faint breath of movement on her side as the younger woman flew for her in a blaze, followed almost immediately by the older shade. They both reached Daphne at the same time, determination in their faces, terrifyingly human.

Again, Daphne was powerless to stop the attack. As she

watched the last tendrils of smoke drift into the air, any satisfaction gained just a minute before was ebbing away.

"I guess that was just a lucky one," she told Phillip, who hadn't yet joined in the attack.

Daphne sighed.

"Again."

The scenario repeated itself over the next hour. Despite the frequency with which the attacks came, Daphne could not get used to the sight of the shades passing through her as if she herself were air. At least by the end of the hour, she was successful at deflecting one shade a quarter of the time.

As she headed for home, Phillip trailing behind her voluntarily while the rest drifted off to seek a quiet place deeper in the woods, Daphne allowed herself to feel more confident about her abilities than she ever had before. The practice had gone much better than expected, and as long as she practiced every day in the coming week, Daphne hoped she would be much better prepared for any dyszoons that came out of the Veil on Halloween.

A small sense of security dulled the sharpest edges of her worry and fear, the weight of her task less heavy than it had been. It could be done. She could fight dyszoons. Between her and Claire, they'd banish the creatures back to Hell quickly.

And then deal with the Veil.

Daphne allowed herself a grim smile. It was a start.

16

THE FOOTBALL GAME

Daphne noticed a gradual improvement over the next few days as she practiced each morning and after school. A breakthrough came Friday morning, when she was able to repeatedly deflect two shade attacks in succession.

Still, Daphne could not be sure her efforts to improve her ability to fend off an attack would be enough. The memory of the dyszoon she'd fought in the woods was like a bad dream she could not shake off, setting a high bar she had not yet reached. But shades, although they couldn't entirely mimic dyszoons in battle, were her only hope of improvement.

That evening, Daphne walked with Jessica past the football bleachers halfway through the first quarter to choose seats. She had not attended a game in years, but Jessica had invited her to the playoffs and made no mention of Veronica being there. The thought of spending time with her best friend without inane chatter was worth the price of the boredom.

"There's Taylor." Jessica pointed.

They recognized a group of girls sitting a few rows up near the center of the field. Daphne was glad to see Beth, who was wearing a jersey of one of the Falcons football players, sitting with them.

"Hey, Daphne! Hey, Jessica!" Beth waved.

"Hey!" Jessica answered cheerfully. "Mind if we sit by you guys?"

Daphne sidled in first on the available bench behind the group. The others had had the foresight to bring a blanket to drape over the hard seat, a green-and-white fleece with falcons.

A few middle-aged parents on the row farthest up screamed, "TOUCHDOWN!" The Long Haven Falcons scored the first points of the game, and the players in green lined up for the field goal. The home side of the stadium clapped.

"Score!" a man shouted as the football bounced off the yellow pole and spun through. The cheering was more enthusiastic this time. The dance team on the far end of the bleachers began a semisynchronized victory dance. Daphne clapped politely and leaned away from Jessica's enthusiastic cheering.

"Go Ethan!" Beth called in front of them, clapping her hands wildly.

Jessica leaned toward Daphne's ear, phone in hand, and whispered, "Beth just started dating him. The guy who kicked the ball."

"I thought so, with the jersey," Daphne answered. The number on the player's uniform matched the one Beth was wearing. "Who are you texting?"

"Veronica," Jessica replied. "She's wondering where we are."

"Is she coming over by us?" Daphne asked with sudden dread.

"No, she's standing at the end somewhere." During home games, a large group of students wearing jerseys stood at the end of the bleachers to cheer the band players and the nearby dance team.

"I'm going to be taking my cousin trick-or-treating," Beth was saying as Jessica took a picture of herself and sent it. "Otherwise she couldn't go..."

"Oh! That reminds me, there's a Halloween festival next weekend. I think it could be fun!" Jessica said to Daphne, putting her phone away. On the field, the teams broke for a time-out.

"Halloween?" Daphne said blankly. In her mind, Friday was reserved for two things: school, and fighting evil spirits from Hell.

"Yeah, it's at the park. There's going to be a band, a haunted trail, hayride, pumpkin-carving contest, concessions..." Jessica ticked them off on her fingers.

"What time?" If it was too late in the evening...

"I think it's from like eight to midnight or something," she answered, and Daphne's heart thumped unpleasantly. She and Claire had not arranged a time to meet, but it would certainly be somewhere around that time. Yet what excuse could she give not to go?

"Yeah, that could be fun," Daphne said, trying to sound noncommittal. Fortunately, the teams had lined up again and the whistle blew, and Jessica's attention was distracted.

As they watched the game, Daphne wondered what time she would need to meet Claire at the bridge to face down the Veil. If the dyszoons were arriving on Halloween, did that mean the stroke of midnight, noon, or during the time bleeding into November first? They would no doubt discuss it on Saturday.

The first half of the game passed in a dull blur, and it became clear the Falcons' first touchdown had been an anomaly in their performance. Halftime arrived, with a seven-point gap between the two teams. The crowd began to disperse, including Beth and her friends, to get concessions. Daphne stayed behind with Jessica, who was trying to diet and feeling conflicted about her self-denial.

A slow-moving throng of people passed in front of them. Among them appeared Ashley Zhang, shepherding what must be her two siblings, a boy and a girl who looked grade-school age, toward the concessions area at the end of the fenced field. She looked miserable. Most likely she'd been forced to take them to the game, Daphne thought. She could not imagine Ashley coming to cheer on the Falcons for fun.

"Hey, Ashley! *Ashley!*"

Daphne looked at Jessica in surprise at what she felt was a more enthusiastic greeting than the relationship required. For a moment it looked like Ashley would pretend not to hear, but the boy stopped and pulled on the sleeve of her jacket, pointing.

"Oh. Hi," Ashley said. They stepped up to get out of the way of the passing crowd.

"What's up? Are those your siblings?"

"Hi," the girl said, waving. She could hardly be older than six or seven.

"Hi!" Jessica said, now beaming and adopting the cheery voice she saved for children. She loved kids, Daphne knew, feeling rather aloof by comparison. "I'm Jessica. What's your name?"

"Alexa," she said.

"I'm Alex," the boy put in, perhaps her twin and looking eager to be noticed by Jessica too.

Already turning, Ashley nudged them both and said, annoyed, "C'mon, guys, let's get to the bathrooms before it starts again."

"Bye." The girl waved again. They stepped into the crowd and were gone.

Daphne watched them walk down the line, eyebrows raised. "That was awkward."

"Oh," Jessica said, adjusting her coat. "I thought it was fine. Her sister is so cute!"

Privately, Daphne thought anyone else would have noticed the strangeness of the exchange. "Do you know Ashley at all?"

"I had Jewelry with her last year," said Jessica. "We had fun."

"Fun?" Daphne echoed automatically, staring. Ashley was never anything but borderline hostile. "I mean, she always seems kind of moody to me."

"Maybe she is now," Jessica said, shrugging. "But last year she was different."

Daphne couldn't think of a reply that wasn't skeptical. She hadn't known Ashley until this year, and *know* was a strong word. Had they ever even spoken? But *fun* was also stretching it. Jessica did tend to see the best in people, or at least be blind to their faults. Maybe that was it.

Just then, Beth and her friends reappeared, holding food.

"Na-chos!" Taylor announced in a hushed stadium voice, hopping up the benches and plopping down on her blanket. "Want some?"

An expression of strain passed over Jessica's face, and she grabbed a chip. "I shouldn't, but..."

Taylor held the plastic tray out. "Daphne?"

"Thanks."

As they waited for the game to start again, Daphne leaned forward toward Beth as Jessica chatted with Taylor.

"So, how long have you and Ethan been dating?" she asked. On the field, Ethan was at the sidelines, speaking with a teammate. They had rarely talked, but she remembered thinking he was kind.

"Two weeks," Beth said, her cropped red hair shining in the lights. "It's a little hard, though. My mom is really strict." Daphne vaguely recalled some references Beth had occasionally made at lunchtime.

"Does she know you're dating him?"

"Yes," Beth answered in an exasperated way that alluded to some argument. "I told my dad first, and he approved it, so *she* had to. My mom thinks I'm too young to date. Even though she *knows* him because we've been friends for, like, five years."

Daphne thought back to whether she and her mom had ever discussed dating but came up short. They occasionally talked about guys, but it had never been about iron rules for dating them. Not that she had much to talk about, to cause worry. Her thoughts drifted to Nathan. Was he at the game? Should she have invited him along?

"What's your curfew?" Beth was asking.

"I don't really have one," Daphne admitted.

"Are you serious? None?" Beth looked startled, as if unable to imagine such an arrangement could exist. "I wish *my* mom was like yours."

"What does your mom make you do?" Daphne asked, and listened as Beth recounted the various rules she had to follow. Then the game resumed, and Beth turned again to watch the next play.

Bored, Daphne let her attention wander. She reflected on the differences between their moms. Daphne had never thought her lack of rules strange. It was normal to her, but then again, she'd never been the type of teenager to need them. Actually, if she asked, her mom would probably say Daphne was close enough to adulthood, she ought to be smart enough to take care of herself by now.

Her mom gave her a lot of space, Daphne realized. Space to wander in the woods as a sort of therapy from her nightmares and to retreat into her room for hours at a stretch. Rarely prying into what was bothering her daughter, but there if she wanted to share. They did not fight often.

The point gap closed between the teams in the third quarter, but the next went wrong immediately. The opposing team's quarterback broke through the Falcons' defense and ran a full ninety yards to score a touchdown. The crowd on the opposite side stood and cheered wildly. On the home side, there was gloom.

"Well, this sucks," Taylor said, getting up and smoothing back her black, curly hair unsuccessfully. "You guys wanna hang by the concessions?"

The others agreed. Even Jessica had grown bored with a lost game, though if the Falcons could score two more touchdowns and prevent the other team from scoring again, there was hope for a victory, however unlikely. Daphne could not find it in herself to get enthusiastic either way.

Together they walked toward the blacktopped area, where a large number of students were already gathered, Jessica looking in vain for Veronica in the bleachers as they passed. Taylor went to greet someone as they stopped near the fence, while Jessica began to text. Although she didn't care about the outcome, Daphne looked out toward the field with Beth, who still loyally watched the game in support of Ethan, and took out her phone. Holding it upward, she steadied the shot toward a stadium light. The effect was neat—a fuzz of white around each bulb, bright against the dark sky.

"I think the game is *that* way."

Daphne turned around. Nathan was walking toward her with a friend she recognized from one of her classes, a fellow senior named Dominic. Heather's voice came, unwelcome, out of memory. *He's being distant with his friends.* She shook the thought away.

"I didn't know you were here," she said, pleased.

"I didn't know I was coming until halftime." He shrugged.

His dark-haired friend hadn't bothered to join their conversation but looked with a sour expression toward the field, clearly unhappy the Falcons were losing.

"Do you like football?" Daphne asked, putting away her phone.

"Not really. Cross-country's my sport." He pointed a thumb behind him. "But Dom wanted to go. He's on the team with me."

"Oh—I think he's getting concessions," Daphne said, watching Dom's back retreat toward the building.

Nathan turned. "'Course he is."

"Jessica dragged me here too."

At the sound of her name, Jessica looked up from her phone. "What's that? Oh, hey, Nathan!" She smiled and returned to her phone eagerly, and Daphne looked at it with a suspicion she hoped would turn out to be wrong.

They stood next to the fence and turned at the sound of whistling. Daphne wasn't sure what was happening on the field, but Beth was still watching intently. For once, the silence felt comfortable rather than excruciating.

"You know, I like Polaroids," Nathan said with a side glance at her.

"What?" Daphne turned away from the sight of the distant ref.

"Well, it's not an *actual* Polaroid," he explained. "It's an instant camera. Not the low-quality ones, but then I have a few film ones I use sometimes. I have one that was my great-grand-father's—"

"Wait, you collect cameras? You do photography?" Daphne

said, amazed that they had something she liked so much in common.

"Not really," he said in a self-deprecating way. "I like to develop photos, but I don't think I'm very good at taking them, I mean, not as good as you probably are."

"I didn't know that!" she said. "That's so cool, the developing, I mean."

"It's more of a hobby," Nathan said, now rubbing the back of his neck self-consciously. "I'm really not that good, but I like the physical side of it, I guess. I'd like to see your photos."

"Well, I'd like to see *your* photos," Daphne teased.

"Only if you show me yours first," he said, so deadpan that Daphne broke off with a laugh. At that moment, Nathan's friend returned, carrying a salted pretzel in one hand and a hot dog in the other, which he bit in half.

"Want some?" Dom said thickly, holding out the pretzel enticingly. He swallowed. "We wouldn't want you to *faint* again," he added tauntingly.

Nathan's face whitened, then flushed with embarrassment.

"I'm just *joking*. That's what Coach said, right? You've gotta eat more," he said, and punched Nathan lightly on the shoulder with the hand holding the hot dog as he passed them to watch the game through the fence.

There was an awkward silence.

"You—" Daphne broke off, not sure what to say. All at once she recalled how ill he had looked the day after he missed school, pale and strained. He had mentioned practice—did he faint that week?

But there was no time to say more, since someone had just literally bumped herself into Jessica, giggling. Daphne's stomach sank.

Veronica wore a black headband over freshly highlighted hair and a borrowed jersey, like Beth. Two black lines were drawn on her cheeks. Daphne knew immediately why she'd arrived just then, when she hadn't bothered to seek them out before: she had finally worked up the courage to meet Nathan.

"Hey! I got your message," she said, and looked up, her eyes resting on Nathan. "Are you guys watching the game?"

Too late, Daphne realized that if she had kept talking to Nathan, Veronica's arrival might have gone unnoticed. But now she was the focus of all their attention. The move had worked.

"Not really," Jessica said. "We're just hanging out."

"Well, it looks like we're going to lose anyway," she said, flipping her long hair over a shoulder and then looking at Nathan curiously, as if uncertain why he was there but too polite to ask. He was looking at them both, retreating into shyness. Daphne felt like she was a spectator in the stands, waiting to see how a play would pan out.

"Veronica, have you met Nathan?" Jessica said, barely hiding an amused, knowing smile.

"No. I don't think we have any classes together, do we?" Veronica said to him, friendly. Daphne knew the question was a ploy.

"No, I don't think so," he answered, still shy, like Daphne often was around new people.

"I think I've seen you, though," Veronica said. "Are you in sports?"

"Yeah, I'm in cross-country," Nathan said. By his tone, Daphne sensed him growing more comfortable and felt a flash of irritation.

"Cool, my older sister was in cross-country, but that was, like, a long time ago. She's ten years older than me."

"My older brother did it too," he said. "Do you run?"

"Me? Ha, no! I used to do softball. When does your season end?"

The conversation continued like this for another minute,

and after standing there, unable to contribute, Daphne wandered unnoticed to the fence, annoyed, to observe the teams, which were now much closer to their end of the field. How had she been cut out so easily?

Beth and Dominic were still watching the remainder of the game intently. Jessica chimed in whenever Veronica needed help keeping the conversation going, beaming like a proud aunt over the situation. Daphne looked at the field without really seeing it.

One of the players, she saw, was out of place. A misting figure was standing in the end zone, a helmet resting under his arm as he faced the field. His uniform was undoubtedly Falcons, but of an outdated design. He was of small build for a player.

Daphne grasped the fence with both hands and focused on reaching a phantom arm toward the shade across the yards of lit grass. His form was clearly visible in her mind. She tapped the padded shoulder. The shade turned.

They locked eyes. Behind him, a shrill whistle sounded. Players sprang into action, the Falcons' defense trying to head off the offense. The other team was only yards away from victory, seconds on the clock. They were wriggling figures in the background. Daphne saw only the shade.

He looked at her with a serious, turbulent expression, his back to the field on which he'd once played. Around them, spectators screamed and yelled.

A whistle sounded. A jubilant player carrying the football burst through the shade. Gaze broken, Daphne shifted her focus from him in time to notice the game was lost, that around her those who cared about the game were groaning about the defeat.

"Well, that sucks," Dom said.

Daphne searched for the shade, but he was gone. She felt

strange. Exactly a week from today, she'd be on the bridge on Laurel Road, waiting for dyszoons. For others, this was just a normal Friday, but not for her. She was apart.

At that moment, she was Daphne Cole, surrounded by her classmates and friends. But she could not stay in that spot forever. It was already moving past her.

"Daphne, are we going?" Jessica called. Nathan was rejoining his friend, leaving behind a happy-looking Veronica. Daphne glanced at him, reflecting on Dom's offhand comment about practice. It was probably best not to mention it again.

"Yeah," she said, pulling out of her reverie with an effort. Behind her, the final kick of the game was easily done and over with.

They were parked on the opposite end of the stadium. Daphne followed the evacuating crowd and kept close to Jessica, whom she was giving a ride. Nathan and his friend were not far behind. She heard Veronica say something to him. Heard him respond like they were already half good friends. Gritting her teeth, she willed the depressed crowd to move faster.

What was bothering her, she couldn't quite place. Wasn't it a good thing, if Veronica and Nathan became friends? She imagined Veronica later at home, busily dissecting every moment she'd had with Nathan and adding them up to see if they amounted to anything.

Someone jostled into her. Perhaps what bothered her, at least in part, was that Nathan was failing to see Veronica for what she was. Even so, wasn't it good if he met more people? Yet Veronica had already replaced Daphne as Jessica's best friend—she felt a pang at admitting this to herself so plainly. Would the same thing happen with another friendship Daphne was beginning to value?

It was irrational, Daphne told herself firmly. He could be friends with both of them, and with whomever he wanted.

As long as it isn't Veronica. Despite herself, Daphne smiled. She was worrying about this too much.

Daphne dangled from the bridge, her fingers stretched and white as she strained to maintain her grip on the rocky edge. She could not muster the strength to push herself up, or indeed, do anything.

Beads of sweat ran freely down her face and vanished into the heat of the air. Lava flowed like a golden arm between protruding, needle-sharp rocks under her feet. Despair rose in her at the numb uselessness of her fingers, her impending death.

A poisonous red sky loomed overhead, streaks of flame cutting through it like claw marks. She would not last long without help.

At this thought, a familiar figure appeared over her, clad in black.

"Claire!" She almost wept with relief. "Claire, help me up!"

"I can't, Daphne," Claire said solemnly, pity on her face. "You have to be the one to do it."

"I can't," Daphne pleaded. "I can't do it."

"I'm sorry." Claire turned away.

"No, wait! Help! *Please!*" But the psychic had gone. Daphne looked down at the luminous river. She was going to die.

"Daphne." Her head shot up again as her mother came into view with a worried and hurt expression. "What did you do?"

"*Mom!*" Daphne said breathlessly. "Mom, I can explain!"

"You lied to me, Daphne," her mom said. The venom in her voice felt like a slap.

"I'm sorry! Just help me up. *Mom.*"

"This is your punishment," her mom said, shaking her head, and walked away like Claire had. Daphne was once again alone.

"No, wait, Mom! *Mom!* Come back! Don't leave me! I'm sorry! I'm so—"

She was weeping now. The air was so hot. All feeling left her fingers. They were dead, brittle, ready to crumble. What was the use in delaying the inevitable?

A great fiery rock burst from the lava below and exploded overhead with a sound like a cannon. Ash fell like scorching rain. Daphne bent her head in an attempt to shield herself, burning flakes falling on her hand. She resisted the urge to shake them off and instead waited for the ash to die, gritting her teeth against the bright pain.

Another figure appeared.

"*Nathan!*" Daphne cried out in relief. "Help me up!"

"Why, Daphne?" His tone was different, hostile. He looked down at her with a look of disgust, betrayal on his face.

"What?" she breathed, sweat now pouring with abandon down her face from the effort of holding on.

"Why did you keep this from me? Why didn't you tell me about my sister?"

"What?" she said again, fear turning the sweat on her face cold. Her best bet was ignorance.

"MY SISTER!" Nathan screamed, his face contorted with hatred. He stomped away.

"Nathan! Wait, I'm sorry!" It was too late. He had gone.

Daphne was alone. Everyone had left her alone to die. She pushed her hands into the rock with all her might, rising one, two inches, then nothing.

"Come *on!*" Daphne screamed in desperation, trying to muster the strength again. "Come on, you stupid—" The stones were growing warm. She looked down again at the fiery river and realized her soles were melting.

The outline of a dark figure loomed above her, cast entirely in shadow. Whether it was male or female was impossible to tell.

"Please, help! Who are you?" Daphne rasped, throat dry. The figure moved forward. It was made of blackness. She was struck by a stinging fear as it got closer.

"Please..." Daphne begged, barely audible. "Help me." The figure seemed to contemplate her in the silence. Gently, two hands reached toward hers, and Daphne felt a flash of hope. With icy fingers, it grabbed her wrists, and with inhuman strength, pried her hands away.

Daphne fell. Fell into the abyss, where the long needles waited to embrace her. The dark figure loomed from the bridge, and its evil, inhuman laughter echoed all around her. It was coming from the fire itself.

17

BATTLE PLANS

Fallen leaves crinkled under Daphne's feet. The woods were full of the sharp scent of them. Many leaves still clung to the branches, dark in the night. Cold air was a welcome change from a night that had been full of flames and screams.

Daphne was afraid the noise had woken up her mom, whose bedroom had been devoid of its usual snores that morning. Normally, she did not scream loudly enough anymore to do so unless it was the nightmare of her dad, which had returned for the second time last night. It was going to be difficult to pretend her nightmares were getting better if that kept happening, Daphne reprimanded herself. She needed to keep it under control.

The darkness, deepened by clouds, was suddenly oppressive. Turning on a small flashlight, Daphne swept the harsh light over her surroundings and impulsively chose a small path that led to a neighboring property she had permission to walk on. It had been a while since she'd traveled it. She stepped over a fallen tree.

The cold wind grew stronger. Daphne pulled her jacket

tighter and continued walking, leaves crunching underneath
her boots. So far no shades had crossed her path, and no awareness of one brushed against her mind. Wherever they were,
they were far away.

In a few hours, she would be able to tell Claire about her
progress. Daphne found herself looking forward to it. Two
weeks had passed since last they met, and the battle was looming. Plans needed to be made. In the meantime, practice was
essential. She was eager to share the progress she'd made so far.

A quarter of an hour passed since she'd set out on the path.
Daphne had not yet turned back, impulsively following a
narrow new path paved by deer. The woods on this side were
deep. The path turned, and Daphne glanced ahead.

Her stomach dropped horribly.

At first glance, Daphne could see it was a woman cowering
in terror. Fingers clutched both sides of her head and melted
into dull brown hair. Her gaping mouth shrieked silently in
awful terror, contorting the rest of her face. Eyes, mere slits,
fixated on a sight unseen.

It was clear the woman was a shade, but she did not mist.
She was almost colorless and partly broken into shards, like a
cracked mirror. The pieces pulsated and flashed with violent
light.

The woman continued to tremble, to scream without
sound. Daphne could not tear her gaze away from the fractured
shade's terrified face. Its agony seared into her memory. She
tried not to think about what had happened to make the woman
scream in terror like that. Had she died at that very spot?

Daphne lowered her gaze to the shade's trembling knees
and forced herself to step forward, when she would rather have
run away, trying to reach for the presence of the shade.

There was no presence. Daphne tried harder, feeling her
way across the space between them until she should have

touched the woman's form, but found nothing. Felt nothing. The woman was still screaming, flickering with faulty light. Unreachable.

The word brought to mind a memory of the cemetery, when Daphne had first learned about shades. Some would be unreachable by perceivers, Claire had said, even with their ability to touch spirits. *Some stay because they are simply too traumatized by the manner of their death.*

Daphne had not paid much attention to this at the time. Slowly she lowered her hand, feeling sick. The woman's legs quivered with fear, and Daphne backed away. Even if she tried, she could not help this shade.

Daphne walked quickly back down the path. The part in her, in everyone, that was drawn to the scenes of accident and horror led her to look once more at the horrible face. Its terror was unmistakable. Daphne was sure she would see it in her nightmares, even as she silently vowed to never venture there again. The fractured woman would stay broken.

Daphne drove into the driveway of a small house next to a field and parked next to Claire's car. The psychic was standing next to it with her hands folded together, waiting. She looked tan.

"Hello, Daphne. Thank you for meeting me out here," Claire said.

"No problem," she answered, taking in the yard. It was full of trinkets—silver orbs held by frogs, spinning metal fans in bright colors, and garden angels in wood-chipped gardens. "How was your vacation? I didn't really ask when we talked."

"Excellent. It was very nice to see my sons."

"How many kids do you have again?" Daphne followed as Claire began walking toward the back of the house.

"Three," Claire said, fingering her gold-and-silver moon

necklace and the three diamonds set into it. "All of them live in Miami now."

"Do you miss living there?"

"A little, perhaps, for my sons, but Long Haven is a nice enough community, and the cost of living is less. I don't miss the humidity."

They walked past chimes, which clinked gently together with a mournful sound. Daphne shivered. "Did you have a psychic business in Miami?" she asked. Curiosity tugged at her again, to know more about Claire's past.

"No. I helped with my husband's business, as a secretary mostly. Two of my sons run it now. Retirement didn't quite suit me, so when I came here and saw the building was for sale—"

"Wait, you *own* the building?" Daphne said without thinking. She hadn't considered Claire was anything more than the owner of the studio.

"Yes, and I could renovate it how I wanted for my shop and live upstairs. When I officially retire, the dress shop in front is very eager to tear down the wall and expand."

They turned around the corner of the house. The backyard contained a clothesline, a small patio, and a barn-shaped shed, toward which Claire led the way.

"Why do you have to feed your friend's cats?"

"Sylvia's in Jamestown investigating a haunting," Claire said. "She asked me to take care of them."

"She's investigating—?" Daphne asked, bewildered. "Wait —she can't see shades, can she?" The only perceivers she knew of were Claire and herself.

Claire laughed. "No, but the paranormal fascinates her, so it's sort of a hobby she does with a group now and then. They like to travel around with their equipment and see if they can determine whether the place is haunted, pick up strange sounds, that sort of thing."

"Does Sylvia know you can see shades?"

"No," Claire said. "I've known Sylvia almost since I moved to Long Haven, so nine years. She helps me occasionally at the studio."

"What about your family?" Daphne asked, hoping she sounded casual.

"They know," Claire said simply, stopping at the sliding shed door. It would have been a hard thing to believe, Daphne thought with a desperate curiosity. She could not deny it would be a major load off her mind, if her mother knew about and accepted her abilities.

"Are...we going in?" Claire made no move to slide open the door.

"In a moment." The psychic turned to look at her. "You should know—there are more than cats in here. This shed has attracted a few shades as well."

"It's haunted?" Daphne asked, then realized that although she hadn't paid attention until now, she had indeed sensed the presence of the shades as they approached. It was a strong presence, just on the other side of the door. She thought of Sylvia traveling to investigate a place that might not have any ghosts when there were shades in her backyard.

"Just so you're prepared," Claire said with a nod. She gripped the handle and pulled. Unsure whether to help or not, Daphne backed out of the way as the door slid open to reveal the dark interior of the shed, which was full of tools, a lawnmower, odd pieces of broken furniture, and straggling bits of straw.

Daphne peered closer into the gloom and gave a start.

There were at least eight shades inside, filling up the space. One man's legs were hidden in the lawnmower. Claire joined her.

"Like I said."

"Why are there so many?" Daphne asked, a little uneasy at the scene. She was used to shades by now but had never seen so many crammed into such a small space. They stirred in the light.

"It's quiet and hidden, I suppose," Claire answered. "I've noticed shades seem to like such places, or else precisely the opposite, like the ones on Main Street." Daphne recalled the shades in the woods around her house and wondered how many more she would encounter on her walks. Claire's observation aligned with her own.

The shades' faces were turned toward them, watching. There would be little room to walk in without stepping through some, but Claire stepped forward confidently.

"Move," she briskly ordered the ones nearest the door. They shuffled out of the way, standing in the workbench or other machinery to make space for Claire but apparently reluctant to leave altogether. Daphne followed and stopped just inside the shed, casting a glance at the shades nearest her, a mixture of men and women wearing different sorts of clothing she could only partially place in their times.

Claire opened a plastic container of dry cat food in the corner and scooped a large amount into a container on the gravel floor. A skinny black cat emerged from its sleeping spot in the corner, where a few old blankets were piled, rubbing repeatedly against Claire's legs. Daphne ventured in cautiously. Even with the space given to Claire by the shades, the shed was crowded.

"I found out my house is haunted," Daphne said, glad to have the chance to finally tell someone about it.

"Really?" Claire glanced up in interest. "Do you live in an old house?"

"Yeah, that's why my parents bought it originally, for the history. He said his name is Phillip, and he's a World War II soldier," Daphne said. "But he was in this loop gliding up the stairs, and he wouldn't respond to anything I said until I sort of pulled him out of it. Was that what you meant when you said shades had different levels of awareness?"

"This shade would be one example of it, yes. Most shades are like Robin, or Heather, but there are some, like yours, that merely repeat one action until someone like us pulls them out of it. It's a different way of carrying out their thoughts, I suppose. They act it out." Claire opened the gallon of water on the counter and poured a little into the water dish next to the food, which was busy being devoured.

"That's what I thought," Daphne said, eager to share her theory, "because he kept mentioning a girl named Violet. I asked my mom, and she said there was a Violet who lived in our house in the forties, but I don't know if that's the Violet he keeps talking about."

"Hm. It's possible," Claire answered.

"I guess I'll find out more once Phillip wakes up a little more, assuming he does," she said, more to herself. "He was pretty confused after I pulled him out of his loop. I'd like to know how he died." Daphne glanced at the crowd of young to middle-aged shades standing idle around her, wondering how each of them had passed and what their reasons had been for remaining behind.

"If he knows," Claire pointed out reasonably. "Shades can't always remember how they passed, especially if it isn't the reason they stayed."

"You'd think they'd find it important," Daphne said. Claire chuckled, bending down to stroke the cat.

"Perhaps to the living, but to the dead, it hardly matters."

"So how many cats are here?"

"I'm not sure. They come and go," Claire said. "The ones Sylvia catches, she takes to the pet shelter." The memorial donations for Heather's funeral had gone to the pet shelter, Daphne remembered.

A dusty antique dresser stood against one wall. Something had once struck the mirror above it, forming a crater that cracked the glass into shards.

"I saw a woman in the woods who looked like that," Daphne said quietly, her own reflection split into pieces, a dozen pale gray eyes. "And she was screaming."

"A Fracture," Claire said solemnly, straightening.

"Is that one of the unreachable shades?"

"Yes. Not a pleasant sight, but like I said, some shades are traumatized by how they died."

Daphne didn't want to reveal how troubled she was by her encounter with the Fracture, not when Claire seemed to have a calm acceptance for it all, no doubt something that had come through decades of experience. But the screaming woman's face was burned into her memory: the gaping mouth, the horrible eyes filled with terror at a sight unseen. Daphne didn't want to imagine how it had happened, or whether it had happened at that spot. Had it been murder? A hungry predator? She wrenched her imagination from sinking into all the horrible possibilities.

With a final look at the cat, Claire returned through the parted sea of shades to Daphne's side. The spirits filled the open space.

"When did you first begin to see shades?" Daphne broke the silence. Though she was afraid the question was too personal, Claire appeared to consider it thoughtfully, frowning.

"I think...I was perhaps thirteen when I realized I was seeing people that no one else could, and then these people would vanish. This was in Arizona."

"What did you do?"

"Well, at the time I was terrified I was going insane, seeing hallucinations, along with the nightmares. My uncle had gone to an asylum for seeing things—though for genuine mental health reasons—so naturally, I worried I'd caught what he had." Claire gave a side nod, but despite this casual gesture, Daphne knew, however many years had dulled the pain, it must have been a bad time. She could relate, having had her own turbulent period around that age less than four years ago.

"The people I could see only grew clearer over time, and I'd even begun to speak with them after some came up to me," Claire continued. "Eventually, after a few months, I accepted they weren't hallucinations but spirits of the departed."

There was something missing to the story. "You didn't have someone tell you what you were seeing?" Daphne asked.

Claire shook her head. "No. As I've said before, you are the first person like me I've met—at least that I know of," she said. "I began perceiving after my uncle was committed, and perhaps it was because I was so terrified that I would begin seeing things like he did, I began testing myself just to make sure. I would try my hardest to see something that wasn't there, just to prove to myself I couldn't. Instead, I began to see shades."

Daphne was struck by the loneliness of it. Of accepting one's abilities but doing so alone. There was a special type of bravery in it. Those few hours between seeing the shade in class and seeking Claire out had been agony enough—the prospect of bearing the burden for months seemed impossible.

"Do you think there are many other people like us?"

"To our extent, no. Perception exists on a spectrum, which might allow some to see things out of the ordinary, but logic is a powerful suppressor. If you see something in the corner of your eye, it's a trick of the light, not a shade. I suppose you can go your whole life without learning to see them, even if you have the potential."

"So I might not have ever seen shades if you hadn't told me," Daphne said, watching a misting man walk through the dresser so only his upper half was visible. She couldn't get used to these sights.

"Perhaps," Claire said. "You have a logical mind, Daphne, but a powerful eye nonetheless. You have a talent for noticing things other people don't, shades or no."

Daphne thought of the photos on her bedroom wall. Her mind that always overanalyzed.

"Claire," she said. "This other person, who's widening the Veil. You said before they would have to be like us."

"Yes," the psychic answered, worry passing over her face. "But like I've said, there are many things I don't know. I'm afraid we won't find out more until Friday night."

Daphne's stomach flipped unpleasantly. It was Saturday. Halloween was next Friday. That was all the time they had. A week from now, they would know how it had all turned out.

Knowing she had asked the question before but wanting to be sure, Daphne said, "Do you really think the Veil will widen on Halloween?"

"Yes, I do," the psychic said firmly. "There can be no other reason why the person who widened it in August has waited this long, other than they're waiting for an important date to do it. So unless something happened to them, which I'm not counting on, the Veil will widen in a week."

"Will we be able to sense it when it happens?"

"Most definitely. There will be no doubt. It's no small thing to widen a passageway between Earth and Hell. We will feel it."

Twisting her bracelet, Daphne turned toward the open shed again. The shades had become used to their presence and were no longer staring. "What time should we meet?"

"If we are out there by eleven, that should be enough time.

In my experience, the time when shades become the most restless is in the few hours between late Halloween night and early in the morning on November first."

After a few moments of silence, Daphne became aware Claire was watching her closely.

"It's okay to be afraid, Daphne," Claire said. "But I'll point out you are more skilled than you feel right now."

"I've been practicing more. It's getting easier. I think." But would it be enough?

"Just consider how much you have already learned. Another week is plenty of time. And anyway, I'll be there."

The long-healed bruise on Daphne's shoulder seemed to ache. "I'm just...worried about injuries. The dyszoon I faced was fast and really strong. And if I can't deflect even stronger ones—"

"Don't think I've underestimated the danger I've put you in, Daphne," Claire said. "But I will say it again: you don't know your own ability. Sometimes, it takes facing the things we fear and dread for us to realize the depths of our own strength. Or as my husband used to say to our boys, you can only practice so long before it's time to step out in front of a crowd to see what you're made of." She laughed fondly.

Daphne did feel afraid. However, the horror of the coming battle didn't feel quite real yet, even though she'd faced a dyszoon before. It was more the fear of the unknown. "I guess I'll just practice as much as I can until then."

"That's all we can do," Claire answered.

Daphne nodded, then reached for the handle to slide the door shut. To her surprise, Claire laid a hand on her arm.

"Wait, let them do it," Claire said, nodding toward the gathered shades.

"But it's heavy." Daphne stared, remembering how Robin in the cemetery could not move even the flowers on the grave.

"All of them together, they can," Claire answered. "I would like you to see."

Incredulous, Daphne turned to the shades.

"Close it," she called. The shades sprang into action and disappeared into the corner. Disembodied hands poked through the metal wall to grasp the edge of the sliding door, an eerie sight.

Slowly, to Daphne's astonishment, the sheet of metal moved as the misting hands pulled. The door slid steadily. It was shut halfway, closing off the darkness within. It did not stop once.

Together, they watched the door slam shut.

Daphne returned home, head full as she shook off her shoes in the entryway. The faintly glowing form of Phillip was visible in the space between her and the kitchen, curling mist rising from his still shoulders. He turned toward her as she approached.

She considered him thoughtfully. In the week since she'd woken him, the shade had not spoken much and still was unable to answer her questions about who Violet was, until she had given up asking him. While invaluable during her practices, Phillip had not proved himself to be a great conversationalist.

"Was Violet your girlfriend?" Daphne asked him directly.

His face tightened, as usual. "I must see Violet. She's dying."

Daphne sighed. Maybe she should just give up the matter and take him to the woods for another practice battle. Obviously, she couldn't mention Violet's name and expect to get any other response. Unless she just needed to change her approach?

"Okay. Who is..." She closed her eyes briefly. "Who is your girlfriend?"

Phillip looked at her blankly. She took this to mean he did not have one, and was disappointed her theory was wrong. He had not come back for a girlfriend.

"Okay, who is...your sister?" Daphne tried wildly.

"Alice," Phillip answered promptly.

Excitement flooded through her. Was the solution so simple? Daphne looked carefully at his face, in one way only a few years older than herself. "Who is your mother?"

"My mother," he said seriously.

Daphne resisted the urge to laugh and ran a hand through her dark hair. But she was running out of ideas. If Violet wasn't his girlfriend, sister, or mother, then who was she? Violet had been ill. Dying. Phillip likely had been burning with the desire to see her but had been unable to do so. The woman had to be important.

Daphne looked up quickly, wondering why she hadn't thought of it before.

"Who is your wife?" she asked.

Phillip stared at her, mist trailing off his body, holding his long rifle around his shoulder. Daphne leaned forward on her toes. His face grew clear.

"Violet."

The resulting explosion in her mind was like fireworks. The pieces of the mystery were fitting together in her mind, forming a story more complete than with any other shade she had met. Violet was his wife.

Why had he been in a loop? It could only be guessed. Daphne pictured an alive Phillip imagining himself walking up the stairs to his wife's deathbed in her childhood home, over and over, forever separated. Even as he faced his own demise across an ocean, his last thoughts were of his young wife, who was also facing death, her own battle. If he survived the war, there was no knowing what he would find at his return, or if she would still be there to say goodbye to.

"Thank you, Phillip." Daphne stepped past him. The shade remained in his spot, forever stuck on that pivotal day in 1944.

18

DECISION POINTS

On Thursday, Jessica had a proposition.

"I totally forgot about the Halloween festival tomorrow! Do you all want to go?" she said to the table at large.

Daphne had also forgotten about the festival, which Jessica had told her about during the football game.

"What is it?" Veronica said skeptically, as if it weren't anything she could possibly be interested in.

"A Halloween event at the park," Jessica explained. "There's going to be a band, concessions, this giant pumpkin carving, some contests, games, a haunted trail that's supposed to be super scary, a hayride put on by the fraternity...It starts at seven and goes until midnight."

"Oh. That could be fun."

"What do you think, Daphne?" Jessica said.

"I'm..." the word she was going to say was *busy*, but she suddenly had a pitiful mental image of herself lying nervously in her room, with only Phillip awake for company, until the time came to head out to the bridge.

What was more, Daphne hadn't thought of a way to

sneak out of the house late at night. Her mom might be asleep but could wake at the sound of the starting car, or be simply not able to go to sleep. The festival would provide the perfect excuse to be out late. Although it went past the time she was scheduled to meet Claire, she could always just make an excuse to leave their group before eleven, if it came to that.

"I'm up for it," she finished, though immediately wondered if she wouldn't regret it when the time came.

"What about you, Beth? Taylor? Maria?"

Beth pursed her lips in apology. "I'm taking my cousin trick-or-treating."

"Oh, that's right."

"I have to go to my dad's this weekend, sorry," Taylor said regretfully.

"I'm hanging out with my boyfriend," Maria said.

"What about you, Ashley?" Jessica called, undeterred. Ashley was hunched over her lunch tray, her face half-hidden by a sheet of frizzy black hair, but her fork was merely poking at the food. She gave off such a wall of moodiness, Daphne wondered at her friend's courage in trying to break through it. "Do you want to go to the Halloween festival with us on Friday?"

The fork stirred slightly. "No," Ashley said in a tone that seemed almost angry. She didn't look up.

"Oh," Jessica said with strained politeness, and seemed at a loss for words at such a blunt refusal. There was a long, awkward pause. Veronica stared at Ashley with raised eyebrows.

"Is there a cost to get in?" Daphne hurriedly said to Jessica.

"No, I'm—I'm pretty sure it's free," she replied, her voice still rather high.

"What's free?" a voice broke in. Nathan was suddenly

standing behind Daphne with an empty lunch tray, and she twisted to look up at him.

"A Halloween thing," she explained.

"Yeah! Do you want to go?" Jessica said, all trace of upset now gone, or at least put aside. Daphne admonished herself: why hadn't she thought to ask him? But the thought of doing so made her feel shy. She wasn't as bold as Jessica, who, though undoubtedly working on Veronica's behalf, seemed to have taken a liking to Nathan in any case.

He looked surprised to have been asked. "I wasn't trying to—"

"We don't mind! You can bring some of your friends, and then we can all meet up?" Jessica pressed.

"What is it?" he said, sounding hesitant. He glanced at Daphne as if for reassurance. She smiled at the obvious detail Jessica had forgotten to include.

"Kind of like a festival, with a band, vendors, a haunted trail, and—hayride?" She looked to Jessica, who nodded vigorously. Daphne chanced a glance at the unusually silent Veronica, who was listening raptly to their conversation, looking anxious to participate but overcome by her own shyness.

"That sounds fun," Nathan said, nodding. "I could bring some of my friends."

"Good, then we'll have a group," Jessica said. "You wanted to go, Veronica?"

"Of course!" she answered brightly. Daphne realized Veronica hadn't given a definite answer until then. She groaned inwardly. The evening wouldn't have been much fun anyway, with the prospect of the Veil hanging over it, but with just Jessica and Nathan, it could have been passable. Now Veronica's inclusion would bring a different vibe to their group: not only would she hog Jessica's attention, but the night would probably be spent watching her attempts to flirt with Nathan.

But there was no backing out now that Nathan was joining them, as the person he knew best in their group. She was not a flaky person. It would be strange to say she couldn't go, without a good excuse and when she had just accepted the invitation. And besides, the Veil shouldn't prevent her from living a normal life. Or the dyszoons...

A sickly, low-burning panic sprang up, a warning sign. Daphne managed to smile and say bye to Nathan, who left to carry his tray to the kitchen, then excused herself and walked quickly to the bathroom. The fluorescent lights were too bright, and if only she could mute the echoing chatter of the lunchroom...*Stay calm.*

Daphne swung open the door with relief. Mercifully, the bathroom was empty. She entered a stall and shut the door, leaning a forehead against the cool green metal. She felt lightheaded, sounds and sensation oddly distorted and distant. *Breathe*, she repeated. *It's okay. Breathe. Feel it. Let it go through.*

A minute later, the bathroom door opened. Daphne pulled her forehead away from the metal, sighing. She needed to pull herself together. The girl chose the stall farthest away.

The worst of the panic had subsided. Daphne felt weak and shaky, as if she had just fought the dyszoon again, but she could get through the rest of the day.

The other girl flushed, and Daphne felt compelled to do the same to the empty toilet and leave her stall rather than suffer the embarrassment of the girl wondering why she was taking so long. Opening the door, she saw Ashley Zhang was washing her ink-stained hands at the sink.

Their eyes met in the mirror. Daphne settled for a small smile that was not returned. There was the awkwardness of two people who recognize each other but don't care to acknowledge the fact if it can be helped. She settled at the second sink and began to wash her own hands, agonizing over whether she should try to make small talk but feeling the opportunity fall away with every long second. But what would they even talk about? They had Euro and lunch together but had never exchanged a word. Ashley was the moody girl at the end of the table.

They settled side by side, the air stretched and silent except for the rush of running water, which always ran ice-cold. Ashley seemed, as usual, to bristle with untapped anger. Daphne finished quickly, given her hands were already clean, and passed Ashley on her way to the hand dryers.

The sound was loud, obtrusive in the strained silence. They were uncomfortably close, and Daphne averted her gaze, wondering why Ashley was taking so long to wash her hands. Maybe she was attempting to get the ink off them. She finished drying and turned to go.

"You think you're so great, don't you?"

Daphne froze. "What?" she said, turning.

She was taken aback at the expression on Ashley's face. Her eyebrows were sharply furrowed, teeth almost bared. Every inch of Ashley's face showed the utmost loathing, as if she wished Daphne a painful death. Her hands were balled into fists on either side of her overlarge sweatshirt, wet where she had wiped them. Although a full head shorter, she seemed to grow tall on fury alone.

"I said you think you're *better* than everyone else!" Ashley said loudly, almost spitting. Daphne stared. A spark had gone off in her brain, making her unable to comprehend what was happening. Ashley's uncombed hair almost crackled with electricity. The tap was still running.

"What are you—"

"It's all about you, isn't it?" Ashley spat, looking more demented than ever, and Daphne recalled the self-portrait Beth had hung in the glass case outside the art room; she was struck by how similar the expressions were. "You're so much *greater*. More *worthy*."

Daphne gaped at her, then glanced helplessly at the closed door. Obviously something was wrong, and if she could only run and get someone, the school officer—

"Just because your *dad* died, you think you're so *tragic*," Ashley spoke again, taking a step forward until they were within arm's reach of each other. Daphne's head whipped back to face her. "Just because he's a so-called *hero*."

The bell rang, but Daphne could hardly hear it over the thundering of her own pulse.

"Stop it," she said quietly. Bewilderment had vanished, and the cause of Ashley's bizarre eruption ceased to matter. The bell, the stuck tap—all of her attention was focused on Ashley's voice. The corners of Ashley's mouth lifted, as if she knew she had finally struck true.

"Don't want to talk about your daddy?" she said in a low voice, mockery dripping from every word. "I bet he got a medal, and a memorial, right? Seeing as they give one even if it's your own fault, as long as he kicked the bucket on the job, it doesn't matter if he was a lousy firefighter—"

Without conscious thought, Daphne swung her open hand and slapped Ashley hard across the face.

Fury gave way to shock as her hand touched the other girl's cheek. A sharpness that was like rage, yet biting cold, flashed through Daphne. It was something beyond anger she sensed inside Ashley. She stared blankly, her hand lowering slowly. What she had felt—

The tap unstuck. At the sudden silence, a bubble burst. Reality rushed in, and with it, shame. The expression on Ashley's face was something like triumph, the faint imprint of a hand now visible on her cheek.

In a daze, Daphne turned and left the bathroom. Crowds of people still pushed through the hallway, but luckily she was in the back, and no one paid attention to her as she joined it. Everything was a blur of movement and talk, and she was just a shadow behind it all.

Then Daphne was at her locker, but she knew she wouldn't be going to her next class. Illness—that's what she would tell them at the office. It was remarkable, though she felt nothing, how much it felt like everything. Daphne gathered her books and swung her backpack over her shoulder. Students walked to their next classes, a world apart.

"Hey! Where are you going?"

Daphne jumped. She had forgotten Nathan now walked with her after lunch, and for the first time, she regretted it. Too late, she remembered to try and hide her expression. At least her eyes were dry.

Nathan's eyes widened. "Hey, are you okay? What's up?"

"I—nothing. She just...said some things," Daphne answered distantly, looking down at the floor as a ghostly rage welled up inside her again.

"Who did?"

"Ashley." The feral face appeared before her clearly. "She was really angry for some reason, and then—then she said—"

Abruptly, Daphne broke off with a shake of her head, willing the memory to go away until she could be alone to deal with it. It could not be here. She could not break down in front of Nathan, who had already seen more to her than she had ever wanted. Already, she hated that he was seeing her this way and knew her face must look bone-pale.

"I-I need to go home," Daphne said, trying to inject normalcy into her tone, and took a step toward the office.

"Sure," Nathan said, looking confused but evidently forgoing further information for now. "I can go with you—"

"No," she said quickly. It was difficult to keep herself together. "I'll be fine, I think I just...need to go home." The desire to get away from school as fast as possible was making it difficult for her to not break into a run, and she attempted a smile. "Talk to you later?"

He nodded once, seeming to understand but not liking it. "Yeah...sure."

Not giving him time to say anything more, Daphne smiled again, then turned and walked as fast as possible to the office.

Her legs moved in time with the swinging bench on the front porch of her house. Time passed distantly, neither fast nor slow but simply there and not there. Only the sun marked it was moving, as it had the last few hours.

With half a mind, Daphne looked at the bracelet she held in her hands. Its thin silver band caught the light, and the owl at the top frowned upward. Again Ashley's expression floated before her eyes, shame tearing through her with the same sharpness as when Daphne had slapped her. There was no room left for curiosity about what ability this revealed. Only it seemed Ashley's turmoil ran deep.

The gravel crunched. Daphne looked up at the sound, heart beating wildly, and straightened at the sight of her mom's car returning from work, which honked in greeting. Nerves clenched her stomach. But it was time—the conversation couldn't be postponed any longer.

Her mom returned from the garage and walked up the steps, carrying her work bag. "Hello, O dearest daughter, how was your day?" When no response was given, she paused and looked closer, her gaze piercing in a way that was reminiscent of Claire. Daphne knew her expression was being expertly read. "What's wrong?"

She paused and gathered herself. "Mom," Daphne said with forced steadiness, and clenched her hands together against the nerves. "I need to talk to you about something."

"Okay," her mom answered after a moment, with a small nod that seemed more for herself, and settled onto the bench. "What do you need to talk about?"

Daphne steeled herself. "Dad."

A flicker of surprise crossed her mom's face. Evidently that wasn't what she had been expecting. "Okay," she said in a guarded tone.

Daphne hesitated, then forced herself to talk. "I was just remembering...about how he used to come to my room whenever I had my nightmares, even when he had just come off duty and he was really tired..." She rotated the bracelet in her hands, considering the night terrors that had not gone away with age like they were supposed to. Nightmares where she ran in slow motion from a hungry clown with smeared red lips and skeletons climbed up the basement stairs, pulling her toward them with their own gravity.

"He was better at getting you back to sleep than I was," her mom said in a careful tone.

Nodding, Daphne resumed. If she didn't think about it too much, it was possible to talk. "I always felt he could fight them off for me, whatever my dream was." She remembered falling asleep against a muscled arm while a deep voice read a story, a sense of safety lingering that kept the dreams away the rest of the night. On the few nights he was at work, her mom took up the task, but it was not the same. "Then, I was embarrassed later..."

"You felt you weren't a kid anymore and you didn't need your parents to comfort you," her mom said matter-of-factly. "You were eleven. That's normal."

"I know. But I think...what bothers me..." It was difficult to say what she must. "That's the last time I felt close to Dad," Daphne admitted, a tightness growing around her eyes. "I remember he looked hurt when I told him I wasn't a baby anymore. Then I always felt like he couldn't accept I was growing up."

A sigh came from her mom. "I remember the arguments. You were a lot alike."

Daphne looked up. A sheen covered her mom's eyes. "That was the problem, I think. But I felt like he didn't understand me. And that's what I regret."

"He still loved you," her mom said quietly. "Even if you had trouble relating to each other."

The bracelet flashed in the sun. A final gift. "When he gave me this," Daphne said, looking at it, "that's my last clear memory of Dad, before he died."

It was a Valentine's gift, a little more than a month before her fourteenth birthday. Her dad had handed over a folded piece of cardstock decorated with firefighter stickers and hearts, the limit of his artistic ability. Inside was scrawled, "Love you Owl-ways."

Then from behind him he'd pulled a smooth black box, which she'd opened to a silver bracelet decorated with an owl, her favorite animal at the time. She'd loved it instantly, giving him a last, if somewhat awkward, hug.

In three weeks, he was gone.

"Most of the time, I feel like I've moved on, I've gotten used to it, but then other times it's like it just happened—" Daphne felt a hand close over her own. For a while they were both silent, and she fought to control the raw emotion welling up from the hidden parts of her soul, and the dark period she'd deliberately forgotten that was now breaking through to the surface.

Daphne could not recall hearing the news for the first time

but knew at some point she was told her dad had suffered a heart attack while responding to a fire. That he had rushed into the burning house after a report there was a girl still inside, one that turned out to be false, and he had fallen through a floor that gave no warning of its collapse, into the burning basement. And though he was immediately pulled out, the damage was done.

She'd worn the bracelet every day since. Life had eventually fallen into a new normal, but some days it seemed like a façade, a poor attempt at recreating the real life they'd had.

"That's normal, Daphne," her mom said, and squeezed her hand, her own cheeks wet. "Believe me."

"But shouldn't I be over it?" she said desperately.

"No, you won't ever be 'over it,'" said her mom with another squeeze. "Things get better, of course, and feel normal again after a while, and life moves on, but at certain times, it will come back to you strongly."

Daphne wiped her face. She had spent too much emotion in the last six hours. "Is it—is it like that with your mom?"

Her mom smiled sadly. "Yes, I still think about her every day. It's a little different since she died when I was twenty, not thirteen. I still feel that grief, but enough time has passed that it's nice, not painful, to remember her," she said. "Though it was always hard, knowing she would never see me graduate college, or get married. That she wouldn't see you."

After a pause, she added, "That might be why you feel worse about it now. You're in your final year of high school, and he won't get to see those changes, and that's hard." She turned to Daphne earnestly. "Do you know you're the strongest girl I know?"

Daphne smiled, but she thought the same of her mom, who was so strong herself. Both a chronic worrier and the funniest person she knew, who had gone through so much tragedy and yet remained whole.

"I feel so...guilty sometimes about how much I put you through, afterward, when my nightmares became worse," Daphne said. "I didn't think about it at the time, but you had everything else to deal with, and I was just another burden—"

Her mom gripped her hand again. "No," she said firmly. "That's exactly what I'm here for, and I never want you to feel guilty over it. If you weren't a burden, I'd have no opportunity to show you every day how much I love you, Daphne. And that goes both ways."

Daphne couldn't find the words to speak, but in the meantime, she was content to rock the bench. Her mom spoke again.

"You've been having the dream about your dad dying?" she asked directly. And looking into her mother's eyes, Daphne knew that, in this, the time for evasion had passed.

"Twice," she answered truthfully, and saw confirmation on her mom's face. "But...I don't think it will come back anymore."

"Okay," her mom answered after a pause. "But if it does, you don't have to keep it from me. And for the record, you can always talk to me about your nightmares. Always. And your dad, for that matter. I'm not a frail Victorian lady. I can handle it. I *want* to handle it, all right? That's what mothers are for."

"Okay," Daphne said in a small voice.

"Good," her mom said briskly. "I've been thinking something's been up, these last few weeks."

A sudden cold came over Daphne, bringing her back to her present situation. Here was the perfect opportunity to tell her mom about her abilities, and the other half of her problems.

But Daphne knew she couldn't. Resolve came unchallenged, as if it were a decision that had long been made. Not only would she have to explain her abilities, but also that she was willingly walking into a dangerous situation. She didn't want to combat any attempts to talk her out of it. If there was one thing she had inherited from her father, it was a sense of duty. To finish the job, no matter the personal cost.

She slipped the bracelet back onto her wrist.

"It will get better, in time," her mom was saying. "I promise."

Daphne turned to her and managed a small smile. Talking about her dad had been difficult, and though she did not feel better at the moment, she knew that one day she would. That burden had lifted.

The other could fill its place.

19

HALLOWEEN

Daphne's first resolution on Friday was to apologize to Ashley.

She searched for her before school, then at lunchtime, but Ashley's usual spot was empty. Daphne was disappointed, but the looming prospect of what she was to face soon occupied most of her mind. Despite her dread, Daphne felt a strange calmness about the situation, the recognition that she had prepared as much as possible and there was nothing left to do but deal with it.

In the brief break between lunch and seventh period, Nathan stopped by her locker as usual.

"How are you doing?" he asked in a slightly lowered tone.

"A lot better, thanks," Daphne answered as she swapped out materials for the rest of the day, hoping her upbeat tone would lay any concerns to rest and diffuse awkward questions.

"So what happened?" he asked, leaning against the lockers.

"Nothing," she said hastily. "Me and Ashley just had a fight. I don't even know how it happened. She said some things —" Daphne shook her head, forcing away the memory. Some words were better left unrepeated, the main reason she had not told her mom about the incident. Besides feeling ashamed about losing her temper, Daphne would have to explain why, and she didn't want Ashley's words to hurt anyone else.

"Are you guys friends?" he said, looking surprised at the possibility.

"No—honestly we haven't really talked before. I think she's just going through some things, I don't know."

Nathan nodded, and wordlessly they set off down the hall together. "You know, I've had a bad feeling about her," he said after a few moments of thoughtful silence. "I mean, I guess I don't know her, but she always seems...angry."

"Yeah, I get that vibe from her too," Daphne said. "I think Jessica was friends with her last year, and she was better then. But anyway, I'm going to try and talk to her on Monday."

"Good luck with that," he said skeptically, and Daphne smiled despite herself, noting the relief on his face that she had done so. They reached the door to the history classroom, and she turned to say goodbye. "I guess I'll see you tonight?"

"Yeah, I think Dom was going too. Looking forward to it." He smiled and walked away. Daphne was suddenly glad she was going to the festival after all.

As she entered the history classroom and spotted Veronica, she wondered what the night would bring with all of them together. Her eyes roamed over to Ashley's empty seat. She would apologize Monday, she told the guilt that rose in her.

Tonight, however, she had bigger things to worry about.

At half past seven, Daphne put on sneakers and tightened the laces with forced calm, glancing up at the wall of photos in her bedroom to seek the picture of the bridge on Laurel Road. The time had finally arrived. It did not seem real.

She stepped into the hallway. Phillip stood near the

hallway mirror, his preferred spot. Something was off, Daphne could tell immediately as she took in his restless stance, the sharp turns of his head.

"Phillip?" Daphne drew closer to the mirror only she was reflected in. The shade's normally calm face was drawn into tight, anxious lines. His misting hands tightly gripped the rifle, and his eyes darted around, alert, as if he expected the enemy to burst into the hallway at any second.

"Phillip," she said, attempting to step in front of his line of vision. "Phillip, what's wrong?"

The shade didn't respond but continued his restless scan of their surroundings. Daphne opened her mouth and then closed it, thinking hard. Phillip was a spirit. Was it possible he knew what was coming? Was he able to sense when evil drew near? In that case, there could be no doubt.

Tonight was the night.

Daphne took one last, wary look at Phillip and descended the dark stairs.

"Are you headed out?" her mom's voice called from the softly lit living room. A moment later, she appeared in the arched entrance.

"Yeah," Daphne answered simply, hands self-consciously in her jacket pockets.

Her mom appeared to have noticed the dread on her face, adding somberly, "It will be fun. Don't let Veronica get you down, okay?"

"Okay." Daphne attempted to smile. Her mom only knew a small part of what was worrying her, but it was necessary. That much she had decided.

"How late do you think you'll be?" A curfew was never set, a fact Daphne was grateful for, particularly on this night.

"The festival goes pretty late, and then we might go out to eat or something," Daphne answered with deliberate vagueness. The festival ended at midnight, but before then, she would be out by the Veil, bracing herself for what would come out of it. The next time they saw each other would be after the battle.

Her mom nodded. "Be safe," she said, unaware how fitting the farewell was.

Unable to think of anything to say, Daphne walked the rest of the way down the stairs. "I'd better get going."

"All right, have fun," her mom said sternly, then added, "Don't get crr-azy!"

Daphne rolled her eyes in amusement and turned into the entryway, impulsively grabbing a handful of candy from the trick-or-treater bowl and stuffing the pieces into her pocket as she stepped onto the porch. A line of gourds her mom had undertaken to gut were spaced apart on the railing, lit from within by tealights. They were too far away from the road to be appreciated by drivers, but festive for the rare trick-or-treaters who might have stopped by.

Daphne paused to take one last look at the house, which, lit with golden light, had never looked so safe from the horrors that awaited her. Phillip was undoubtedly continuing his furtive watch upstairs.

Would it have been better to skip the festival and stay? But Daphne knew, when it came down to it, she could not stand waiting alone with no real distraction. This was the right decision.

Shrieks lit the night as Daphne walked toward the booths and games that made up the heart of the festival. The sun had long set, and lights and noise beckoned in the distance.

"You can do this," she muttered to herself. "Have fun. Be normal."

A child-sized skeleton passed, carefully guarding a caramel apple in its hands. Daphne glanced around. A large number of vendors, food trucks, and even a few rides were set up, moving with an alluring light. A thick crowd wove their way between these. Another shriek pierced the air from the twirling ride, followed by the energetic beat of a drum from a large tent.

A raucous cheer greeted a chord from an electric guitar. Daphne checked her phone. Jessica had not yet answered her text, and in the crowd, it would be difficult to find her. They had not set a meeting place, not knowing what to expect.

A gap in the crowd opened. Through it, Daphne spotted Nathan standing by one of the games and fought her way toward him with relief.

"There you are!" he said with a wide smile that sent a sudden warmth through her despite the chilly air. "I just got here. Where are the others?"

"I don't know, I'm waiting for Jessica to text me back. Where's Dom?"

Nathan shrugged. "He couldn't make it." Daphne suppressed the urge to roll her eyes again—although she barely knew him, Dom did not impress her as a great friend.

One of the game operators was watching them expectantly. Nathan nodded toward him. "Do you want to play?"

"Oh. Okay," Daphne said, inching toward it skeptically. "How does it work?"

The operator answered. "It's simple—all you have to do is throw the ball"—he held one up—"and try to knock over one of those milk bottles." He pointed to three bottles stacked together on three tables behind him. "If you can knock all of them over, you get the biggest prize."

Above them was a halo of stuffed animals, and Daphne's eye settled on a row of cute, multi-colored owls with large plastic eyes.

"I'll try for one of the owls," Daphne said. The game operator handed her the ball after taking payment from Nathan. With Nathan's eyes on her, she was anxious to hit well and cringed as the first ball she threw whizzed over the top of the stack.

"All right, good try," Nathan said good-naturedly, clapping in encouragement. "Next ball's all yours."

Daphne quickly threw it. The ball hit the table and bounced off.

"Almost!" the. game operator said, handing her the third ball.

"All right, don't watch me," she said, aiming. It was harder than it looked.

"Ah, so close," Nathan said as the third ball tumbled to the ground. Daphne stared at the undisturbed bottles, disappointed. She really had wanted an owl.

A ping sounded from her pocket. Daphne pulled out her phone to see Jessica had finally responded. "They're by the band," she informed Nathan. "Want to head over there?"

They made their way toward the music. Pumpkin lights and plastic skeletons decorated the booths. They passed a mystical-looking woman laying out tarot cards for a captive audience. Daphne couldn't help wrinkling her nose in distaste, thinking of Claire. Even though they got along far better than she could have ever expected, Daphne's opinion on psychics hadn't changed. Anyway, it was never discussed between them. She wondered if Claire was doing something special at her studio for the holiday.

Veronica and Jessica were standing outside the periphery of the tent, watching the band play. Approaching them, Daphne noticed Veronica was wearing nicer clothes than she'd been at school, and she had curled her long, highlighted hair. Comparing herself in a dark jacket and jeans, Daphne felt a twinge of jealousy. She wished she were as effortlessly elegant as Jessica, as pretty as Veronica.

"Is Nathan showing up?" Jessica asked her, after they greeted each other.

"He was just behind me," Daphne glanced over her shoulder, bewildered. However, Nathan was nowhere to be seen. "Maybe he stopped somewhere?"

"We can wait," Jessica said reassuringly. "Let's watch the band, it's pretty good."

The band played through two more songs before calling a short break. Although Daphne kept an eye on her phone, she did not receive a text from Nathan. Had something happened?

Veronica left for the bathroom, but Daphne was reluctant to leave the spot, sure he would show up any moment. Sure enough, no sooner than Veronica left did he appear in the crowd, looking harassed. Daphne went to go meet him.

"Where did you go?" she asked.

In answer, he held out a purple stuffed owl from the bottle game. Daphne took it, amazed. "You went back again?"

"You just seemed really disappointed." He shrugged but looked pleased. "It took longer than I thought."

"It's probably rigged," she answered, still astonished as she poked one of its plastic eyes. "It's so cute, thanks!"

"No problem," he said, grinning widely. Daphne returned the smile, feeling very light, more so than she had in weeks. Reluctantly, she walked back to the band, wishing it could have been just the two of them walking the festival. She gave the owl a final pat and stuffed it in her jacket pocket without much difficulty, wanting to keep it to herself.

"How come you're not in costume, mister?" Jessica said at their approach.

"Because you're not wearing one either?"

"Good point," she said, laughing. "Veronica said there's

these really cool jack-o-lanterns by the bathrooms. Want to walk over there?"

They worked their way through groups of people, a crowd that mostly ranged in age from thirteen to parent-aged, and at least a third in some sort of costume. Finally, they spotted Veronica, who brightened at their approach. Behind her were a dozen elaborately carved pumpkins, one with leering white teeth, another dotted all over with glowing eyeballs.

She said hello to Nathan. Daphne was amused at the shyness in her voice, while at the same time remembering how hard it had been for her to talk to him at first. Feeling the lump from the stuffed owl in her pocket, she softened. Maybe she was being too hard on Veronica—after all, Jessica liked her. She couldn't be all bad...

"Jessica, look at this one!" Veronica said gleefully, pointing at a carving with a grotesque, almost demon-like expression.

"Gross!"

While they took photos of it, Daphne glanced up at the moon, which was neatly split in half. She wondered what Claire was doing at that moment.

"Too bad it's not full," Nathan said, looking up, too, while the other two became excited over a pumpkin that had been carved into a carriage and posed for photos.

"And orange," she said. Their eyes met, and Daphne forgot where she was. The contact only lasted a second, however, before they were interrupted by a request to take a better photo of them with the carriage.

They wandered the booths. A small crowd had gathered around a table covered with many different handmade sweets— candy-topped cookies, dirt cups, popcorn balls, and cake pops. Daphne itched to buy something, although she couldn't help thinking of all the candy she'd emptied out of her pockets in the car. She decided on a cake pop shaped like a candy corn, passing over the cakes resembling spiders.

Jessica looked longingly at a caramel apple coated with colorful sprinkles. "Is it healthy if it's an apple?"

"It'd be hard to eat," Daphne pointed out, biting off the orange part of the cake pop.

"True..." Jessica said wistfully.

They continued through the grounds. Although enjoying the sights and the fact that Nathan walked by her side, to Daphne it was like there was a veil separating her from the surroundings, hampering her ability to enjoy them fully. Luckily, Jessica could talk and joke, filling any silence or awkward pauses. Veronica was quieter than usual. While this was an improvement in many ways, Daphne herself became almost mute as the night lengthened toward the inevitable. At least Nathan seemed to be enjoying the evening, she noted with relief.

At half past nine, they made their way to the haunted trail, the part of the event all of them had truly wanted to see more than anything else, and waited their turn around a bonfire built up by the college students who had organized it. Jessica shuddered excitedly at the sound of a shrill scream from within the woods.

"Ready?" Nathan asked Daphne as they were finally led to the trail entrance.

"Of course," she said, wishing she could have come up with something more witty.

A yellow sign nearby warned trail-goers of a zombie outbreak and stated the woods was a quarantine area. Cautiously, the various small groups ventured into the woods, leaves crunching beneath their feet.

"You guys go ahead," Jessica said, clinging to Veronica's arm. "I *hate* going into the woods at night. It's creepy."

"I think that's the idea," Daphne answered, keeping the sarcasm out of her voice. She thought of her many hours wandering in the woods at night. Zombie outbreak or no, dark woods no longer frightened her. But no doubt the haunted trail would bring surprises.

"C'mon!" Veronica said eagerly. "I'll go first." She linked arms with Jessica and forced her along.

For a full minute, they followed the jack-o-lanterns into the forest, until they had traveled far enough to lose sight of the festival. Daphne, walking with Nathan, felt safer for his presence. Yellow tape had been strung between some of the trees. They passed a handful of bones.

Despite herself, Daphne's unease grew the longer the trail went without any surprises. She expected someone would jump out at them at any moment. As they moved along, a recording of a calm, authoritative man's voice played from the trees.

"Please be advised this is a quarantine area. All unauthorized personnel should leave immediately...Do not initiate contact with a zombie. If contact cannot be avoided, shoot the zombie in the head...If bitten, proceed to the nearest biohazard containment tent, where you will be treated for the contamination..."

With a bullet, Daphne thought. Something brushed the leaves to their right.

"Did you hear that?" Veronica said quickly.

"It's probably a zombie," Nathan said in a teasing tone, leaning toward her. Daphne glanced at him quickly.

"Oh, well, in that case." Veronica straightened, though her arms were still linked with Jessica's.

They turned a corner in the marked path. A figure wearing a white biohazard suit stood up from examining a body covered in a white tarp. "Hey! You shouldn't be here, this is a quarantine area!" he said in panic.

A dark figure moved up ahead and disappeared into the trees.

"Sorry," Jessica said awkwardly. They moved forward along the path, the worker watching them go.

"Hey, you don't want to go that way! We haven't found them all!" he said loudly. "One of us has been bitten already!"

Daphne shivered. Though cheesy, the worker had felt eerily real, but the only way was forward. They left to the sound of him repeating the warning to the two small groups behind them. She braced herself and marched ahead of Nathan along the pitch-black path, lit only by the jack-o-lanterns. Low, suspenseful music grew as they moved forward. A large tent was in the distance. Jessica giggled nervously, a sound echoed by a girl in one of the nearby groups.

"I wonder if they're—"

With overly dramatic roars, three zombies leapt toward them from in front and behind. One of them wore a red-stained biohazard suit with the helmet missing. Daphne stepped away instinctively and bumped into Nathan. Jessica screamed and began to sprint up the path with the other fleeing groups, dragging Veronica with her far away from the zombies. "C'mon!" Veronica yelled as she passed, and took Nathan's hand, which was nearest, and pulled.

"Daphne!" Nathan yelled, but missed her hand as he was forcefully dragged away. Daphne took a step to follow, but the zombies growled and moved closer, surrounding her, closing the gap to escape. She suppressed the urge to scream and, ducking her head, plowed forward underneath the outstretched arm of the nearest zombie. A painted hand touched her shoulder, but she shook it off and sprinted up the path until she reached the tent, heart racing.

The others were nowhere in sight, no doubt having gone inside the tent already. It was eerie to be alone in the dark, a glitch in the established rules of haunted trails. Daphne was slightly resentful at the way she had been left behind, even though it had not been on purpose. She focused on the next obstacle blocking the path.

White plastic decorated with more yellow tape and a quarantine sign marked the entrance to a large, makeshift tent that thrummed with music, a light strobing from within. Daphne looked to her left, wondering in a moment of weakness if it would be possible to bypass the tent altogether. Her heart leapt at the sight of a figure half-obscured in the trees—someone watching to make sure she didn't do exactly that?

However, the man didn't move. "Hello?" she called to him. As she drew closer, Daphne's first instinct was that he was not one of the college students; he wasn't wearing a biohazard suit or any zombie makeup. Daphne peered around the trees for a better look.

An old man with a trimmed white beard and wearing a cheap suit jacket stood near the tent. Mist rose off his shoulders and faded into the air. Daphne stared at him curiously. She had not met many old shades.

He did not answer her greeting but shifted restlessly from foot to foot, staring furtively around him, as Phillip had done earlier. It was like he expected someone to leap out and attack —and not a zombie.

"Hello? Who are you?" Daphne tried again, stepping closer. He stared into the trees. "Who are—"

The change was sudden. The shade looked abruptly at her and grasped her arm with a spotted, misting hand.

"*It's coming,*" he said hoarsely.

His intent gaze was close to hers. Startled by the change,

Daphne took a step back, his cold fingers melting through her arm.

"I-I know," she told him, backing away farther from his taut face. "I know."

She'd taken too much time already, even if it was only a minute. Stopping at the entrance again, Daphne took one last look at the old man now obscured by a tree. *It's coming.* She looked at the biohazard sign. The tension of the trail had broken, and she was just a lone person standing around props in the woods. Artificial horrors, compared to the real ones that would be arriving soon. *It's coming.*

It was time. Time to leave for Laurel Road and face down the Veil, even if she was a little early. But first, she needed to get through the tent. Daphne inserted a hand into the gap and brushed aside the plastic entrance.

She was, at first glance, alone, but Daphne didn't trust this. Light flashed more intensely, and it was difficult to see through the cascading smoke and the sheets of white plastic hanging from the ceiling, breaking up the space. Daphne glanced around the large interior for the exit.

As she did, a black-clad figure emerged silently from behind one of the hanging sheets. Heart jumping in spite of herself, Daphne turned the other way and saw a second figure had emerged from a corner. Their movements were strangely jerky in the strobe, their dark arms reaching toward her—

Daphne twisted around. The light was dizzying, the smoke obscuring everything. A feeling of stupidity mixed with her rising panic. How hard was it to find the exit? She strode forward and swept aside a hanging sheet. It was impossible to tell which way she had come in now. The figures were moving in on her just like the zombies earlier, and once again she was left to fend them off alone.

Daphne stumbled toward the tent wall and pushed with a

hand. It didn't give way. All of the walls looked impenetrable, and she could not even tell where the entrance had been. A gloved hand reached for her shoulder. She felt so dizzy...

"Daphne!" said a voice, and she turned and automatically grasped the outstretched hand. A moment later, she was stepping through a slit in the tent she was sure had not been there before, and outside into the dark. Daphne dropped the hand and looked at the trees, blinking away the white spots in her vision.

"Thanks," she said to what she could see of Nathan. Feeling embarrassed about her panic, Daphne quickly added, "Where are the others?"

"Not far ahead," Nathan answered reassuringly, waving a hand up the trail. "Sorry you got left behind. I didn't realize it until we were in the tent. I thought you were just behind us."

"Sorry, I got held up by a zombie."

"Happens to the best of us."

Daphne laughed, any residual resentment fading, and walked briskly with him up the trail, blinking the last of the spots away. The sooner the trail was done, the better. Her dizziness had improved, but next time, Daphne resolved to walk around the tent instead.

They found the others huddled by a tree.

"There you guys are! Thought we lost you," Veronica said. Her arms were folded and her eyes were on Nathan.

"Are you okay, Jessica?" Daphne said.

Jessica was staring at the ground, her mouth tightly set, looking unusually pale. "Yeah," she said after a delay, as if testing whether she could speak without being sick. "The strobe lights made me dizzy. Next time, I'm going around it, I don't care."

"I got dizzy too," said Daphne. "How much farther, do you think?"

"Not that far," Nathan answered, to her relief. The sooner they were done, the better.

They banded together again, jogging toward the sound of screams and the roaring of a chainsaw.

The end of the trail came quickly, with a few more scares.

"Congratulations, you didn't die," a girl in a biohazard suit near the exit drawled lazily. "Enjoy the rest of the festival."

"Thanks," Nathan said to her, and turned to the others. "That was better than I thought it would be."

"Yeah," Jessica answered in a rather high voice. "Yeah, it was fun. The hayride isn't haunted, right?"

"No, it's just a hayride," answered Veronica, smirking.

"Do you guys want to get something to eat before we go?" Jessica asked. The color had returned to her face. "I want a pretzel, but I don't want to eat it all by myself."

"Sure," Nathan said.

Daphne checked the time on her phone. The trail had taken almost an hour, and it was now half past ten. She would have to leave soon in order to get to the Veil by eleven. By the time they got a pretzel and went on the hayride, she could be very late—and she had promised Claire.

They set out across the grass toward the main part of the festival. The old shade's warning rang in her ears. *It's coming.* Daphne thought through scenarios in her mind with increasing urgency. What excuse could she give to the others?

She retreated quietly to the back of their group and only half listened to the conversation, not even caring about the way Veronica was trying her best to have Nathan's full attention, the horrors of the trail apparently having melted away any remaining shyness. The others didn't appear to notice Daphne had become very quiet. The fun of the night, unexpected though it may have been, was now behind.

Eating was the last thing on her mind, but Daphne thought it might be strange not to get anything at all, so she ordered a small soda at the window of the vendor they stopped at. Her throat felt dry, and it might help her stay alert.

Daphne sipped the soda without tasting it and watched the crowd as she waited for the others to get the pretzel, still debating how best to leave. Maybe she could say she wasn't feeling well and needed to go home. It was an easy solution. She could blame the strobe tent.

Jessica was now flirting with the young vendor. Daphne's stomach squeezed—it was time to make her excuses. She would just have to—

In a stroke, all sound was extinguished. The distant band stopped playing, and the others continued talking, their mouths now moving silently. A rush of cold swept over Daphne, drowning all thought. As if in slow motion, the paper cup slipped from her icy fingers.

The cup hit the ground and burst open, soaking her shoes. Sound, as quickly as it had disappeared, returned in full force. Someone shrieked from a nearby ride. Nathan turned around from laughing at something Veronica had said and glanced down at the dropped soda, still grinning.

"Aw, what happened? I'll get you another—" Nathan looked up at her face, and his smile dropped slightly. "Daphne? What's wrong?"

Daphne barely heard him. She was staring at a point past him. It couldn't be. It was too soon. Too—

"Daphne?"

She looked up, realizing for the first time he was talking to her. The soda seeped into her socks, unacknowledged. Nathan's expression was growing more serious, his frown deepening in concern. Behind him, Jessica and Veronica were taking the pretzel eagerly, having noticed nothing. Only Nathan had happened to look her way at precisely the worst moment.

"I—"

She had to leave. Nothing else mattered.

"I have to go," Daphne heard herself say. She turned and walked away, then broke into a run, pushing her way through the crowd, not hearing what Nathan called after her. A small part of her knew it looked strange, that it would require explanation, but she could not care yet. A proper excuse would have to wait.

It had begun.

20

THE BRIDGE

Daphne sped down a deserted road in the dark, noting that the speedometer had risen well above the speed limit. There were no cars to be seen as the landscape grew hillier, wilder, outside of town.

She fumbled with the phone in her jacket pocket and, with one eye on the road, called Claire.

The phone dialed. "Pick up! Pick up!" Daphne yelled in desperation. "Claire, pick up!" An automated female voice told her to leave a message. Cursing, she hung up and chucked the phone onto the passenger seat to join the owl she had wrenched from her bulging pocket, its eyes wide and innocent. Adrenaline pounded in her temples. And, if she were being honest, fear.

A detached sense of terror loomed like a monster in the shadows around her car. It was terror unlike anything Daphne had felt before, and only her focus on the road kept it at bay. She could not give in to it. Not yet.

Laurel Road came into view. Daphne slammed on the brakes and jerked the wheel to the left without heeding the stop sign. The phone slid off the passenger seat and fell to the floor, lighting up with a text. She ignored it.

Yellow headlights parted the darkness and just reached the trees lining the road on either side, their tops faintly lit by the half-moon above. Daphne was conscious of passing this way a hundred times on a different night when a creature had prowled the dark toward another girl. One who had not survived.

Her progress seemed horribly slow. Nearly fifteen minutes had passed since the rush of cold had swept over her. That was fifteen minutes for the dyszoons to come out of the Veil, to disappear into the surrounding dark. How would she and Claire be able to find them?

Daphne reached the hill and shuddered to a stop. The Veil was clearly visible even against the dark sky. To her horror, she saw it had almost doubled in size, like a pupil dilated in the absence of light. Radiating evil.

Daphne tore her gaze away and exited the car, slamming the door shut. Her senses were sharpened by fear. Besides the Veil's appearance, there was an ominous sense of nothingness. But just like in the strobe tent on the haunted trail, Daphne didn't trust she was alone. She glanced once down the dark road, hoping Claire's car would soon appear.

Daphne jogged down the hill. It felt terribly long, this slow descent to the bottom. The only sounds were her hurried footfalls and heavy breathing, the silence around her stretched like a rubber band. Daphne focused on this silence, reaching out for any sign of a dyszoon. Again, there was nothing.

The ground leveled out and Daphne pounded to a stop, short of breath. A stitch pinched her side. She glanced again at the Veil, the only sign something was amiss.

Daphne considered her surroundings as she rotated on the spot, eyes adjusting to the moonlit night. She felt wrong-footed in the quiet after hastening to arrive. Had the dyszoons already left and fled into the woods? Should she begin searching in there? Uncertainty stopped her. It was difficult to think clearly, when at any moment, the silence could split open.

C'mon, Claire. The psychic would know what to do. Together, they could form a plan.

Daphne paused to take in the Veil's size. Someone had done this. With a chill, she realized that person could be watching her, maybe from the woods. It was almost as if she could sense the shape of them. Could feel them move closer, impossibly fast.

She sensed it a moment before it came.

Instinctively, Daphne fell to the road as a black shape detached from the darkness and hurtled over her head with a piercing sound of rage. Daphne brushed hair out of her face and shot to her feet, heart pounding in her throat, just as the black shape returned for another blow. There was no time to think.

Her arms flew out automatically, just as they had done so many times before in practice. The creature hit an invisible barrier and bounced off.

Daphne bent over, aghast at the force of the single hit, much like a boulder smashing against a wooden shield that only just held together. This dyszoon was much stronger than the one that had weakened in the woods after striking Heather's car. It was straight from the Veil and would not be banished back to Hell so easily.

The dyszoon quickly recovered and flew toward her like an oversized, shapeless bat. Daphne felt the pure force of its hatred toward her in one breathless thought before striking again.

A sword against ice, but with a fatal crack. The dyszoon

exploded into black dust, which settled as if drawn magnetically to the ground, seeping into the cracks of the asphalt.

Daphne realized she was breathing short to the point of a panic attack and took a shuddering, calming breath. She had defeated a dyszoon. She should be happy at the victory, but it frightened her how hard the battle had been, even when it lasted less than a minute. There had been barely time for thought, only instinct.

A wave of cold, much softer than when the Veil had opened, swept over her again. Daphne watched as another dark shape hurtled out of the pupil that was the Veil. The hairs on the back of her neck rose.

Planting her feet in the middle of the road, she braced herself for the coming attack just as another shape followed its fellow. Her mouth turned dry. There were two dyszoons at once. But—she had prepared for this.

The first made a beeline toward her. Daphne blocked.

Again it was not enough. The dyszoon was thrown back with the hit, but not enough to be extinguished. Daphne staggered with the blow and registered that its fellow was flying toward her. She didn't bother to raise a hand as she mentally struck it, but the hit was sloppy. The dyszoon screamed as its trajectory was deflected from where Daphne was standing. It was only provoked.

Daphne realized how weak she really was against them. *Just these two. Just these two and then I'm done,* she thought, but fear was clouding her mind, fanned by the hatred she sensed spilling from the creatures. Hatred that pierced like needles, pushing despair into her veins, feeding on any strength until it seemed to grow into its own entity. *Fighting is pointless,* it said. *You're too weak. You're nothing. Give in to us. Become like us.*

A dyszoon was hurtling back for another attack. Weakly,

Daphne struck out at it and staggered again at the strength of it. Her knees hit the asphalt, despair rising. All that practice, and it was still not enough. She was too weak, she was failing. A dyszoon flew toward her crouched form. It was over—

A car gunned over the hill and flooded the scene with light. Before Daphne had the chance to think, it sped to the left of the road and lurched to a halt. Hope surged in her chest as she recognized the red car as Claire's.

It's not over.

The spell of despair broke. Fierce determination flooded in its wake. Daphne stood up and struck out at the attacking dyszoon, an ax through glass. The creature shattered at her touch. Its dying shriek pierced her ears and was gone, black dust enveloping her and then evaporating into nothingness.

Daphne whirled toward the final dyszoon but saw it had forgone attacking her to swoop toward Claire's emerging figure.

"Claire, look out!" she screamed.

Her heart leapt to her throat, but Claire flung out a careless hand, and the dyszoon was gone.

There was no time to celebrate. Daphne turned with horror just in time to see two more dyszoons fly from the Veil. Claire joined her, and Daphne registered dimly that she wore a costume headband. They did not stop to talk.

The two dyszoons reached them, attacking one-on-one. Daphne deflected hers and saw Claire do the same in the corner of her eye. Repelled, the dyszoons shrieked in unison and curved in an arc for another ambush. With Claire by her side, Daphne felt the last of her despair leak away.

Another breath of cold came over her, but Daphne didn't turn to see the next dyszoon soaring out of the Veil. All of her attention was focused on striking out at the dyszoon as it returned multiple times to attack. She and Claire were being forced farther apart, and Daphne could not spare any time to see how she was doing.

She repelled the dyszoon again just as the latest one soared in to join it. Not expecting another attack so quickly, Daphne struck out erratically. The dyszoon was only slowed down before it hit her squarely in the chest.

A force like a giant kickball knocked Daphne backward onto the asphalt. Breath left her lungs. For several long seconds, the shock of the impact made it impossible to register anything except the fact she was alive. The dyszoon had been slowed down enough to prevent any damage other than a future ache. Daphne comforted herself that dyszoons could not harm the living like they could their surroundings.

There was no time to recover. A black shape hurtled toward her head, and in the next split-second, she rolled to the left.

The asphalt exploded where her head had just been. Shrieking, the dyszoon soared upward again. Daphne rolled and leapt unsteadily to her feet, only just taking in the new pothole in the road.

The dyszoon returned. Daphne struck out with her free hand. A rain of black dust showered over her without sensation. She turned unsteadily to face the last dyszoon, still dazed from her fall.

Claire was suddenly by her side. Together, they struck the shrieking black creature as it swooped toward them. It was no match for their combined hit. Black dust suspended bizarrely above them and fell like evaporating sand.

Daphne stared at the spot where it had disappeared. A new stillness, all the more so because there were no more dyszoons, settled on the night. It was over. She could hardly comprehend it. Hours of practice, and it was over in a few minutes.

"You did it, Daphne." Claire turned toward her then,

smiling with pride. Behind her, the motor of her still-running car could be heard, its headlights partially lighting the bridge.

Daphne felt wobbly. The soda she had drunk earlier threatened to make a reappearance. Gently she bent over and put a hand on one knee, trying to steady the trembling. The other she placed on her chest, which, like her shoulder from her first encounter with a dyszoon, would likely be bruised. Adrenaline was slowly fading away, though not enough to feel relief yet.

"It was close," Daphne said, concentrating on the ground. "If you hadn't turned up..."

"You did well. Either way, it's over." Claire looked toward the bridge, and the Veil, taking in its new size with an expression that made Daphne feel nothing was over after all.

"Did you feel it open, or did you just get my message?"

"I missed the message," Claire said, turning away from the Veil. "I was at the studio when it happened, and then I rushed out here as fast as I could. I hope you weren't alone too long."

"You only came a minute after me." It had seemed much longer, in the tautness of her fear and the quickness of the battle. They had defeated six dyszoons, the most they had predicted.

"Luckily, Sylvia was helping me," Claire said, "and she could take over."

"Do you think there's any in the woods?" Daphne asked, slowly straightening. The nausea was passing.

"No. I only felt the one come out. There was a long gap until the second. I believe we're safe."

"Good," Daphne said shortly.

"Are you all right?" Claire asked, observing her with concern. "I couldn't always watch. Were you hit?"

"Yes," Daphne answered. "But I think I'll be okay," she added hastily at the alarm on Claire's face. Tiredness had seeped into every muscle. Adrenaline had left, leaving her feeling weak. "I'm just glad it's ov—"

A terrible sweep of cold cut off her words. Automatically, Daphne turned toward the bridge. With Claire, she watched, entranced, as a black shape hurtled out of the Veil. It was immediately followed by another, then a third. Seven dyszoons flew up into the sky like black blemishes in the night sky. One shrieked. Daphne's hair stood on end at the sound, at the number.

They settled into battle stances even as she felt doom settle on her heart. There were too many. They could not fight off so many dyszoons at once—it was impossible.

"Claire," Daphne said shakily, "I don't think I can—"

She turned and was jarred by the intent expression on her mentor's face. Daphne recognized the look: shrewd, calculating. Like options were whipping around the psychic's eyes, fast as the dyszoons in the night. Settling on one.

"Of course," Claire mumbled to herself, then bounded toward her.

"Claire, what—" Daphne instinctively took a step back. But Claire seized her left arm, pulled it straight, and gripped it, viselike, with her own right hand.

For the second time in her life, Daphne felt as if a lightning bolt surged through her veins and lit her brain on fire. It was an indescribable sense of power, of invincibility. Her senses became sharp, clear. Somewhere in her mind, Daphne was aware that Claire was giving a lot. Much more than in the cemetery. Too much. And yet seconds passed and Claire's grip remained firm, every line on her face etched with fierce determination. Giving away her own strength. Giving them their only chance.

One of the dyszoons pelted toward them from above. Daphne closed her eyes to the stillness that enveloped her, feeling the form of it approach. Then, she tore from Claire's loosening grip and struck out at it with a defiant scream echoed by the dyszoon as it exploded into nothingness. In the corner of her eye, Claire stumbled.

There were still half a dozen creatures left. Daphne turned her focus to them, and as if sensing her new power, the remaining dyszoons screeched and flew toward her from every direction. They had decided to attack her as one rather than divide their forces. Daphne could sense all of them. Just minutes ago, this sight would likely have immobilized her with terror, but now they were easy.

They were nothing.

Daphne threw up her hands, and the creatures pelted one by one into the invisible barrier she had created around herself, the sensation like fists knocking against a pane of glass. She winced at each hit, startled by the closeness of each formless creature that threw itself against it yet bounced off. It was like she was at the center of a cylinder shield that held in place around her.

The dyszoons darted around her, and through the shield, Daphne could again feel the force of their intense hatred toward her as they screamed and snarled. Their anger at the shield, at her presence, at her existence. They pelted into it again and again, with more fervor, growing enraged with each failure to penetrate it. Her hair flew as they soared by.

Due to their speed and number, it was difficult to keep track of them. Daphne knew she could not hold the shield forever. Already the energy Claire had given her was waning, the effort of keeping the shield in place more difficult with each passing moment. But how could she fight them without dropping it?

As if they could sense this thought, the dyszoons' hits decreased, then stopped altogether. They were still flying around her, half a dozen blurs circling tighter around the shield, each in its own ring. She was encased in a cyclone of black. The second the shield broke, all of them would strike her at once. If one could bruise, maybe six could kill.

Her hair lifted in the wind from their movements. Daphne closed her eyes. She needed to think. Claire's energy was fading away, but power still flowed to the tips of her fingers. Dyszoons encircled her, waiting for the instant the barrier was down. Time slowed. With her eyes closed, she could perceive all of them.

They were nothing.

Her eyes opened. At the same moment, Daphne pushed out at the black forms around her with as much strength as she could muster. The dyszoons scattered as if caught in an explosion, flying in all directions. Yet this only bought her a few seconds; already they were recovering to make another assault, their high-pitched shrieks full of anger and promising death. She was ready for them all.

The first dyszoon reached her and turned to dust at the force of her touch. Daphne perceived another form hurtling toward her and spun around, striking out. It shattered into sand.

Daphne struck out at a third dyszoon, but it was a difficult hit, even as it dissolved at her touch. Claire's energy was leaving, the sense of invincibility and power fading and being replaced by exhaustion. But still two more raced toward her.

With two swipes of her arms, Daphne struck out at both in succession. They deflected, shrieking in rage. One returned, and she struck again. It turned to dust, its final scream quivering in the air. The final dyszoon soared toward her.

"Don't," Daphne told it, and struck.

Dust floated around her and was drawn magnetically toward the ground. Daphne contemplated it for a few seconds and then glanced down at her pale hand. It was trembling uncontrollably. The last of Claire's borrowed energy had finally faded. Still, it did not matter. All of the dyszoons were gone.

"Claire..." Daphne said, looking up at the Veil. The pupil looked down on her silently. She could hardly believe it. They had done it. It was over. She laughed, full of disbelief and also the beginning of elation. "Claire, we did it, we—"

A strange, gurgling, choking sound. Daphne froze. Slowly, tentatively, she turned around.

Claire stood near the edge of the road. Her body was convulsing, limbs shaking violently. Foam spilled out of her upturned face. Daphne looked at her in horror, comprehension coming with the force of a tidal wave.

Seven dyszoons had hurtled out of the Veil. And she had defeated...she had defeated only—

Claire had given away a lot of her strength. It was a risk. She could not defend herself from an attack. Which meant, if there was one dyszoon left—

She was possessed.

21

THE OTHER PERCEIVER

"Claire!"

Daphne sprinted forward. Claire's body stepped back clumsily, as if to get away, and snarled at the sky.

Running had given Daphne the illusion of purpose. Even though she was closer, Daphne realized she had no idea what to do next. Helplessness swallowed her as she took in Claire's convulsing body. The dyszoon inside could be harming her in some irreversible way, and yet Daphne could only stand there, watching. But she had to do *something*.

The creature's form was visible to her. Somehow, she needed to get the dyszoon out. But how? And what if it injured Claire? But the alternative was undoubtedly worse.

Daphne lifted a shaking arm and tugged at the dyszoon. A horrible shriek of fury came out of Claire's mouth. The psychic looked demented, eyes rolled up in their sockets. Her body jerked. Daphne's panic rose to a fever pitch.

"Claire!" she shouted, and tugged at the creature. A black form rose out of Claire's mouth and retreated back inside. The dyszoon would not let go so easily.

"C'mon!" Daphne tugged again. Claire's body jerked violently and her head fell forward, spitting foam, arms flopping. It was a terrible sight. "C'mon!" She could not get it out. Claire was going to die if she could not get it out. "C'mon!" Daphne tugged again weakly, but Claire's body only jerked and choked.

"C'MON!" Daphne screamed, feeling like a madwoman, tugging with each yell. "C'MON!" Black billowed out of Claire's mouth and retreated back inside.

It was no use. Daphne bent over, watching Claire shake, and sobbed. Another feeble tug did nothing but make the dyszoon scream again. She could not do it, could only watch as it destroyed Claire from the inside. A dyszoon would claim a second victim.

Anger coursed through her and stilled her shaking shoulders. There would not be another, Daphne vowed. She would never—never—let another person die or another family be torn apart because of a dyszoon.

A terrible shriek sounded again from Claire's mouth, as if the dyszoon sensed the determination growing in Daphne's chest. Panic was not going to help the situation. She swallowed and closed her eyes, if only to block out the image of Claire's body as it shook and choked, as if controlled by a sick puppeteer.

Daphne forced down the terror of what would happen if her attempt failed and focused on the dyszoon inside of Claire; she could feel it quivering inside. She latched onto it and tugged. The dyszoon screamed. A black mass emerged and wrenched itself back in. Daphne tugged again. The creature almost lost its grip this time. She paused and tugged again, screaming, with all her might.

A dark mass erupted from Claire's mouth and catapulted into the air like a slingshot. Released, the psychic collapsed in a heap. Daphne reached for the dyszoon again and struck.

It shattered at her touch, a final shriek reverberating off the still trees. A stillness came over the night. An empty quiet.

Daphne allowed a second to register this before running to Claire's body, which lay on its side. "Claire," she shouted, falling to her knees next to her, and turned the body over fully. "Please, please."

The psychic's eyes were closed, but her mouth was open slightly, the residue of foam dried around it. A pebble was digging into Daphne's knee, but she did not bother to move. For the first time, looking at Claire's face bathed in the light of the moon above, she was struck by the fact that Claire seemed truly old. The psychic's red hair contrasted sharply with the deathly paleness of her weathered skin, which was more sunken and drawn in dreams than it was when she was awake.

Her mind numb, Daphne laid a trembling finger on Claire's neck.

A pulse, faint but present, beat against her fingers. Hope sprang like a tiny flame.

Claire was alive. Daphne let out a shaky laugh and collapsed back into a seated position, not bothering to wipe the tears on her face. Claire was alive. The gamble, her own inattention, had not cost the psychic her life.

Daphne buried her face in her hands and laughed again. If she didn't, she might have burst into tears instead. Claire was okay. She would have to recover, but she would be okay. The dyszoons were gone, and they would talk about the Veil later. There would be a later. Daphne glanced toward the bridge and immediately scrambled to her feet.

They were not alone.

Lit distantly by the headlights of Claire's car, a figure stood shrouded in shadow in the middle of the bridge, directly underneath the widened Veil. It was late at night, Daphne thought. There wouldn't be people out here, unless...

Daphne glanced at Claire in hesitation. What would the psychic advise her to do? There were no more dyszoons, but the person, whoever they were, could still harm her in other ways. She had no weapon.

She turned toward the bridge and, bracing herself, started toward it. The figure did not move, but Daphne knew it was watching her. Her pulse quickened. She could sense everything ahead would be decided by what happened between her and the person who stood on the bridge in the dead of night.

Daphne stepped onto the stones. Her quiet steps were heavy in the silence as she approached the figure, still difficult to make out even in the artificial light. The person was short, that much she could tell, with long hair.

Several yards away, Daphne stopped, frozen by the force of her recognition. Her right hand tingled.

It was Ashley Zhang.

For several long moments, they stared at each other. Daphne knew her face must look white, shocked, but if anything, Ashley looked bored. She was wearing the same baggy sweater as the day before, and her black hair was even more wild and uncombed.

"So," Ashley said, "I see you got rid of my dyszoons."

The pause was long, each girl surveying the other in the dark. Daphne's thoughts crackled. "Your dyszoons," she repeated at last. It could not be true. It could not be Ashley who had widened the Veil.

Ashley shrugged. "Well, I let them out."

The smug expression on her face was completely at odds with what had just happened. Disbelief filled Daphne. But as if in answer to her doubts, a vivid image arose from her memory of Ashley's almost feral expression in the bathroom, screaming of madness. And then as Daphne's hand struck her cheek, that sharp sense of something like evil—

"I thought you might be like me," Ashley continued conversationally. They might have been talking about school. "Ever since that stupid 'spider' in class. I could see the shade by you— I thought maybe you had seen her. Then you were here before..."

"You widened the Veil," Daphne stated, still numb with shock. "You're the one who let those dyszoons out in August."

Ashley's smirk deepened. "Obviously," she answered with a roll of her eyes Daphne could make out even in the dark. Anger surged through her, the only emotion that seemed to penetrate the numbness. Her mind seized on it.

"Why?" Daphne said, quivering with the anger. Ashley's nonchalance, like yesterday's rage, was provoking her. "What was the point?"

Ashley's smile was condescending. "The *point*—?"

"I defeated all the dyszoons, and they didn't hurt anyone." Claire's body convulsed before her eyes. "You failed."

"The dyszoons were just a test," Ashley said, and to Daphne's satisfaction, she sounded annoyed. "They weren't there to *do* anything."

"Then why let them out? Why widen the Veil?" Daphne said, an ache in her chest that wasn't just caused by the dyszoon's hit. "The shade from class—did you know she died that night? Those dyszoons killed her."

Ashley gave a start, the smugness in her face receding. "What?"

Daphne frowned. Was it really possible that Ashley didn't know? "Heather Grey. She was a year above us."

"Heather Grey..." Ashley said with a blank look and then cocked her head, smug again. "I think I had a sweater that color once."

Anger surged through Daphne again. "So you don't even have a purpose, then," she said wildly, wanting to provoke Ashley in turn, if only to see the smugness disappear.

"I have a purpose you're too stupid to even think of!" Ashley retorted.

At the childish outburst, confusion overcame Daphne's anger. Not over the fact that Ashley could be capable of letting out the dyszoons, but that she had acted alone—and was sticking around to tell Daphne about it. For the first time in their conversation, a sickly dread welled up in her. A warning that might have come too late.

Neither of them spoke, and the outburst dwindled into silence. Ashley's fists were balled, and some of the feral expression from yesterday had returned. Above her, the widened Veil hung still and menacing. An abomination in the sky.

None of it made sense. What purpose could Ashley possibly have in expanding the Veil? Especially when the Veil had been dormant for so long, maybe beyond both of their lifetimes. If she was really acting alone...

"Why did you widen the Veil?" Daphne said warily, looking above.

"Because the world *sucks*!" Ashley spat, unhinged torment and disgust in every word. "Everything is falling apart. It'll show you. It's going to bring a new order."

"It?" Daphne said, bewildered. "The dyszoons?"

"No, not *them*. It's—" The word died in a choke. Ashley lurched forward as if sick, reaching a hand to her throat.

"Ashley?"

She choked again, lurching. Daphne went cold in recognition.

Ashley's body began to jerk violently, just like Claire's had. It shook and flopped back and forth, as if in the throes of a

seizure. Daphne stared at her, at a loss. It couldn't be a posses-
sion, there were no more dyszoons—

Abruptly, the jerking stopped. For several long moments,
Ashley stood still, bent forward stiffly, a sheet of hair hiding her
face. Then, slowly, she straightened, lifting her face. Her eyes
had rolled back, leaving only white.

A piercing terror cut through Daphne. She wanted to run,
to bolt, but her feet seemed to have lost the ability to move.
Ashley's mouth opened, and a terrible voice spoke. One deeper
than the earth, harsh as spiked steel.

"DAPHNE...COLE..."

The sound reverberated like an earthquake and cut through
her like piercing needles. Daphne bent over, slamming her
hands against her ears. The sound was like the full presence of
that portion of what she had felt after slapping Ashley, of evil.
She was drowning in it.

"What are you? A dyszoon?" she shouted, hoping somehow
that talking would distract it and ease the force of its terrible
presence.

A wave of laughter crashed over her. Daphne pressed her
ears tighter and, in desperation, pushed against the sound like
she would a dyszoon. To her surprise and relief, the force of its
presence receded enough to allow her to look up at Ashley's
form, still and terrible against the backdrop of dark woods and
sky. The puppet mouth moved with the voice's words.

"I am much greater than the creatures I command," the
voice growled in sadistic amusement, its voice like a chalkboard
being grated upon. Ashley's mouth leered. "I am a demon,
older than the world itself."

"What do you want?" Daphne said to Ashley, to the thing
that had taken control inside. That may have been doing so for
a long time. The leer widened, and then the mouth moved
again, the voice coming out of it jarringly deep.

"I was impressed tonight. You are stronger than the girl, who has been—shall I say—*worn out* by helping me." Ashley's body shook roughly, like a limp doll. "You are stronger than her, though less willing," the deep voice continued. "I can change this. I can forge a new connection between you and this useful path of mine. With your help, I can rise and leave this prison."

Ashley's scathing words in the school bathroom, before Daphne had slapped her and felt the demon's presence, drifted back to the surface of memory. *You're so much greater. More worthy.* Daphne had been distracted by the anger and loathing etched into Ashley's face, but there had been another emotion there—was it jealousy? Maybe she had seen Daphne as a rival, had been told by the demon she was easily replaceable, even after all of her efforts to expand the Veil. Why else would she risk being exposed? The thought of rejection had made her reckless.

Daphne realized she was still covering her ears and lowered her hands. The demon couldn't possibly think that she would accept the offer—not when she had just defeated the dyszoons.

"Why would I help you?" she asked.

"Your world is coming to ruin. It needs a new order. Let me show you—"

The bridge and Ashley vanished. Daphne collapsed to her knees and clutched her head again as a stream of visions passed over her eyes. Evil after evil was committed, person against person, unchecked, unabated, like a wave that could not be contained. It was horrible, it was too much, all hopeless—

Daphne screamed and the vision broke. Her eyes were streaming, and she wiped at them with a sleeve, taking a shuddering breath. The visions were already fading from her memory, but a sense of despair lingered.

"Can you see the state of your race? I could change this, with your help. Together, we can accomplish much—"

The bridge disappeared once more. Before Daphne's eyes danced a startling, breathtaking vision. Large crowds of people were gathered in every city on Earth, crying out in misery and pain. She saw herself at the center of it, powerful, a balm for humanity. The feeling burned in her. She could help them all, the whole world, if only she accepted the offer. She *would* accept, and help others. Save them, yes, just like her father had—

His face blazed before her like a torch in the darkness. It was a lie.

"*No!*" Daphne screamed. The shining vision of herself shattered, replaced by the dimly lit bridge. Temptation to accept, so strong a moment ago, receded. "*I won't!*"

Her mind was clear again, temptation gone. The demon was looking to rule the earth for itself only, for evil. It was not looking to help people, only to harm them. The illusion was just that—an illusion.

Her breaths came short, like she had just run a sprint. She had come perilously close to the edge.

Ashley's mouth curled upward in a dangerous smile. "You won't? You are stronger than I thought, to have resisted. No matter; I can still use the girl."

Ashley's body jerked forward a little, as if volunteering.

"This is just the first test, Daphne Cole. My dyszoons are not the only thing you will have to battle. My inferior will pave the way for me. I look forward to hearing what you make of it."

The presence vanished. Immediately, Ashley collapsed into a heap and did not stir. At the same moment, a truck appeared around the bend in the road on the opposite side, speeding toward them.

Before Daphne could think about getting Ashley's crumpled figure out of harm's way, the truck screeched to a halt to the right of the body. She lifted up a hand against the intense glare of the headlights, which were blinding to her after being used to the semidarkness for so long. The door opened, and a tall figure stepped out of it. It was impossible to identify in the darkness, but Daphne felt a sense of familiarity, somehow.

In a few seconds, the figure had lifted Ashley up and carried her to the back seat, its face hidden, and climbed back into the driver's side.

With another loud screech, the truck reversed and violently U-turned. It was vanishing into the darkness. Daphne ran toward it uselessly for a few steps and stared at the spot where it had gone, knowing only by the fact Ashley was no longer there that she had not imagined it all. It had happened so fast.

The bridge was silent once more. She gave the distant road a final look and then, urged by the part of her mind that still worked, ran to Claire's unconscious body.

22

FALLOUT

"Claire...Claire..."

For several minutes, Daphne knelt by Claire, gently shaking her arm, to no effect, and resisting the urge to collapse and fall unconscious too. Exhaustion, kept at bay by adrenaline and the necessity of staying awake into a night dragging into the small hours, was creeping in. She only left once, to turn off Claire's car and glance again at the dark circle in the sky. It was now nearly twice its former size. She turned away. They could deal with it later.

Lifting Claire was out of the question. She was too heavy, and Daphne's own body felt like dead weight, being shuffled around relentlessly and ready to collapse at the first opportunity. Plus, she knew enough about accident procedure to know more harm could be caused by moving Claire without knowing the extent of her injuries. What if something was broken? There was no way of knowing what damage the dyszoon had caused, not unless Claire woke up.

What could she do? The weight of helplessness was almost too much, and Daphne would rather have curled up and cried.

But she could not give up. There had to be something she could do.

Her phone was in the car. Daphne realized that if all else failed, if Claire would not wake, she would have to call an ambulance, or perhaps her mom first. The thought of the awkward questions made her panic rise. Claire *would* wake up. She still had a pulse.

Daphne stared at Claire's too-pale face with a growing sense of guilt. It was her fault the psychic was like this. She had forgotten her in the exhilarating rush of energy coursing through her veins.

Energy...

The solution was suddenly obvious. But how was it done? What did she have to do? Hesitantly, Daphne pulled back Claire's sleeve and gripped her cold forearm, spotted with age, with her right hand.

Nothing happened. Daphne closed her eyes, mind sinking into the bliss of sleep, but she forced herself not to give in quite yet. The last of her strength was needed, both for Claire and for herself to get home. She concentrated on that strength and willed a small burst of energy to leave her body, to pass into Claire.

A hot trickle ran from her arm to her fingers. Daphne thought, blurrily, she was succeeding. She sank further into the dark bliss of sleep.

Claire stirred, and immediately Daphne let go of her arm. "Claire!" she yelled in shock. "Claire, are you all right?"

The psychic mumbled something incoherent, her eyes still closed. Then suddenly they popped open, white light from the moon shining in their depths. Claire turned her head. "Daph... ne. It worked." They closed again.

"Claire, Claire!" Daphne shook her again, and Claire's eyes opened slowly. "Are you hurt?"

"No...Don't...think so." Claire swallowed and fell asleep once more. Daphne watched closely, but Claire appeared to be fine. Relief flooded her.

Leaving the psychic to rest, Daphne stumbled up the long hill to her car and steered it carefully into the middle of the road. She waited a full minute by Claire's side again before shaking her awake. "Can you stand?" she asked, and Claire nodded sleepily and put most of her weight onto Daphne. She bore it as best she could, and clumsily, they walked the few feet to the open passenger door.

"Watch your head."

It missed the ceiling by an inch. Daphne buckled the seat belt over Claire's limp form and slammed the door. Claire's car was still by the bridge, miraculously unharmed. It would have to be retrieved later. For now, let the rare passerby question why it was parked on the wrong side of the road, abandoned.

Exhaustion did not allow Daphne to think much beyond getting Claire and herself home. It had never been more difficult to keep moving, when she would have happily lain down and slept and dealt with the consequences later. The clock on the radio announced it was almost two in the morning. Only a few hours ago, she had been at the festival. Already the memory was as distant as if it were another year, another life.

The rest of the journey passed in a blur. Daphne reached the studio and found it was unlocked. She left the door open and returned to Claire, bracing herself for the difficulty of carrying her inside, but this time Claire was able to carry more of her own weight, even as she leaned heavily on the arm around Daphne's shoulder. Together, they shuffled across the lamplit sidewalk and through the door. Daphne helped Claire lie on one of the couches and dismissed the idea of collapsing on the other. She needed to get home. Locking the studio door behind her as she left, Daphne returned to her car and turned onto the empty street.

It was almost like no time at all until she was walking through the front door of her house and stumbling up the stairs, cursing as she tripped. The door to her mom's bedroom was just ajar.

Mystique lay in the middle of her bed, curled happily like a fluffy black pillow. "Move over," Daphne told her blearily and lifted up the sheets. The cat took the cue and leapt onto the floor with a jingle, having long since learned that nights on Daphne's bed were violent affairs.

An instant later, sleep claimed her.

Strange dreams bordering on nightmare came in the night. In a landscape of gray and shadow, a tilted white obelisk fell and shattered into dust. The dust descended into the form of Phillip, who curled abruptly as if shot and transformed into a crescent moon. The moon rotated and became the sneering mouth of Ashley, which grew and darkened into a black hole Daphne hurtled toward—

Many hours later, she awoke. By the light streaming through the window, Daphne could tell it was late afternoon, and she checked the ancient alarm clock on her nightstand: she had slept more than twelve hours.

Still, she felt tired, as if it would take a week of sleep to recover. Daphne settled back again and gingerly rubbed her collarbone. There was a gentle ache at the touch, but nothing more. The dyszoon hadn't done much damage, but her mind had the vague impression she had been recently hit by a bus. Or perhaps that was what waking up after severe exhaustion felt like. Claire was undoubtedly worse.

At the thought, Daphne grabbed her phone from the nightstand but then paused. If Claire *was* worse, having been possessed, she would need the rest. It was not an issue to wait a few more hours. Daphne let go of the phone and settled down again.

Almost immediately, she bolted upright.

The festival. Her abrupt, unexplained departure. Nathan's expression, as he turned and saw hers—

Cursing repeatedly, she seized the phone and turned it on. One of the texts displayed was from Jessica, but Daphne opened the one from Nathan. It was strange to feel a greater sense of urgency about explaining her departure to her friends than to deal with all that had happened last night, which was arguably more important. But no longer faced with the prospect of the Veil opening, ordinary things now couldn't simply be put on hold because they were not evil spirits from Hell.

Daphne scanned over the few brief texts from Nathan, which amounted to *You okay?* and *what happened?* and a final bedtime *?????* Biting her lip, she read Jessica's: *Daphne!!!!! Did you get sick or something girl? Nathan thought so...Text me!!*

At the mention of Nathan, Daphne paused to consider: what had she looked like? The way Nathan's face had dropped was the only clear spot in the blurred moment after the Veil had expanded. And he had seen her face, full of unmistakable terror. It was not the face of someone about to be sick, but no other explanation was possible. Daphne looked at the time again and hastily began to craft a late response to both, explaining she had been almost sick, and had been sleeping ever since. With Jessica she joked maybe she'd caught the zombie virus, but she felt reluctant to do the same with Nathan. He had seen her face.

She squirmed as she hit the send button. Would he believe it? But what other explanation could there be? She thought of the owl he had won for her, no doubt still lying on the floor of her car.

Daphne lay down again and wondered if the growing cloud in her head was the beginning of a cold, when the phone rang. With a lurch, she saw Claire was calling and answered it.

Claire's voice sounded faded, raspier than normal. Daphne felt a pang of guilt as she listened that lasted long after she hung up, even after the psychic's short assurances that, other than the obvious, expected pains, she was all right. They would find a time to meet in the next few days, when Claire had recovered more. When they both had.

Jessica's reply to her text came in, swift and sympathetic, and a plea accented with exclamation points to feel better. It was the second text from Nathan that Daphne stared at for a full minute. *Sure, hope you feel better.*

Sure. What did that mean? Was that sarcastic? Did he believe her excuse?

You're overthinking, she told herself. Nathan wasn't sarcastic typically. Her mom would say it was a typical guy response, that the message could be taken at face value. But Daphne wondered why it bothered her so much. It was impossible to reveal the truth—yet she still felt Nathan deserved better.

Daphne realized she must have fallen asleep again, because it was dark when her mom came in "to make sure you hadn't died." It seemed she had come down with a cold after all, and she weakly replied to all the questions about her time at the festival. Guilt panged her chest, aching both from the dyszoon's hit and the weight of all she couldn't say. There was so much her mom remained in the dark about, but that was the way it had to be.

The lingering effects of exhaustion from a month of dread welled up from her soul, keeping her in bed the next day and home from school on Monday. It had been a long time since Daphne had slept so many hours without any nightmares, or indeed any dreams she could recall. Maybe the horrors of her waking ordeal with the dyszoons and the Veil meant they were kept at bay for now. It was a reprieve that did not come often.

When not asleep, she relived the battle again and again. Every word of the conversation on the bridge was dissected. Daphne burned to discuss it all with Claire, realizing large parts of the night would need to be filled in. Claire did not yet know about the demon, or Ashley's role in it all.

After many assurances Daphne would be fine, her mom left for work at the library, and Daphne was alone when Claire called again, wanting to meet in the afternoon.

A few hours later, Daphne parked her car in the side street next to the studio and got out, squinting against the sunshine. It seemed unnaturally bright, given the darkness of everything that had happened.

She stopped outside the entrance and peered into the studio. The lights were off. She tried the handle and found it was unlocked. The bell jingled as she shut the door, bringing a heaviness of silence. The perfumed room was gloomy despite the natural light coming from the window, leaving patches of sun on the floor.

Daphne walked to the curtain separating the front room from the hallway and pushed it aside. The light in the office was on.

"Claire?" Daphne called. "Are you here?"

A round of coughing answered her. "Sorry—yes, come in, Daphne. Could you lock the door?"

Daphne walked back to the front door and turned the bolt.

"I unlocked it for you," Claire said when she came back, "but I don't want anyone coming in. I'm taking a few sick days."

She certainly looked sick, Daphne thought as she examined the psychic. Claire was wrapped in a heavy shawl and wedged behind the cluttered desk. Her nose was red; the wastebasket next to the wooden swivel chair was half-full of tissues, and a mug of tea steamed on the desk. Something whirred underneath. Looking down, Daphne saw a small machine was blowing hot air at the psychic's feet. The room was stuffy.

"Shouldn't you be resting, then?" Daphne asked, standing at the doorway. There was nowhere to sit in the cluttered room.

"I'm fine. I'm not seeing clients, but I still have business things to take care of I thought I'd better get to."

Guilt wormed up in Daphne's stomach. "How are you?" she asked anxiously.

"Sore," Claire answered bluntly, and put a free hand on her hip. "I ache all over, but that's been getting better. Anyway, let's go to the other room. There's nowhere to sit in this mess."

Claire was in a worse mood than Daphne had ever seen her, but that was understandable. She decided not to offer help as the psychic slowly got to her feet, but at her request unplugged the hot air machine.

"Do you want some more tea?" Daphne asked, noting Claire's mug was empty. "I can make some."

"Thank you. Make some for yourself, if you like."

Daphne got out of the way so Claire could get through the doorframe and quickly brewed two mugs of tea. When she walked to the other room, Claire was already in her chair, eyes closed.

"Here you go," Daphne said, setting the refilled mug down onto the coaster. She felt another pang of guilt, looking at Claire, and was anxious to help in any way. They'd both

suffered from the battle, but Claire's discomfort was undoubtedly worse. She had been possessed. That was Daphne's
fault.

"I'm sorry," she said humbly, sitting down.

"For what?" Claire opened her eyes in surprise.

"For letting you get possessed. I knew you wouldn't be able
to defend yourself after you transferred your strength, but—"

"Daphne," the psychic said, fixing her with a familiar stern
stare, "I don't blame you in the slightest. There is no one to
blame for my getting possessed, except the dyszoon, I suppose."

"But I should have watched—"

Claire held up a wrinkled hand. "No. There were more,
many more, than we were expecting, and your attention had to
be on them. In fact, one of the things I wanted to say to you is
how...proud I was, and am, at how well you were doing."

"What?" Daphne said, blinking.

"I am. I helped in the only way I could, and only because
the situation was beyond reasonable expectation of your abilities at this time."

"But I still should have—"

"And if I don't blame you," Claire broke in, louder, "the
only person getting in the way of forgiveness is yourself."

Daphne bit off her next sentence, but then smiled at
Claire's unrelenting sternness. The worst of the guilty knot was
unraveling. If Claire didn't blame her, why should she? Maybe
her conscience was being overly sensitive to her own faults,
ever since slapping Ashley...

Ashley. Claire didn't know about that yet, but it filled
nearly every waking thought of Daphne's. Of what had
happened, and where it had yet to go.

There was much to be discussed. Daphne filled Claire in
on the particulars of what had passed between her and Ashley,
and what the demon had told her. It took a long time, and

another refill of tea, to get through it all. Claire sat in silence for long periods, frowning at a spot in the distance.

"So this demon," Daphne said, "it opened the Veil in the first place so it can have a passage to leave Hell, but it wasn't until now the Veil was wide enough to let anything go through."

"Because it's found a helper now," Claire added. "You said she was a classmate of yours? How well did you know her?"

"Not that well. She sat at the same lunch table as me, but she was always moody and by herself. Only I should have known, after—" Daphne broke off, feeling heat touch her face, but related the slap and the evil she had felt inside of Ashley, though she hadn't known what it was at the time. To her relief, Claire didn't offer any sort of reprimand, only nodded.

"The thing is, I don't think she was always that way," Daphne said, anxious to hurry forward on the topic in case Claire changed her mind and started lecturing. "My friend Jessica—she's the one who did the reading with me when we met—she said Ashley was different last year. Like, normal. Do you think she's possessed by the demon in some way?"

"Not...possessed," Claire said thoughtfully.

"Maybe brainwashed?" Daphne suggested. "She would have to be, don't you think? If she's not possessed."

"That would be my thought, if Ashley is different than before, like you say. But how it happened, how this demon found her, and was able to communicate with her..." Claire broke off, shaking her head. "As I've said before, there is evil at work in Long Haven. But luckily, for a time at least, there's still much to be done to widen the Veil enough to allow this demon to pass through. What that entails, what kind of things it will make her do"—Daphne felt a sickly sense of unease—"I don't know, but it gives us a little time. You don't know who was driving the truck?"

Daphne shook her head, remembering the speed at which the figure had arrived and carried Ashley away. The memory was already blurred—she had been exhausted. "It was too dark. I think it was a man, but I don't know for sure. His lights were too bright, on purpose, I think."

"Well, it seems there's another enemy we can look forward to meeting," Claire said with a dry tilt of her head.

Daphne smiled faintly, but she had trouble thinking of Ashley as an enemy. She wanted to admit to Claire the pity she felt. It was strange, knowing Ashley was responsible for their current predicament, for Heather's death, but Daphne recalled her face on the bridge, every inch screaming of madness beyond reason. It was not the real girl—she was hidden under the demon's influence. If that was possible to strip away, could Ashley come back?

They could only speculate how the demon had recruited Ashley. Maybe she'd been ensnared by some version of the shining lie shown to Daphne, one where she could help the world, or simply live in one without suffering. The powerful promise of that vision could have then blinded Ashley to the evil of its source until it was too late and she became a worse version of herself—one without any hope, except in a lie.

Daphne swallowed. That was one part she had left out so far, of what the demon had offered her in that breathtaking vision. How, just for a moment—

"There was something else the demon said," Daphne began hesitantly, and went into detail of the vision. When she was done, she waited with dread for how Claire would react.

"I knew it was a lie," she hurriedly explained, seizing the pause. "But when I saw it, the things I could do, I was so close to accepting it—"

"Evil shows us possibilities, not consequences," Claire said, leaning forward. Daphne saw with relief she wore a kind expression. "Don't feel bad that you were tempted, Daphne. Being tempted is in itself not a sin. You almost accepted the offer because, like with wanting to help Heather, you saw a chance to do good. That is your nature."

"I guess I just wanted to believe I could change things." It felt important to explain, to vindicate herself.

"That is how ideas often begin—with good intentions," Claire said. "Whether good things come out of those intentions is a test of time. Just as with helping shades. Still, I believe now you were right to help Nathan."

"You do?" Daphne said, surprised Claire would say something so opposite to her consistent warnings.

"Was I right to warn you of the dangers? I think I was, but what state would the world be in if we only helped others when there was no risk of being harmed ourselves? There are entire jobs based around the concept: rescue workers, police officers..."

"Firefighters," Daphne added quietly.

"Exactly. And in my bitter old age, I seem to have forgotten. It's a selfish way to live."

Daphne nodded shortly, unable to answer, but she sensed none was needed. Although she didn't necessarily need Claire's permission to help shades, it was a relief to have her support. It was true there were many shades she could not help —their problems were from too long ago. But if she could help a few, that would be better than nothing.

She thought of the complications of helping Nathan, but also of the small ways he had improved. It was true he had helped her as well. Already she valued the friendship they had. Whether Heather would be able to move on soon, Daphne didn't know.

Her eyes drifted to the gilded, oval mirror on the wall above Claire, its glass old and warped. Words cast aside in the wake of the battle and the appearance of the demon returned.

"Ashley—the demon talking through her—said something to me at the end," Daphne said, staring at the mirror without seeing it as the bridge came into view, with Ashley's rolled eyes and the oddly angled body that had lost control of itself. "It told me its 'inferior' would pave the way for it, or something, and it looked forward to seeing what I would do with it. Do you think it meant some type of dyszoon? Like a stronger one that'll be fully formed?"

She looked at Claire's face then and saw it was grave and worried. A thump like a fist of doom hit Daphne's heart.

"Claire? What do you think it meant?" she said, a lukewarm dread filling her stomach like poisoned tea. Claire didn't answer straightaway, her mouth set firmly in a line. Daphne looked at her anxiously but did not interrupt.

At last Claire spoke, carefully and deliberately, staring into the air at some future only she could see, lurking in the shadows of the room. "About demons, I know only a little. Only what I have seen in nightmares." Claire closed her eyes briefly, as if remembering. "But I do know they are not all equal. Some are very powerful, much more so than other demons, who would be seen as lesser."

"Inferior," Daphne answered intently, the meaning becoming clearer.

"Yes." Claire nodded, turning to meet her eyes, a dark sky against the gray moon.

"So when it said its 'inferior' was coming to pave the way for it, it meant..."

"A demon. An inferior one, yes. But inferior does not mean weak."

Daphne frowned, struggling to understand this new enemy. "But how do you defeat a demon? Would they be like a stronger dyszoon, like I said? And we would just have to..." She let the words trail off, at a loss.

"I don't think so," Claire said. "As perceivers, we can both command good spirits and fight evil ones. But demons aren't spirits."

"So we might not be able to fight it?" Daphne said.

"I don't know," Claire answered. Her lips were pursed again. "If not, we will have to find a different way to defeat both this lesser demon and the one you met, eventually. But that will have to be solved with time. It could be years; it could be months. In the meantime, we must deal with the present situation the best we can."

The fallout, Daphne thought. There was no pretending things would be as before. She gripped her mug tightly. "Now that the Veil has been opened more, dyszoons can come out at any time now, right?"

"Yes," Claire said, setting down her empty mug with a sigh. Daphne's heart sank even as what she had already feared was confirmed. "I'm afraid so. It may be some time, maybe a long time, or not very long at all. It will depend on how well the dyszoons are able to travel through. But the only thing we know for certain is that they will come."

Daphne absorbed this, the uncertainty of their situation. She was so used to Claire having the answers, but it appeared the psychic's knowledge was now running out. They would have to walk blindly together into a future neither of them could see, only guess.

She nodded curtly at the unspoken task. It would be her responsibility now, along with Claire, to battle whatever came out of the Veil, whether it was one, three, or a dozen dyszoons at once. They no longer had the luxury of knowing when that would be, or how often. It could be at any time, and she would have to be ready, lest another person die. Daphne was the best responder. It was her duty now.

She looked around the room. So much had changed here, been discussed. Remembering how it had been when she first entered, it was strange now to feel comfortable: to look at the woman across from her not through the lens of her profession but as a person. As a friend.

"Claire, you don't have to tell me, but what did it feel like?" Daphne asked quietly.

Claire didn't have to ask what she meant. "All I remember...it was cold, but it was so cold it felt like fire. And I felt..." She closed her eyes and put a hand on her face, covering one eye. Daphne looked at her anxiously, not knowing what to say. After a moment, Claire removed her hand, unsmiling. "I understand better what it means to be a dyszoon, and I believe I was right in saying it's a special kind of agony, not an escape from it."

They drank in silence for a while. Daphne's head was full. The terror of what was coming was edging over her like a darkened cloud, yet she felt the beginnings of resolve. One battle was over, and another would start soon. It could be a long time until that happened, like Claire said, or not very long at all. She would just have to be ready when it did.

But in the meantime, there was something she could do.

23

THE CEMETERY AGAIN

Daphne drove underneath the metal arch and up the narrow road past a field of headstones.

The strange sense of unreality that had come during her last visit swept over her again as she exited the car and paused with one hand on the open door, facing the descending sun inching toward the hill she knew Robin must still haunt.

She ignored the feeling—this time, she would not dream of her father.

Purposefully, Daphne made her way along the rows, hand closed over the results of her feverish research of the last few hours. Straight from Claire's studio, she had driven home and taken out her laptop. Claire's permission to help shades had sparked an idea, one that could also provide an outlet for the restlessness of having done nothing but rest the past few days. The desire to do something in the midst of the unknown.

Her mom, luckily, had an account for an online archive of newspapers that could be keyword-searched. Uncertain of how Robin spelled her name, Daphne instead searched for the only date she knew: September 1967. The month Robin, the shade now looking toward the growing sunset, had died.

Finally, in the late September archives, Daphne found with excitement what she was looking for: a report of a tragic night in the cemetery. A young woman's body found. What Claire hadn't known, however, was that there had been a second body. A man, at twenty-three only a year older than Robin. Pursuing any follow-up story, Daphne discovered that a later autopsy confirmed the deaths had been overdoses.

But he hadn't joined Robin in haunting the cemetery after death. He had moved on. She had remained.

The shade spotted Daphne. Robin was no longer faded like last time but was as clear as any other shade. Her starved-looking appearance, more pronounced in hollowed cheeks, made her look older than she really was, or had been while living. Long, misting hair cascaded to her waist. Mournful eyes in the rapidly dimming light watched Daphne approach.

Remembering the last time they'd met, Daphne felt it strange now to imagine there had been a time when seeing shades was difficult. They were everywhere now, and Daphne could avoid seeing them no more than the headstones surrounding her.

"I think I know why you stayed behind, and I want to help, if I can," she told Robin, without bothering with a beginning. The shade considered her but did not speak. Daphne pulled out her phone, which contained the results of her research and the other side of the story.

Robin had a son.

The obituary mentioned she was survived by her mother and a child named Gabriel. And that was where the story ended, in print at least. Daphne had resumed her search online, feeling almost feverish as she entered Gabriel's full name into different databases and sorted through the repeated names, trying to confirm the real one, the right age.

Keeping those profiles handy, Daphne had paired his name with the local high school, with no hits. It was possible he had moved. Then she tried words like *drug* and *overdose*. The search turned up an obscure donor list with his name on it from two years ago, for a drug program in the state, and Daphne's pulse quickened. Could it be the same?

It was only half an hour ago that Daphne, in a rush of exhilaration, felt certain she had found him.

"Did you stay for Gabriel?"

At the sound of her son's name, Robin expression sharpened, as if the balance of her world and consciousness had righted in that moment. Then it became drawn and mournful again. Behind her, the sun was setting in a blaze of orange wreathed by clouds.

"I thought maybe he was the reason, so I tried to find him on the internet—if you know what that is." Daphne broke off, collecting herself. "So I looked for him, and—and I found him." She withdrew the phone from her pocket and showed the screen to Robin, whose eyes tore from Daphne to look.

"That's what he looks like now," Daphne said. On the screen was a photo of an aging but distinguished-looking man, wearing a suit as he accepted a service award for his active fundraising work for an opioid addiction program. "From what I read, he does a lot of charity work with his wife, and they have four kids—" She scrolled to the next photo of a vacation on the coast. "Those would be your grandkids, and then he actually has a grandkid, too, but I couldn't find any pictures—"

Daphne lowered the phone. Robin had been silent the entire time, her eyes transfixed on the photos, and now she looked up. Uncertainty gripped Daphne—what happened now? Was it enough to know the facts?

"Your son is okay," she told the shade. "You don't have to stay behind for him anymore."

The last sliver of sun dipped behind Robin. Their surroundings sharpened in the twilight. Daphne watched the shade's face, which had shown no change.

"Gabriel is okay," Daphne told her, then, feeling it was somehow right, added: "Be at peace."

Robin's eyes closed. Nothing happened, but then Daphne saw that the mist rising off the shade's body was expanding inward and floating away in a personal breeze. Little by little, the shade dissolved into smoke. A final, tired sigh resounded in the air, and Robin was gone.

A sense of peace hovered. Daphne stared at the spot where Robin had been and stood for a while as the last pink haze of sunset faded into the darkening sky. Only then did she turn and make her way back along the headstones, surrounded by the dead, but none of them ghosts.

24

UNFORESEEN

Daphne felt well enough to go to school the next day. It was strange to be surrounded by chattering people who didn't know anything about what had happened on the bridge and to be doing something as normal as school when the threat of evil loomed.

At her locker, she glanced down the hallway toward Nathan's locker and saw he was not by it. Was he still suspicious of her excuse for leaving the festival, or was she overanalyzing everything? If only they had the chance to talk—

"Daphne!" someone screamed, and then the next moment, she was being squeezed to death. "You're back! I missed you!"

"I missed you too," Daphne gasped, rubbing her side as Jessica loosened her death grip. In the distance, Veronica beamed in greeting and turned back to her group before she could see the quizzical look Daphne gave her. Did Veronica feel friendly toward her now that they had hung out together outside of school?

"So, are you feeling better?" Jessica asked, quivering with excitement so her gold earrings swung. "I haven't seen you since the festival! Nathan was wondering where you were yesterday."

"He was?" Daphne asked, her heart skipping half a beat.

"Yeah, I told him you were still sick. You've missed stuff!"

She got the sense Jessica was not talking about schoolwork. "Like what?"

"I just found out, like, ten minutes ago, you'll never guess—it's about Ashley!" By now Jessica was practically quaking.

For an irrational instant, Daphne feared the school had somehow discovered what had happened on the bridge. "What?"

"She ran away!"

"*What?*" Daphne said again, startled. "What do you mean?"

"She's gone!" Jessica said, evidently pleased at the reaction to her news. "I heard it from Olivia, whose mom is friends with Ashley's mom. She ran away on Friday, left her phone and everything." Jessica's voice suddenly lowered, and for the first time became more serious. "I guess she left a note saying she was sick of her life and wanted to start over somewhere—but she wasn't going to off herself or anything like that," she added hastily, misinterpreting Daphne's expression. "But Ashley didn't own a car, so they think she might have had help, or driven off with someone."

"Wow," Daphne said automatically, but her mind was whirring with this new information, new pieces falling into the gaps. Ashley would have needed an excuse for going...wherever she was being taken. Painting her departure as voluntary would mean the search for her would be less urgent than a kidnapping, lessen any media exposure. But it was true—Ashley had had help.

"So *that's* why she didn't want to go with us to the festival.

She was planning on running away!" Jessica said, with the air of having solved a great mystery.

"What? Oh, yeah, she must have been planning it," Daphne agreed, though secretly she thought it was partly due to the fact that Ashley was not friends with them, whatever Jessica's relationship had been with her last year.

The bell rang. Daphne hastily opened her locker and Jessica bade her goodbye. As she yanked books and notebooks off the shelves, Daphne realized she hadn't given any thought to the two little siblings who had been with Ashley at the football game. Or that Ashley even had a family, and didn't lurk in a dark cave somewhere after school. Should she tell someone about the truck, at least?

But even so, she had little useful information in tracking Ashley down. The truck had come and gone so quickly, and it was so dark, she hadn't noted the license plate or model. It was impossible to tell what the rescuer—or kidnapper—looked like. Plus, it would require too many explanations about why she was there on the bridge, in the dead of night.

Daphne looked again at Nathan's empty locker. If only she could have a chance to talk with him.

A part of their conversation from last Friday drifted back to her. The regional championship for cross-country was later in the day. He would not be at lunch, their only period together. She would have to wait until tomorrow, unless...

An idea sprang into her head, a sudden decision. He had invited her to watch him once, hadn't he?

The regional championship was taking place at a wooded park outside of Long Haven. Daphne hurried out of school after the final bell and followed the instructions on her phone. She had never been to a meet before and didn't know what to expect, but knew she probably wouldn't make it in time to see the start of his race.

She arrived at the park and slid her car into a space. Tents and barriers were set up in the distance, and it was cold. Daphne drew her gray coat shut and marched against the wind toward the chattering crowd lining the running path, miraculously edging her way to the barrier a couple yards from the finish line.

"Is this the guys' race?" she asked a friendly-looking woman standing next to her.

"Yes," the woman answered. "Should only be a couple minutes now."

Despite the wait, there was an infectious sense of excitement. Like the others, Daphne leaned forward for a better look down the running path, waiting for the runners to appear.

Sure enough, in a few minutes, the crowd farther down erupted into cheers echoed down the line, and every face was turned toward the runners sprinting into view. Two led the race by several yards. Daphne craned her neck around the woman's shoulder and recognized one of them.

Nathan, wearing green shorts and a tank top with a number plastered across it, sprinted toe-to-toe with another boy in blue.

"Go Michael! You're almost there!" a spectator shouted.

The crowd screamed encouragements at both runners. Daphne squeezed her fingernails into her palms, the urgent frenzy of the crowd infecting her. Both runners were running flat-out now, but Nathan was just a half step behind. The gray-haired coach standing near her was frantically gesturing.

"Push, Nathan! You almost got him!" his deep voice boomed above the screams.

The runners were nearing where she was standing, and the drumbeat in her chest reached a peak.

"Go Nathan!" she heard herself scream.

Whether he heard or not, Daphne didn't know, but suddenly, Nathan was head-to-head with the other runner. They passed her spot. The finish line was feet away. In the final moments, he sprinted ahead across the white line. Victory was made by a second.

She exhaled and, forgetting her own problems for a moment, joined the crowd in cheering wildly. Other runners were quickly following behind and finishing their races. Daphne saw the coach clap Nathan on the back.

He was being hugged by a woman who must have been his mother. By the emotion on her face, Daphne guessed she was an easy crier. At the sight of a gray-haired man nearby—his father—Daphne unconsciously turned away. Nathan she was used to being around, but she didn't feel ready to meet the parents of a girl whose death she had witnessed a hundred times. And when she knew that, at that moment, their daughter was wandering the halls of her alma mater.

Daphne turned and settled for watching the rest of the runners cross the finish line, all looking worn out, before walking a short distance away. A quick glance revealed Nathan had disappeared, perhaps to cool down.

She was starting to regret her impulsive decision to come. It felt awkward now to have come alone, without a plan, even if she had technically been invited. The race was finishing up. She glanced over at the finish line and checked the time.

"Daphne?" said a voice.

She almost dropped the phone.

"Nathan!" Daphne said, a jolt of nerves flipping her stomach. He was standing before her, carrying a water bottle and looking pale in the cool air. His wavy hair was stuck up more than ever and rimmed with sweat.

"Did I scare you?" he said, eyebrows raised in amusement.

Daphne rolled her eyes and put her phone away.

"I didn't know you were coming," he said, now frowning a little. "You weren't here before the race?"

"I only got here in time to see you finish," Daphne explained, worried now that her presence was weird. "That was really good. It was close."

"Thanks. I was tailing the other guy the whole race," he said. "But then my game plan is to push at the end."

"Your coach looked a little worried."

"Yeah." Nathan smiled. "He's like that. We're pretty close, though. He helped me a lot, after..." He trailed off. Daphne felt a stab of awkwardness—while he had never explicitly mentioned his sister's death, it was open knowledge at school. "I almost didn't do cross-country this year, but he told me I'd regret not staying my last year, and I should keep busy."

Daphne smiled. In the following silence, she scrambled to think of something that wouldn't sound dumb, but her mind was distracted. Nathan's appearance brought, with a sudden vividness, the night of Halloween and the sweep of cold, and his face as he took in hers. She had not seen him since, and his brief text had been their only conversation. Had she imagined the skepticism?

Nervously, Daphne tucked her hands into her jacket pockets, uncertain now where to look. It was as if question marks hung in the air. She felt a new restraint between them that was bitter, foreign. But maybe it was imagined. Her mind scrambled with how to broach the topic.

"So...how was the rest of the night? Halloween, I mean, with the hayride and..." Daphne broke off and kicked the grass, pretending to see something interesting in the distance.

"Good." She saw his shrug in the corner of her eye.

"Jessica said it was fun. I wish I hadn't had to leave."

"What happened, anyway?" Nathan asked. She looked up and saw his face looked curious, with a touch of the bewilderment she had witnessed just before leaving. It was a hard face to lie to.

"I just felt really light-headed, so I thought I was going to be sick," Daphne said lightly, as if it were an everyday occurrence. "The strobe lights made me feel weird."

"Oh. Why didn't you text back?"

"I didn't see them," Daphne said, with a pang of guilt, though it was technically true. "I really didn't feel well enough at all to look for you...so I left. I'm sorry."

"Oh," Nathan said again. "It's just, when I saw your face—" He broke off, as if shaking off a disturbing memory. Daphne's stomach squeezed. No doubt some of the terror she'd felt had shown in her expression, and the way she had acted afterward—

Luckily, a sneeze erupted.

"Sorry," Daphne said, wiping her streaming eyes. "I'm still a little sick."

Nathan's face cleared. "It's okay." He grinned suddenly. "But you should get that checked out—you might have something serious."

"Oh, shut up," Daphne answered with a smile. He grinned wider. The tension, real or imagined, had broken. In its place, a warmth appeared near her heart that felt comfortable, but also excitingly new. It spread and tingled the tips of her fingers. She liked being by him, Daphne realized with sudden clarity. Really liked it. Was it possible he felt the same—?

"Hey, look at you!" came a familiar voice. Daphne stared as the girl appeared, seemingly out of nowhere, and wrapped an arm around Nathan's back. "You're all sweaty, ha ha ha!"

"Veronica. Hi." Daphne blinked in confusion. A spark had gone off in her mind, making it difficult to comprehend what was happening. What was Veronica doing at the race?

"Hey, Daphne!" Veronica said, seeming to be genuinely friendly. Her face glowed. "You came to watch?"

"Yeah, I thought I—" Daphne began to say, though hardly knowing what.

"Where did you go?" Nathan asked, looking at Veronica and making no move to get out of her embrace.

"The bathroom. It's *way* over there," she said, gesturing with an arm.

"That's my coach," Nathan said, his head turned toward the sound of his name. "I've got to go, but you're staying for the ceremony?"

"Of course!" Veronica said brightly.

He turned away with a quick goodbye to Daphne, who flashed a smile that left as he did. Veronica beamed after him and bounced once on her heeled boots. She was fashionably dressed in a new-looking coat in a luscious shade of green. Daphne suddenly felt drab by comparison, her fingers curling around the fraying gray threads on her cuff as she turned from Nathan's retreating figure.

"So..." she started, but the words trailed off. A sickly feeling was brewing inside her. What had just happened?

Veronica tore her own gaze from Nathan and giggled, full of a giddy excitement. "Well, you probably guessed already, but...me and Nathan are dating!"

Daphne froze. "You're what?"

"I know! It was only *official* today, but..." Her face flashed with a thought. "Oh! But don't tell Jessica yet, I haven't had the chance. I want to tell her in person!" She giggled again, no doubt at the thought of her friend's future delight.

"Sure..." Daphne said vaguely. Their surroundings felt distant.

"So are you sticking around?" Veronica said, gesturing with

both hands toward the field. "There's still the awards ceremony—"

"That's okay, I was just dropping by," Daphne said quickly.

"Okay, well, see you in school, then!" Veronica waved at her cheerily and practically skipped away, and Daphne watched her rejoin Nathan, saw his arm wrap around her waist...

Feeling numb, Daphne walked blindly in the direction of her car. Somewhere, a team broke into cheers, and the sound reached her in a haze. She opened the door and slumped into the driver's seat, staring at the wheel. The warmth she had felt had long vanished into cold.

It was stupid, really, to care. It was petty, compared to everything that had happened in the last week. But at that moment, Daphne felt as horrible as she had on the bridge. Nathan was dating Veronica. Somehow, it was a fact, one she could not comprehend. Nathan was dating...Veronica.

She started the car and backed out of the parking space, the revelry of the meet reflected in her rearview mirror as she pulled away. Nathan, for whatever reason, had given in to Veronica's absurd attentions. But against Daphne's will, there was a part of her that understood. She had never really considered before how intoxicating it was to be noticed.

In Daphne's imagination, she pictured them on the hayride while she rushed toward the Veil, Jessica discreetly choosing a hay bale farther away and leaving Veronica and Nathan to share one. She saw Veronica taking the opportunity to tease and flirt and flip her long, beautiful hair over a shoulder, to touch his shoulder playfully, and later follow up with messages...

The stuffed owl he had won for her, now on her bedside table at home...Would things have gone otherwise if Daphne had stayed? The thought struck her with an element of truth.

She might at least have prevented the relationship, might have sat next to him instead. A brief vision flashed in her mind, of Nathan's arm wrapping around her waist instead, whispering in her ear...

But Veronica. How could Nathan choose to be with such a person? She was catty, and shallow, but through the numb anger came an uneasy truth. She had convinced herself others saw Veronica the same way she did, when of course that wasn't the case. Her own prejudice, her inability to perceive anything beyond her own views, had made her oblivious of any hint.

She thought of Nathan's face, full of laughter at something Veronica had joked about seconds before the Veil opened. And she was pretty, Daphne admitted wryly. That probably helped.

Daphne drove automatically, not knowing her destination. She didn't want to go home quite yet.

Either way, it didn't matter anymore. The path before her was never so clear as it was now. Others could carry on leading normal lives, falling in love, but for Daphne, there could be no more illusions. The path had been laid the moment she learned about the Veil, and her full attention would have to be on the threat at hand. She could not be distracted from it.

Would Heather be able to move on now that her brother had found happiness? Happiness...

Daphne had a duty now. Her dad had understood that, when he'd rushed into a burning room to save a girl who wasn't there. There was personal risk, yes, but it was necessary. And as Claire had said, what state would the world be in if there was no one to take up such a risk? A threat was coming, had already come, and Daphne was the best person to combat it. It was her path. One she would take alone.

She exited the car. The destination had been reached without conscious thought, but of course it was the perfect place to go. Her fate was tied here.

The Veil stretched ominously in the sky. Daphne stared back at it, leaning against the hood of her car and gripping her thermos of cold tea from the morning. Memories of the battle flickered in her mind, the screech of tires echoing.

Who had taken Ashley, and where was she hiding now? Daphne felt uneasy about the use to which her classmate would be put, all in the name of fulfilling the demon's goal. But Ashley, like Daphne, had chosen her path. At some time in the foreseeable future, those paths would intersect. Whether or not they could continue after that remained to be seen.

And the demon, if it managed to travel through the Veil... Daphne did not want to imagine what that would be like. It was unthinkable. She could not fail.

But a more immediate threat: the dyszoons were now free to come out at any time, dangerous to anyone who happened to cross their path. Whether there would be many was unknown. The only thing for certain was that they would come. But Daphne knew one thing.

She would be ready.

ACKNOWLEDGMENTS

A writer's journey starts out alone, but it doesn't end that way.

I'm grateful to the following people God has placed in my life:

My college critique group, whose feedback and encouragement helped shape the story for the better: Audrey, Elizabeth, Amanda, and Dr. Rybak.

My beta readers: Ranie, Leah, and Kelly.

Andrew. Without your enthusiasm, this novel would have remained unpublished.

A final thanks goes to my family for their love and support, long before any words were written.

ABOUT THE AUTHOR

Kaylin Wise was born and raised in Wisconsin. She doesn't believe in ghosts but loves a spine-tingling tale. This is her debut novel.

instagram.com/kaylin.wise

www.ingramcontent.com/pod-product-compliance
Lightning Source LLC
Chambersburg PA
CBHW050235110726
47898CB00007B/2154